OF
CRIMSON

BY

STEPHANIE HUDSON

Eyes of Crimson
The Transfusion Saga #8
Copyright © 2020 Stephanie Hudson
Published by Hudson Indie Ink
www.hudsonindieink.com

This book is licensed for your personal enjoyment only.
This book may not be re-sold or given away to other people. If you would like to share this book with another person, please purchase an additional copy for each recipient. If you're reading this book and did not purchase it, or it wasn't purchased for your use only, then please return to your favourite book retailer and purchase your own copy. Thank you for respecting the hard work of this author.
All rights reserved.
This is a work of fiction. Names, characters, places, brands, media, and incidents are either the product of the authors imagination or are used fictitiously. The author acknowledges the trademark status and trademark owners of various products referred to in this work of fiction, which have been used without permission. The publication/use of these trademarks is not authorised, associated with, or sponsored by the trademark owners.
Eyes of Crimson/Stephanie Hudson – 1st ed.
ISBN-13 - 978-1-913769-78-9

I would like to dedicate this book to all those who helped make one of my greatest dreams possible by supporting me through this new venture. To all the people who have had faith in me and believed I would achieve my goals and accomplish my mission. One that was set out to help other self-published authors in getting their wonderful stories experienced through the minds of more readers.

But to those especially who work at Hudson Indie Ink, I can't thank you enough! You have helped make it a success in such a short space of time and your quality of work and dedication is astounding, in truth it is more than I could have ever hoped for. This book is dedicated to Blake Hudson, Claire Boyle, Cathy Hudson, Sloane Murphy, Sarah Goodman and Xen Randell. Thank you all for all your hard work, dedication, and commitment. Hudson Indie Ink would not be the jewel it is without all of you who help make it shine!

WARNING

This book contains explicit sexual content, some graphic language and a highly additive dominate Vampire King.

This book has been written by an UK Author with a mad sense of humour. Which means the following story contains a mixture of Northern English slang, dialect, regional colloquialisms and other quirky spellings that have been intentionally included to make the story and dialogue more realistic for modern day characters.

Thanks for reading x

CHAPTER ONE

THERE IS ALWAYS TIME FOR ANOTHER 'OH SHIT' MOMENT

The King.

It was Lucius!

How had this happened? How had I somehow missed this mountain sized piece of information!?

"That's...This...it...it can't be happening," I muttered making Trice look down at me, as we still continued to stand in the side lines as if waiting for the King...*someone my mind was screaming at me was my boyfriend*...to be ready.

"Dinne worry, Lass, I will tell him I wish tae claim ye..." I heard these words and panic struck me so fast that I grabbed his arm, shook it and looked up at him with beseeching eyes before pleading with him,

"Oh Gods, please, Trice...please don't do that! Don't say a word...promise me...promise me quickly...don't—" I was cut off when the sound of all of the guards that surrounded us all of sudden turned to face me as if a wave of flesh had been commanded. And they had, as one look back to the front of the raised throne and I could now see Lucius motioning with his gauntleted hand for his minions to act.

"Ame—" Trice started to say my name and even that I tried to prevent, not trusting what it could do.

"Ssshh...no, don't even speak my name...just promise me, Trice, please," I said as I knew now my time had come, I had no choice but to walk towards Lucius and all I could think of now was saving a friend's life who had no clue who I was to his King. Which was precisely when all the questions started to hit me...why did no one know? Why, if Lucius was in Hell looking for me, did no one know who I was to him? Why hadn't he just stormed his way down from the raised platform now to claim me? To take me in his arms and make it known to his people who I am to him?

Oh Gods...*Had the witch done something to him?*

This thought struck me paralyzed. The fear of what awaited me being almost too much to bear. Because this wasn't my fairy tale ending where the Prince finds me at last and we run into each other's arms as lovers reunited...*this wasn't one of those stories.* No, this was the story of when the Princess discovers that her Prince wasn't a Prince at all but instead a King in Hell who looked anything but happy to see her.

Which begged the question what was in store for me after I forced myself to walk the length of this vast throne room? After I had made it up those steps, towards someone who was clearly renowned to be a tyrant King.

It was just too hard to imagine. That formidable presence that I knew was getting ever more impatient as the seconds ticked by. I knew when the parallel line of guards all placed their hands upon their sword hilts that my time was running out...it was a warning I didn't need but it rang loud and clear all the same. Especially when Carn'neau stepped forward and said,

"Now is not the time to be foolish human, as I do believe it is your death we are trying to prevent." I frowned at this and couldn't help but ask,

"We?" To this he shrugged his shoulders as if he cared little about the part I had focused on before saying a blasé,

"It seemed more interesting having you breathing."

"Geez, thanks, that was so heartfelt, I am thinking you should have Hallmark cards made." He smirked at this and nodded towards the throne where I had to admit, Lucius looked to be getting angrier by the second. But then, the moment I took my first steps, Trice reacted making me raise my hand a little towards him and shake my head slightly, before telling him,

"Please, Trice…don't." He frowned in confusion so I looked towards his King hoping he would get the hint. He followed my gaze and frowned, obviously now trying to piece together my panic. Because now I no longer had to fear my own death at the hands of a King but instead, I only feared for Trice's and any part he played in trying to save me.

That was why I could never allow Lucius to discover how Trice felt about me. Not if I wanted my friend to survive. Because in all honesty, I really had no clue what Lucius would do, as I hadn't yet really experienced his jealously. Perhaps I was being paranoid…but I thought that the smartest plan right now was to tiptoe around the edge of caution. Hell, even I didn't know what I was dealing with?! It wasn't like Lucius was exactly acting himself right now and down here in Hell, then Gods, but even I didn't know him…*clearly*.

Well, I guess it was time to find out but the closer I got, the less I was starting to want to find out. Because I had to say again, it wasn't exactly the reunion I had envisioned us having when we finally found each other. And well, it was becoming clear to me now that something had obviously happened to Lucius. Perhaps he had been captured by the witch and what I was looking at now was the result of that capture?

Like I'd feared, had she done something to him? This question plagued me with every step I took, as the more space that was cut between us, then the more likely that prospect was looking…as well as the fact that, *he didn't exactly look welcoming*. Hell, but other than the handsome face staring back at me, then he didn't even look like the same man I knew. In fact, he reminded me very much like how he had that night in the silent garden when his demon had come to my rescue.

However, the most startling difference was that now it didn't seem as though he liked me quite as much as he had back then. His scowl said it all and I wasn't exactly looking forward to finding out which words he would choose to go with the look of irritation.

His mighty wings framed the back of where he sat, creating a frightening and imposing backdrop to an even scarier being. The horns that they were attached to were now curled up at a different angle than I was used to seeing. And I gathered that this was to allow for what I supposed was a more comfortable sitting position, meaning that remaining in this form was through choice.

His black and red armour looked as if it had been forged in a volcano before its edges hardened to black steel. Each hammered, jagged plate looked more like lava rock that was still molten and scalding to the touch at its glowing centre, whereas the edges looked razor sharp and smooth before each interlocking piece finished in a deadly point like a knife's tip.

This design was mirrored on his chest plate, as pieces curved up from his sides like spiked horns that joined a single dagger point which came down over his heart. Underneath these plates were four V shaped sections overlapping his stomach and covering his abs, which I guessed offered more movement in its design.

The shoulder pieces were made up of five sections that were

moulded over on a curve to fit the large muscles I knew were hidden beneath. The larger two of these sections held huge jagged horns that reached the same height as the top of his head and they flowed down over the chest plate, covering a good portion of his pecs.

So, on the whole and putting it another way, he looked as if he could have killed me with just one hug! And looking to the side now, was where I found his helmet resting on a stand as though it was the only remains left of some headless demon. This time it was all black, matching that part of his armour that reminded me of a trojan helmet in its shape. This was down to the typical T shape cut out for the eyes and mouth, with a dip at the top that came down over where his nose would be. But that was where the similarities ended, as it came down into deadly points past where his chin would be.

Even the eye holes were menacing, with deep slanted angles and ridges above that looked like a metal frown. The top of the helmet matched the V shaped armour that covered his abs, with overlapping plates that were riveted at the edges. The only part of the design that was like scorched lava rock, were the two massive horns that came out at the sides and went up in a large U shape that tapered to gleaming tips of glowing crimson.

As for his face, it matched the rest of him being that of half demon, half startling masculine beauty that I had been used to seeing on Lucius. The darkness in his veins was present, along with the heated, twin pools of crimson replacing the steel blue gaze that watched every step I made towards him. The talons on his armour clad hand were tapping impatiently against the horns of his throne, and in that moment, he had never reminded me so much of his maker before.

He was utterly terrifying!

So much so, that I actually found my feet tripping over themselves as if failing to work together at the sight. I would have fallen had it not been for Carn'neau's quick actions in taking hold of the top of my arm and keeping me upright. Something Lucius only half appreciated, as the second I was securely upright again, he growled out at him, snarling a few words that I didn't understand,

"Ezebu sinnis!" Although, it didn't take a nerdy scholar to get the gist of it being *let her go or die*, seeing as Carn'neau quickly let me go as if he had been stung by my skin.

A few steps later and soon I was left looking up at the raised platform in a way which must have looked like a terrified deer in headlights. Lucius' crimson gaze narrowed in annoyance before he lifted a heavy looking metal plated hand and jerked two fingers, beckoning me forward. But when I didn't move, being too stunned by the imposing sight before me, and one I never expected to see Lucius at its centre, Carn'neau decided I needed prompting, so he muttered next to me with clenched teeth,

"Go on human, as I suggest not keeping your Master waiting." I turned to look at him and frowned in question...*my Master?*

He motioned his head a little in the direction I should go, and I knew the time had come to face what now looked to be my personal devil. So, I did as instructed, and forced my foot to rise to the first step and basically keep going until reaching the top. Doing all this without being able to take my eyes from my feet, telling my cowardly self that this was so I didn't trip, not because this side of Lucius was actually making me afraid.

Of course, I was lying to myself.

Because like this, and with each step cut down between us, then I was starting to wonder what my fate would be if the witch had made him this way? The moment I reached the top was when I received my answer, as suddenly he stood and his increased demonic height had him towering over me, making me jerk backwards. However, in doing so I was too close to the edge and felt the heel of my left foot lose the surface beneath it, which made my world start to tilt as I started to fall backwards.

Thankfully, I didn't get far, as unlike the first time I was pushed off these steps, it wasn't Trice who saved me, but Lucius. His gauntleted hand snapped out and grabbed me. But then it was as if my life had hit some kind of slow-motion mode as I focused on that dangerous hand coming closer, now wondering if my skin was going to survive this? However, something happened just in time, before he came into contact with me, his talons retracted back enough that when his metal clad hand grasped me, it hurt only slightly. But at the very least, I was happy to report that it didn't shred my skin.

After he caught me, he hauled me to him, and I found myself looking up at him with trepidation clear in my wide eyes, ones that I could feel filling with tears at just the raw beauty looking down at me. Then his free hand came to my face so he could run the back of one silken soft talon down my cheek, keeping the deadly tip pointed back towards himself. I closed my eyes for a moment and felt the single tear escape from beneath my lowered lashes. Then his name barely made it past my lips, and I swear in that moment, it sounded more like a secret prayer.

"Lucius." I opened my eyes to find his own now frowning down at my mouth where he had heard it escape from, before his lip curled in a slight snarl. Then, before my senses could fully register, I was spun around to face the large open space and the sea of demons that were all there, each one still on their knees. There were warriors, full of armour and horned bodies. There were winged creatures, more beast than man and women, of both beauty and vulgarity. An ugliness that went beyond the flesh and from just one look you knew that evil was rooted to the bone. An array of hideous features that showcased more

teeth than skin, more rough than smooth, and more snarls of hunger than just sinister thoughts. It was an ocean of danger, like sharks ready to circle whatever kill their Master was ready to cast aside, and a mere hint of blood was a coiled slither in the water, telling them a mortal meal might just be on the menu.

It was little wonder then why the sight made me shudder and before I could step away, his hand that had once been at my arm, came to collar my neck. I swallowed hard, barely allowed the freedom enough for the function. Not with his metal hand now imprisoning my throat from behind, with his strength evident enough that I knew it would take little effort to snap it. But killing me quick, wasn't in his plans, as I felt him use the hold on me to bring me a step back against him. The tremor in my body was unmissable the second I felt that solid wall of armour at my back. Then as he lowered his head enough to speak directly in my ear, I knew that my earlier question had been answered.

The witch had got to him.

She had done something to him, forced his demon to the surface and right now, one thing became obvious the second he spoke,

It was a demon that didn't like me.

Which is when I realised, there was always time for another 'oh shit' moment, and here it was, something that finally sank in the second he snarled down at me,

"Found at last, my little human."

CHAPTER TWO

EYES OF CRIMSON

The moment I found myself in this dangerous grasp, with a King I clearly didn't know anymore at my back, my eyes couldn't help but search out the only light in the room in what felt like an abyss of darkness.

Trice.

I hated myself for needing, in that moment, the comfort of a life that cared. The one person who gave a shit about my fate, as it was clear that the person who should have felt this way, now currently had my life firmly in his grasp. Because he wasn't being gentle with me, not by a long shot. Or was it just being made worse because this wasn't exactly the first time today I had found myself in this position with a demon's hands around my neck?

However, the moment I found Trice in the crowd, I saw that his intense gaze was locked on me and he looked so torn, I was almost worried that he would do something suicidal and challenge Lucius. So, I couldn't help but mouth silently at him,

'I'm okay.'

Of course, Lucius could feel this, seeing where his hand was placed, and I felt him press harder against me from behind as he looked down at my face. He then looked back up to see where my eyes had been before I was smart enough to lower them. The snarl of anger was felt penetrating through my body as it made his chest rumble. Which was when I couldn't help but whisper my first plea, one I had a feeling was going to be the first of many, with this tyrant King at my back,

"Please"

"At least you haven't lost the ability to please me, in both sight and sound," he growled low, now running a hand first across my belly and then up to my breasts. Breasts that were not only now covered in the sheer material of my dress but also being cupped by a hand of metal...a decisive move, where he was most definitely staking his claim.

"Behold at last, my troublesome little Mortal has been returned to me!" Lucius' booming demonic voice echoed out throughout the throne room and I couldn't help but notice that Trice grimaced before turning his head away in annoyance at his King's announcement. Meanwhile I flinched at the sound making Lucius grumble down at me,

"Easy, my Pet, for you won't get away from me quite so easily next time." I frowned wondering what he meant by this. Did he have a totally different memory as to what had happened between us in the Temple? Exactly what memories had the witch planted in his mind?

"And to ensure such, time for your leash once more, my little Mortal Pet," Lucius stated making me frown in question, which ended in wide eyes when his hand came to the front of me. This was when I saw the true nature of that statement was as literal as his words. Because the armour on his right hand started to turn from solid to a thick, oily liquid that dripped down from his fingers. It flowed from his fingertips in long streams that clung there, hanging like a rope and increasing in both length and thickness as more of his armour liquified adding to it. Then when it reached just an inch from the floor, it started to take shape, starting at the bottom as if it was being poured into an invisible mould.

This happened quickly and before long I could see a length of metal links that made up a chain of the likes I had never seen before. Its links looked more like that of a black metal spine that once belonged to some human sized fish, with each bone shaped section ending either side with hooks. Wicked looking spikes, which thankfully were curled inwards, so I assumed were not to cause damage to his 'Mortal Pet'. This was my hope anyway.

But it was little wonder why the very thought of it had me narrowing my eyes in outrage and this even more so when I was suddenly spun around to face him. Because finding him now holding out the last part of my leash in his hand, I could see what was attached to the end of it, this being of course...*the collar.* I could also see for myself now where the creation of it had been born from as the two shoulder pieces of his armour was what he chose to sacrifice to make it. Not his gauntlet like I first assumed, seeing as his hand had been bare when making it.

I became startlingly aware of his face staring down at me, when I felt the side of his talons raising my chin up so as I was forced to look in the cold eyes of my new Master. This was when he warned in a dark and dangerous tone,

"Cast your scowl elsewhere, Pet, before you receive your punishment for escaping me in front of an audience, instead of behind closed doors like I intend!" he snapped making my eyes widen in shock before I could hold back my secondary reaction when my scowl deepened. I also opened my mouth ready to tell him to go fuck himself when something in his eyes quickly stopped me. It was a flash of emotion that gave way for only a second to the grey blue beneath the blood, and in that moment, I couldn't help but feel as if he may have been communicating something deeper with me.

Besides, even if I had been seeing what I wanted to see and that fleeting moment between us had been nothing but foolish hope, then did I really want to see how far this version of Lucius would go? How far he would go to enslave me in front of his people, all for the sake of throwing sass and saving the face of my ego? The answer was no, I was not that stupid. So, I did as he said and lowered my gaze submissively, despite how hard that was to do, as inside my blood was boiling in rage.

"Good to know all my training was not lost in my absence," he said making me want to growl back at him, but I bit my lip to stop myself, something I think he knew as the bastard chuckled. Then I felt the cool, smooth metal as it was about to be placed around my neck, but something unexpected happened as he paused.

Then that was when I heard it...

A very angry demonic growl.

It was such a dangerous sound, that I couldn't help but flinch. Especially when it was joined by the grip he suddenly took hold on my chin as he lifted my face up to inspect it. This time when my eyes met his, they weren't scowling, but asking him a silent question. It was one however he answered without being prompted to do so by me, as his gaze was solely on my neck. A gaze that hardened in anger, with the ring of metal he had been about to place there, now hanging, at the ready in his grasp, the coil of the spine leash curled on the floor like a skeletal snake.

Then I felt his bare thumb run the length of my neck where he must have purposely made his gauntleted glove seep back, doing so to allow for a gentler touch. Something that he didn't know yet, but the hope this gesture gave me, felt like a lifeline.

"You're hurt, my little Šemšā?" This was said so quietly I swear I almost questioned it even being real, or whether my mind had simply conjured it up for the sake of my sanity. At the same time realisation flickered in his gaze as if he had just remembered something and again anger quickly took its place. Because this was when the comfort of both his touch and his words, came crashing down the second he spoke again, as if masking the soft words spoken before it,

"WHO DARES TOUCH WHAT BELONGS TO ME!" Lucius suddenly roared after first looking up over my head, something easily achieved due to the added height of his demon form. The room beyond instantly stilled and not even the sound of breathing could be heard, which was testament alone to how much his people obviously feared him. I started to turn around so I could see the moment I heard footsteps approach, but Lucius quickly put a stop to this, as he grasped my side and snarled down at me,

"No, you will stay where you are and keep your eyes where I want them, at my feet." I swallowed hard, hating receiving the harsh lash of his words. However, despite my bitter feelings, I did as I was told and continued to look down as I felt the man approach.

"As I said, the prison warden is awaiting your sentence, Šeš." He answered Lucius and I wondered at the name he had used for him or if it had been a name at all. As for the man, well, I still didn't know who he was, but at the very least, I recognised the voice as the one that I had believed was the King when first arriving here. The one who had wanted to see me executed.

Lucius growled at this and when I was certain he had turned his head I braved a glance up at the fake King. Which begged the question…*who was he to Lucius?* Was he some kind of stand in for Lucius for the time he spent topside? In fact, I was almost sure I had heard him mention how someone ruled in his place.

"BRING HIM TO ME!" Lucius roared suddenly, jerking me from my thoughts as the thunderous sound echoed throughout what could have been his entire kingdom. I could just imagine that the wave of fearful, demonic faces travelled much further than the ones in this room, as I wasn't the only one holding myself ridgid. Because, like them, I knew precisely what was about to happen and well, I didn't exactly relish the sight of an execution, despite the demon's crimes against me.

The only commotion in the vast space came from the guards as they dragged in the prisoner at the ready, I had a feeling he was about to lose a lot more than the cock I had teased Trice in saying I had rid him of. I knew when Lucius growled low and menacing, that without looking he was being dragged closer. Of course, it was also obvious by the sound of the demon begging for his life, doing so now by trying to twist the story to his advantage.

"Lies, it's all fucking lies! The bitch was trying to escape, wanting me to fuck her before she attacked me!" I sucked in a breath, raised my head up and opened my mouth about to defend myself when I felt pressure on my lips stopping me.

"You don't have to speak...for his memories will speak the truth for him...and I warn you, my Pet...*he'd better be fucking wrong,*" Lucius warned on another growl. Then, even against his wishes, I couldn't help but raise my head in defiance before I stated firmly,

"He is." This was said despite the metal thumb against my lips. Lucius' eyes sparked a brighter glow of crimson before he grabbed the back of my neck. Then he suddenly pulled my face closer to his own as he dipped his head, telling me from only an inch away,

"Then your reward will be that of an easier punishment,"

he told me, and I opened my mouth to speak. But thankfully I stopped the bite of my reply just in time when he raised a brow, doing so as if silently daring me to dare to push him. Then he got even closer to me and pushed me instead,

"I believe this is where you show your thanks and respect to your Master's generosity." I swear I was close to growling back at him and he knew it as I gritted my teeth and said,

"Thank you, Master." His grin was pure evil and that of a demonic sadist. I couldn't help but ask myself where my Lucius had gone. The one who softly played with my hair until I fell asleep in his arms. The one who indulged my geeky and admittedly, often childish hobbies when playing with Lego and such. The man who made a fuss of my cooking and danced with me as though I was the only person in a room full of hundreds. The man who picked our song, one called 'In case you didn't know' as a way to let me know just how much he cared about me. And the man who took care of me when I got drunk and playfully teased me about it in a sweet way the next morning. This man, the one who now looked lost to his demon, who had told me he loved me and called me his little Šemšā, his Khuba…

His little sun and his love.

Where had he gone?

"She still pleases me," he muttered with that grin still in place as if talking to himself. I couldn't help it, but his words made me close my eyes and turn my face away, making him grab my chin in a rough hold and warn,

"Although that can change, and you would do well remembering that!" he snapped before turning to the man at his side and telling him,

"Rape him of his memories," Lucius ordered all the while still with his grip on my chin, making me flinch in his hold at the crude word he used, making me hate the sound of it coming from his lips. I swear, I was close to tasting bile, that, or blood from biting the inside of my cheek so hard. Something I did just to stop myself from doing something stupid like openly challenging him.

Then the second he let go of me, I couldn't help but turn my face away, closing my eyes again. Something that thankfully, this time he gave me. However, I knew this was only because he had set his angry sights on someone else. The only grace this gave me was that I finally had some breathing space, even if it was only by him taking a step away from me. I just needed to think, and being so close to him like this, being dominated in this way was driving me closer and closer to panic. A useless emotion that I knew wouldn't help me in the slightest right now.

So, I took a deep and calming breath before I braved a look to my side, doing so in time to see Lucius grant a silent order with a nod of his head. This was before the roars of pain started. I couldn't help myself but look, doing so to find the back of the man I had assumed to be King now stood in front of him. He did so with two of the King's personal red guards holding the demon between them, fighting to hold him still.

The jailor's light grey skin now looked even paler, with his hard rock like flesh looking more like crumbling ash. Whatever Lucius' high-ranking subject was doing to him, it looked to be nearly killing him. His hand was in front of the demon's face, obviously with no contact needed other than the inch between them. The hand of what currently looked like a sorcerer, as I could just about see the streams of difference in the air, like when you see the haze of heat blurring the landscape ahead.

Whatever he was doing, the demon soon stopped roaring in pain, and became more like someone lured into a trance or zombie like state of mind. One controlled by a new puppet master, only instead of strings pulling at his limbs, they were pulling at his mind. This was obviously how the man was extracting that part of the demon's memories and I had to wonder, was he stealing them completely or just accessing them?

My answer came shortly after but not before I witnessed a reaction I had not expected, as the moment the man broke contact with the demon, he burst out laughing. I had positioned myself to try and not make it too obvious that I was looking, able only to do so by the higher advantage on the raised throne area. One I had when glancing down over my shoulder at them.

"Well, your little Mortal can certainly be called resourceful if nothing else," the man said still with humour lacing his words, and it didn't take a genius to know where that humour came from, not considering how I had managed to survive the attack. Hell, even without a bedpan in hand to repeatedly hit over the head with, there were too many things to count about that fight that someone would have found funny when looking back.

The demon slumped forward, obviously unconscious for the moment and only prevented from being sprawled out across the floor by the two guards that still had hold of him. I felt Lucius' eyes come back to me and he simply nodded to the floor, as a way to remind me where he wanted my gaze. Then he simply growled out another order, only this time, it wasn't one aimed at me.

"Show me!" The snarl of his words had me doubting that Lucius would find what happened quite as amusing as his subject did. This thought had me sneaking another glance to see how it would work, and doing so just in time to see Lucius as he reached out and grabbed his subject behind the back of his neck. This brought him a stumbled step towards his King, and once secured in his rough hold, they both closed their eyes.

It was in this moment that a silent sigh of relief slipped through my lips, as for the first time it looked as if my Lucius was back in the same room as me. Well, even more so if it hadn't been for the inky veins shadowing his features and the massive body of armour, of course. But there was just something about Lucius closing his eyes that gave him a more human quality. Almost a vulnerable side that was never seen when he was awake. Although, that was before Hell, as at the moment then the word *vulnerable* was the very last one I would have used to describe such a being.

No, Lucius right now was as hard as stone with, unfortunately, what looked to have a heart to match, and a sheer will that could bend iron. But whilst he was busy looking into the memories of what happened in the cell, I chanced a quick glance at Trice. I knew I shouldn't, but in my weakness I couldn't help but find his intense eyes staring back into my own. I also couldn't help but wince when I saw the pain there, pain combined with a rage that was only just being kept in check. This was why I felt the need to do anything in my power to stop him making a grave mistake...*emphasis on the word grave*.

'I'm okay,' I said silently, mouthing the words I knew he could read from my lips when he frowned before turning his face away. He also added to this with a look of disappointment before closing his eyes as if he couldn't stand to see me being treated this way...*but if only he knew.* Should I have told him the truth...should I have told him everything? Maybe now seeing this he would have understood it all a little better, or maybe it would have only made it worse. I didn't know and the hopelessness I felt at the unknown was eating away at me. I just wanted it all to be over and to find Lucius alone so I could discover the truth of what my future held with him. But as for right now, well, it simply felt like I didn't know him.

Not. At. All.

A sinister and dangerous growl was all I needed to warn me

that it was over, and Lucius had seen all he had needed to. I knew this when my quick glance showed Lucius' furious steps taking him directly down to the jailor. Then he grabbed him by his left horn, using it to lift his head up enough to swiftly knee him in the face. I quickly discovered this wasn't effective enough to do damage but that it was only done as a means to wake him up. Clearly, Lucius wanted him conscious for this next part, but then it wasn't all he wanted as his next order was aimed at me,

"Turn around my Mortal and watch the hand of death claim what you were unable to do," he said just as the jailor started to shake his head, now coming around from his unconscious state quickly. As for me, I did as he said after releasing a deep sigh, knowing that there was no getting away from it or the sight of Lucius' brutal revenge. And when I did, the demon shot a look at me and then to the sight of his angry, tyrant King looming over him like death uncloaked. Unsurprisingly, he started struggling to get away.

"No, no! I didn't do anything! I didn't…" Lucius grabbed hold of his horn once more and twisted it enough that it forced his head to the side in what looked like a painful way, making him grimace. However, Lucius' gauntleted hand simply tightened and twisted further before he got closer to him informing him in a dangerous tone,

"Ah, but you did Drude, you just don't remember your crimes, for I had them stolen from you." I sucked in a deep breath the second I discovered what kind of demon he was…*he was the same as Dante.*

Although my guess was that he was a different breed, as he obviously fed from sexual deviancy not just from the dreams of others. The Drude looked immediately to the man who had rid him of those memories. This made Lucius' right hand man smirk back at the same time tapping two fingers to the side of his head, doing so to indicate just exactly where those memories were being kept now. The demon's eyes widened before he shot a panicked look back up at his King.

"My crimes?" he asked in confusion, but it was no use as this was when Lucius nodded for his guards to let him go. Lucius then lowered himself even closer to the demon that was still on his knees and at the same time taking hold of the other horn, so they were both in his unyielding grasp. Once in his hold, Lucius answered him with dangerous calm that was viciously snarled at the end,

"The crime of...*touching what is mine!*" He ended this with a tighter grip before a quick twist in opposite directions was all it took for Lucius to rip both horns right out of the top of his face. This left the demon both howling in pain and with two large gaping holes above his eyes that quickly drenched the rest of his agonized face in demon blood. The demon was then left to slump forward with his shaking hands going to his missing horns. Lucius used this as a chance to issue a warning to the rest of his people.

"Let this be a warning to all as you witness what happens to those who TOUCH WHAT BELONGS TO ME!" He roared this last part as he held the two dripping horns out by his sides, before he cast them angrily aside, making me jump as they skidded along the floor behind him, only stopping at the first step. The demon had hopelessly tried to use this opportunity to try and crawl away, no doubt praying that this would be the end of his Master's wrath. But then the second Lucius' eyes focused on the demon's movements in trying to escape him, they narrowed despite the grin that lay beneath the surface. It was obvious to all in the room that the impending death of the demon jailor was one that excited their King. Because just when I thought that this was punishment enough, Lucius started walking slowly towards the grey mass of muscles trying in vain to get away. Long black, bloodied streaks along stark white marble became a gruesome pathway for Lucius to walk along to get to his prey. But the blood from where his horns had once been that were now being discarded like trash behind him, soon became the least of his problems. Because Lucius soon reached him with nothing more than a few determined strides and was stood over him. He then wasted no time before reaching down to get a firm grasp on the roots of his white hair, using this punishing hold to haul him to his knees. This made the Drude try to twist free, but he wasn't given long to continue to try as Lucius dipped his head and let his demon roar out,

"THE MORTAL IS MINE!"

After this Lucius raised back to his full height so he could deliver the killing blow, which started when his armour became liquid once more. Only this time it flowed down his arm with speed, leaving it bare in three seconds as it became that of a thick and deadly black sword in his hand. One that in his grasp became so much more than just a weapon…

It was a message.

A message delivered as he raised the sword high for all his people to see what happened to those that defied him and touched what was his. A killing blow that came quickly after letting go of the demon's hair for a mere whisper of time. The sword grasped in both his hands before their King plunged it straight down into the back of the demon's neck so that it travelled the full length of his spine.

The dying roar of my would-be rapist didn't last long as Lucius speared him down the centre as if making him ready to be put on a roasting spit. But then he let go of the sword and let the very dead Drude fall face forward with an echoing crack upon the marble. After this he turned to face me and with his bare right hand now held behind him, he walked back up the steps towards me. I watched open mouthed and in shock as the hilt of his black sword, one that was stuck out of the demon's dead, hardened flesh, started to reform.

It slithered from its victim and snaked along the white marble quickly with the sole purpose of returning back to its Master. It did this by reaching up to his awaiting fingertips as though it was being reunited with its body. Once there it continued to flow back up his arm until by the time his feet hit the top of the steps, the last drops of the black liquid was back in place, and reformed once more as the solid plates of his armour.

After this he came straight to me, and said in a stern voice,

"Now, that is how you kill a Stone Drude." And yep, one look at the guy and he was right, that would pretty much do it. After this he grasped my chin to turn my face away from the gruesome sight. One the growing pool of black blood was creating with a Yin Yang effect on the once pristine white floor.

But soon my vision of black and white was gone and a sinister depth coloured my world once more with,

Eyes of Crimson.

CHAPTER THREE

MORTAL PET

"I think my attempt at killing Drude days are over," I muttered before stopping myself, as my hands flew to my lips too late. However, instead of the backlash I had been expecting, he simply raised a brow and I swear I even saw his lips twitch slightly in what I could only hope for was amusement.

"Something that shouldn't be a problem for you in the future and to ensure such…" He paused, before looking down at the discarded chains of my new reality and opening a fist so they obeyed the silent demand. Meaning they shot from the floor in a flash of movement and were clutched in his hand before he continued with his intentions,

"Time for your collar and a fucking leash…*one I should have tied you to years ago!*" After Lucius had pretty much growled this at me, I sucked in a violent breath as I questioned just how close to the edge this game he played was built on a foundation of truth? Just how many words spoken were ones he had always wanted to say but felt too restrained to do so?

I knew Lucius liked control. I knew he was a dominant lover, as well as being the one who liked to call all the shots. And for the most part, I allowed him, for the simple fact that he knew his own world far better than I ever could. Facts I was well aware of, as I was far from numb to the situation around me, even if right now, I wished for it. Because the same could be said for this world, a place I suspected he had to rule with more than just an iron fist but one that held the Venom of God.

"Throw that shit stain out!" Lucius snapped making me jump.

"Well, I must say, I didn't know what was more entertaining, her encounter with him or the execution because of it," the man to his right said with a chuckle, one that died the second Lucius snarled angrily at him before issuing a warning,

"Careful Šeš, for ridding him of life still hasn't cooled my temper in discovering the one who put her there," he said making it clear who he blamed, making the man scoff before telling him,

"And what would you have had me do, allow a snake to lie in wait in your bed, when my belief was justified?" he braved saying in return. I frowned and it was one that only barely matched Lucius', for his was more of a scowl that could have stripped a being of his courage in a heartbeat. Telling me this man was either suicidal or he was more powerful than I knew.

"No, I would have chained her to it!" Lucius snapped back in reply to his question, one that was challenged once more,

"She was believed to be in no danger at the time, a prison that—"

"A prison she was in by your command, one you had no place to make!" Lucius growled back cutting him off by putting him in his place. But whoever the identity of the man was, it was clear he was someone high enough up in the rankings not to feel threatened by Lucius as he argued further,

"And once again, as I said earlier, the reason being for such action was she carries the witch's Hex." Lucius snarled angrily before releasing a sigh of frustration and then ordering me in a stern yet restrained tone,

"Turn around, my Pet." I did as he said, and the moment I looked up to take in the crowd, he barked out a snap of an order,

"Eyes down."

I don't know why this was said, but had to question if it was because he had noticed me looking at Trice before? Did he know something or was jealous? I hoped not, as I didn't think that would mean good things for either of us. And although I knew Lucius wouldn't hurt me, I couldn't yet make that same claim for my friend.

So, after doing as he ordered, I heard the sound of metal clattering to the floor as he had obviously let go of the collar and leash for a second time. I felt my hair being swept off my back and positioned over one shoulder for him to be able to see the Hex for himself. Two things happened after this, and that was a hiss of air being sucked through gritted teeth followed by the rumbling of a growl. A furious sound that became the polar opposite of the gentle touch that followed as his fingertips outlined the marks the witch had made.

Again, *it gave me hope.*

"So now you see why she ended up in your prison," the other man said, and without being allowed to look at him, I could only just make out the sight of him leaning casually against one of the pure white pillars. It was one of many that framed the higher platform, showcasing the importance of who sat upon the throne of bones, of what I guessed was enemies conquered.

Lucius growled low again and snarled,

"You believed me responsible for having this Hex cast?"

"I gathered you still had the use of your own witch and it is a Summoning Hex after all...besides, I think you will agree, Šeš that it has the stench of the witch you had me hunting all over it." He said, calling him that Šeš name again, that was pronounced like you would say 'ceasefire'. But it surprised me to discover that he had this person, whoever he may be, hunting the witch, and I hated to admit it but there was obviously so much I still didn't know when it came to Lucius.

"It was the witch," Lucius admitted making the man then ask,

"Question remains now is why would the witch bother to Hex this mortal girl, who you yourself has claimed is nothing more than a favourite pet of yours?" I stiffened at his words. Lucius also felt it as he still had his hand exploring my back and I swear he could hear my heart pounding in my chest. Lucius' hand skimmed down my back until getting to my waist and giving it a squeeze. After this seemingly tender move I couldn't help but wonder if he was trying to reassure me without words? After all, we had been in this position once before, where he had to pretend not to care in hopes of saving me.

Was this what all this was now?

It was starting to look that way more and more each minute. After all, I couldn't forget the note I found in the basket of food telling me to 'play along'. And well, other than Trice, no one else knew I was a Princess other than the man at my back comforting me with his gentle touch.

I continued to try and convince myself that this was the case, despite the pain his next words inflicted.

"The witch does so to toy with me no doubt...besides, well trained submissive slaves like this one are hard to come by, and I grow tired of the thought of training another, especially when she fits my cock so well." Lucius said as he stroked the top of my head, like…well like a damn pet! Gods, but how I really hoped this was all for show.

"Yes, she must be a very good fucking fit for your cock considering you just near tore fucking Hell apart to find her, and as for training, well then I wouldn't praise the bitch for that too much seeing as she managed to run from you," he said making Lucius snap and he did so by leaving my back in a heartbeat. I sneaked a look to the side to find in that second of leaving me, Lucius now had the man's neck in his grasp and had him pinned to the column he had been stood by with his feet off the ground.

"Be careful, my Šeš, for no one is permitted to speak of my slave in that way other than her Master! Do I make myself clear?!" The man who he had strangely named the same thing he had called Lucius, growled back and his fangs lengthened dangerously before he snarled like a wild beast, all calmness a thing of the past. But Lucius tightened his hold and banged the man's head against the column as his wings expanded out in a show of strength. I quickly looked to the sea of demons to find them all watching this scene play out with great interest. I turned back to do the same after first granting a brief, confused look at Trice who, like everyone else, was obviously questioning the actions of his King.

"Yield to a greater power, Šeš, and remember your fucking place, for I am not the King you once knew!" Lucius threatened making the man grimace in pain as Lucius obviously squeezed his neck harder. But before long he lowered his gaze and his fangs retracted, showing his submission. And well, if there was one thing this scene told me, then it was that whoever this person was, despite his actions, he meant something to Lucius. Because I knew that had it been any other, then Lucius wouldn't have thought twice about just killing him.

After this show of compliance, Lucius let him go and it was a show of strength when the man didn't just drop to his knees as the marks Lucius had made on his flesh looked like burns. However, he just twisted his neck a little and rolled a shoulder as if trying to brush off the memory of his King's touch.

"Now you will tell me of this attack but first..." Lucius paused his demand with what I was soon to find out was in place of another. But this was after walking back over to me and spinning me once more until I was facing him. Then he nodded to the floor and continued his demands,

"...Pick it up." My eyes widened when looking up at the cruelty in his eyes before he added in a hard tone,

"Now"

I swear but if I could have clenched my teeth any harder, I would have felt them cracking. Because the impulse to tell him to fuck off was getting harder to hold back by the second. Yet despite this, I also knew that being hot headed right now wasn't going to help me and it certainly wasn't worth the five seconds of satisfaction it would achieve. I needed to be smart and right now that meant doing as I was told. So, with this mindset, I looked down and started to lower, when suddenly, he grabbed my arm and hauled me back up.

"When you lower to your knees before me, I want your eyes on my own, just like I trained you...now again!" he snarled in annoyance and I gritted my teeth once more, refraining yet again from lashing out at him like I wanted to at being treated like a damn dog! But then being smart about this meant a chance of discovering the purpose of why he was acting this way. The details of which I hoped were explained to me very, very soon.

So, I did as he demanded of me, which meant that when I lowered this time, I did so without taking my eyes from his. And my reward for this was that crimson glow that told me he liked what he saw, despite the charade he was supposed to be playing. I swallowed hard at both the heated gaze that held nothing but carnal promises and the knowledge that there was his Kingdom at my back. Because right then I felt about as far away from the title of his Queen as I could possibly get. Something that left a bitter taste in my mouth seeing as he was the one purposely putting me there. It was messing with my emotions, as trying to rationalise every minute that ticked by was becoming harder to do with every seemingly heartless action he made against me.

Once I was down, he nodded to the demonic looking leash and the second I glanced at it, he tutted, flicked two fingers up and mouthed,

'Eyes'

So, I braved narrowing my own briefly, before feeling out with my hand for the leash, and the second I found it, yelped in pain as it pricked my skin. I wanted to growl at that arrogant raised brow of his, the one that silently challenged me. But instead of cursing his name, I concentrated on the degrading task at hand. Which meant that without looking at what I was doing, I felt around for the collar, thinking this was a safer choice…*despite knowing what it was destined for.*

"*Oww,*" I muttered making him grin sadistically before flicking two fingers, telling me to rise. But then the moment I was up, he took the collar from my bleeding hand and started to stretch it, making it slightly bigger and doing so with startling ease. Then he put his hand through the metal loop, so it was resting at his wrist, which freed up his heavy gauntleted hands. This was done so he could gently shift my hair before he placed the collar around my neck. I knew he locked it at the back the second I heard a click and his hands lifted from my neck.

I raised my hand up to touch it, feeling the inch-thick ring along with the weight of it now laying heavily against my skin. However, I now noticed that due to it being stretched it rested lower than my injury so it would not rub against where the prison guard had tried to strangle me to death...*which meant he cared.*

After this he picked up the leash, obviously not fearing injury like I had, and wrapped a section around his fist that thankfully was enough to cause tension and lift the dangerous spikes away from touching my body. Then he ordered,

"Come, my troublesome little Mortal, it is time to sit by your Master's feet." I swear my eyes nearly popped out of my head at this. But he had turned towards his throne and after a slight tug, I was prompted to follow behind him, like the slave he claimed me to be. But then he continued on a few steps beyond his throne and I was left frowning in question as to what he was planning next? However, one question soon morphed into another as he reached up with his free hand so he could fist the length of crimson material behind his throne. And it was now that it finally hit me where I had seen that image at its centre before...

Lucius' sigil.

How the hell had I missed that from when I first arrived at this Gods forsaken place! I flinched when he suddenly tore it down and dragged the length of it behind him back to his throne where he dumped the mound of it at the foot of his colossal horned seat. Then it became clear his intentions as he nodded down to it and so everyone could hear, he ordered,

"You can sit there, my slave, for we wouldn't want you going numb before your punishment, now would we?" Then he grinned and welcomed the room of sniggers that hit my eyes along with the wave of sound. But then, with a brief look, I could see there were at least three men in the room not looking as amused as the rest.

The McBain brothers.

I didn't know where Vern and Gryph had been before, but they were just stepping up behind Trice, and I could see from here when Vern started whispering something in his brother's ear.

"I said sit!" Lucius bellowed suddenly making me jump before doing as he asked. Meaning that had I had no other option than to lower to the pile of material, that I had to say, was far better than the cold, hard white marble that seemed to mimic the King who owned it.

Although saying that, if he had truly been as cold and hard as he appeared to his people, why care about my comfort at all? And admittedly, had he not been acting like an asshole I wanted to kick in the balls, then I would have preferred his lap. But as things stood, then the reasons for his behaviour had better be good, for I was definitely close to losing my shit, King in Hell or not!

So instead of being allowed to do what I wanted to do, which was slapping him before just walking out of there, I swallowed the urge and sat at his feet like a Gods be damned Pet! And I did this hating every fucking second of it! I was a Draven for Gods sake! I sat at no man's feet and doing so, well…it went so very far beyond the ingrained self-respect in my soul, that I found myself fisting my hands just to prevent myself from lashing out. Something that would grant only a moment of satisfaction and become nothing more than a lapse in weakness and stupidity, for the outcome would not have been worth it.

However, fisting my hand in anger was what made me remember that my hand was still bleeding as I felt the blood trickling down my palm. So, I looked down at the small cut on the pad of my index finger and raised it to my mouth to suck.

Damn leash!

At the same time, I looked at the man who obviously was someone important in Lucius' world and I had to question, was this who he had chosen to rule in his absence? I was sure I remembered Lucius saying something about this once. It would make sense seeing as I had found him sitting on Lucius' throne when I was first marched through those doors. And after what he had said, it was also obvious that at the time I was being thrown into a cell, Lucius had been out there looking for me himself.

Now all I needed was a name to go with the annoyingly handsome face that had accused me of being a witch. He was dressed the same as when I had first arrived, in his cloak style jacket that reached the floor in points at his feet. At first I had thought it was just some kind of black material, but with the shimmer of silver I could now see, then I realised it was from some kind of scaled animal skin of the likes I had never seen. And most likely I never would as it was no doubt from some poor unfortunate demonic beast that had seen his death at the end of the sword I could now see attached to his side.

It was one that was distinctively curved and deadly, being one I recognised instantly as a shamshir. In fact, it was a sword I knew well as my father had many variations in his collection seeing as it was a Persian sword. Its name even meant 'lion's fang' in the Persian language, no doubt due to its distinct shape. It was a one-handed, curved sword that featured a slim blade and had almost no taper until its very tip. I also knew from experience that you had to be very skilled to fight well with it, as it was normally used for slashing an unarmoured opponent.

This was because it wouldn't do much damage against one dressed in armour and whilst the tip could be used for thrusting, the drastic curvature of blade made accuracy more difficult. Hence the need for skill, which was just a hunch here, but I gathered that whoever Lucius had trusted to rule in his place, would no doubt have that particular skill set in spades.

But looking at that sword and then back at his face, I could now see the connection, as his vessel most definitely looked to have Persian descent. Like the warm bronze skin that covered an abundance of muscles, and a shade darker than my sun-kissed tan. It was also the dark hair that was styled back and brushed the tops of his shoulders in its length. The almond shape to his olive green and amber eyes, that spoke of his vessel's heritage. But then, like Lucius, his new vessel would have changed in time after his rebirth, so the way a person looked often meant nothing.

However, it was when I was studying his chosen right-hand man, that I felt a pair of crimson eyes on me. My first clue to this was when the man in question paused what he was saying and looked at me. I then felt the slight tug at my neck and was forced to move with it, which brought me closer to Lucius. Meaning that I was forced to my knees when at the same time he gave me his reason why,

"Your blood is not your own, Pet…*But. It. Is. Mine."* Lucius said, emphasizing the last four words with every tug on the leash that forced me a knee step closer. This continued, forcing me forward until I found myself against his armoured leg, one that mirrored the rest of the layers of plated metal that covered his body. Thankfully, the bend of his knee was the only place that held a dangerous point, so I was spared that uncomfortable experience.

But then he snapped me out of staring at his leg as he held out his hand, obviously expecting something of me and because I wasn't quick enough, he told me,

"I suggest you give me what I demand of you before I decide to slit a vein and quench a much deeper thirst." I slowly looked up at him with wide eyes, at the same time swallowing hard. But I found myself wondering if he would, which was why I was almost tempted to push him. But despite being curious to see what would happen I stopped myself knowing the precarious position my open defiance would put him in.

Because forcing him into action wasn't the wisest decision just then. Hence why I did as I was told, playing the good little pet and placed my bleeding hand in his. One that was quickly lifted to his mouth and before I found my finger in there, he simply ordered,

"Continue." This I soon realised was said for the man next to us to continue in what he was saying before my actions took Lucius' attention away from him. Which meant that during this conversation I also found myself becoming a little snack for a Vampire King. But despite how pissed off I was, I still had to force back the moan of pleasure it created as he sucked my finger into his mouth and pulled what little blood he could from the small wound. I felt the heat invade my cheeks as I was made to sit there squirming and staring out at the crowd, trying everything now to ignore the hungry eyes of hundreds. But it was mainly the pair of angry eyes that was trying to catch my own in the crowd that I forced myself to ignore, as Trice was making it his mission to be obvious.

But then something in this must have occurred to Lucius as he suddenly let go of my finger, before licking at the wound and sealing it. Then he stood and with one swift action, he circled a length of the spiked leash around his hand before pulling it taut, so I had no choice but to regain my feet. Then he declared loudly,

"That little taste of you put me in mind for something stronger, for the blood between your legs will do nicely." I gasped at his crass announcement at the same time he yanked hard enough that I fell into his side. Then he grasped my chin, to force my head back, making me look up at him. This ended up putting us only inches apart as he too had lowered his own head, at least enough that his greater height would allow. The two massive horns at his back, that his wings were attached to, created a looming and sinister shadow over me. I therefore held my breath, as in that brief, dark moment, I thought he was going to kiss me. Especially as his crimson eyes burned into mine, the scorching heat in them having nothing to do with Hell, but only for his desire to have me.

But then, at the last second, he turned my face away so he could snarl into my cheek before biting it. Thankfully, he didn't break the skin, but it stung all the same. However, he then made a show of licking it, and groaning, telling the entire room,

"Mmm, I am going to enjoy biting into this flesh once more." Then without taking his intense gaze from mine, he said,

"Šeš, you have the throne."

After this he let me go suddenly, making me nearly stumble forward and only catching myself in time before falling flat on my face. And well, let's just say that I didn't exactly need to add any more humiliation to the shame train which was full and on its way to mortification town…or should that be the bloody town, one where Lucius was planning on sitting my ass on his dining table, slitting a vein in between my legs and making an erotic meal out of me. And more startling still, what did that say about me if that idea was making me wet?

But then, with a pull of my leash I soon snapped out of it. I had no choice but to start walking as he tugged me along behind him. And despite how demeaning it was, I also knew it could have been worse. I could have been led out of there on my hands and knees, like the Mortal Pet he claimed me to be. Although, when he reached the bottom step, he kicked one of the horns aside and ordered,

"I want those horns dipped in gold and added to my throne before my return, for I have Mortal Pet to reclaim…" He paused and after another tug for me to follow him,

He added dangerously…

"…And a punishment to deliver."

CHAPTER FOUR

HARD PUSH

Lucius walked me down the centre with his wings folded tight to the back of his body. The longer lengths were crossed at the bottom, so they remained raised enough from the floor, stopping them from trailing behind him. I also couldn't help but notice that when the sea of demons parted for us, Trice needed to be jerked backwards. This was thanks to Gryph as he grabbed a fistful of his shirt and yanked him back. Thankfully, this stopped him from doing anything stupid as I could see for myself that Trice had instinctively placed his hand on the hilt of his sword as we went past.

However, I wasn't the only one to see this, as Lucius' keen eye first looked to Trice and then back to the place the angry looking McBain brother had his gaze rooted to...*which just so happened to be troublesome little me.* Lucius snarled angrily their way before snapping back at me,

"Eyes on your fucking feet, girl!" I did as I was told, as I was led from the room, with the last image on my mind being

Gryph and the slowly healing Vern whispering to their brother. This was no doubt trying to convince him not to do something suicidal. And if one thing this little scene told me, it was that I needed to explain things with Trice, and soon. Something that was obviously depending on which Lucius I found myself with once we were behind closed doors. Because I didn't want to get Trice hurt, but I also knew that for me to say nothing, could potentially be more dangerous as his temper rose, and with it, his angry King's.

Gods, but talk about being in between a rock and a hard place, this was more like being between brimstone and a Hell's fortress. One he was walking me through right now and the moment we were on the other side, he gave me a slight tug, pulling me closer to his side. This was so he had the slack of the leash enough to push a pair of double doors open with both hands, making the armour at his shoulders lift and I jumped at the echoing crack of sound.

Oh yeah, *Lucius was pissed.*

These doors were different to the ones I had walked through when first entering his fortress, and it made me wonder how I had missed them when I first arrived. They were situated on the left-hand side and were at least twenty feet high, with each side decorated in a crude puzzle of broken black glass. It was also the ones that before they opened, I had just made out the image of a tall black shard. A symbol I wouldn't fully understand until I would reach my destination. However, it sort of resembled the building itself, only from the outside as it had looked like a group of giant shard shaped skyscrapers all linked together. This was by a network of impossibly high narrow walkways that from the ground had looked more like veins feeding the largest building we were inside now.

Although, once through these doors, it showed the true nature of just how high the buildings were, as it had opened up to a gigantic spiral staircase that was so high you couldn't see the top. Wow, I guess Hell didn't believe in elevators. But then one look at his wings folded at his back, then this wasn't exactly surprising seeing as most wouldn't need them. Jeez, just looking at the number of steps, and I knew it would most likely take an average person a whole day to get up them, maybe more.

But seeing as Hell wasn't exactly brimming over with 'average people' then I guess this wasn't ever a problem. And well, it would most certainly help in keeping low ranking demons in their place, for the demonic opulence wasn't lost on me, even if it was only a staircase.

The startling white marble extended from the throne room into this space that was a mixture of smooth and rough, with the walls being a collection of jagged shards. These all reached upwards like white pointed fingers overlapping the layers beneath. This space was then framed by a giant spiral of highly polished stairs that weren't exactly conventional. In fact, they looked more like shards that had fallen away from the rest of the walls and stopped when they got to a ninety-degree angle. This then created a bridged effect as they slightly overlapped forming a spiral of ledges that created the staircase.

It was utterly stunning.

The space itself would have been big enough to get an eighty-foot yacht inside, with room to spare. I also quickly noted that when looking up the centre, it looked as if you were stood at the mouth of a colossal beast. One that was about to swallow you whole with an endless mass of spiralled teeth. This was because there was no handrail to speak of. And even though I was not the type to be scared of heights, I just knew the higher up I travelled, the more that fear would develop into something that had the potential to cripple me.

Which was why I couldn't help myself when I told him,

"If you expect me to take the stairs, I will be ten years older and completely grey from fear by the time I reach the top." He glanced back at me and I could just make out the slight smirk that graced his lips. Then he rotated his arm, making the leash tighten as it looped his forearm once more. This action suddenly jerked me forward until I had no choice but to go falling into him, making me land hard against his chest. I tentatively looked up at him with wide eyes, needing now to tip my head right back due to the increased foot in height. I also found myself holding my breath as he slowly reached down and banded an arm around my waist before lifting me up. Then I let out a little yelp in surprise when his wings expanded out to their full width and he told me,

"Don't worry, Pet, I don't plan on letting you wait that long for your punishment." This statement quickly took my breath away, both from his words and his actions, as he finished his sentence by abruptly launching us straight up into the air. His hold on me then tightened as his wings tilted us slightly so they were at the right angle to manipulate the air beneath them. At the same time I was still left with my mouth open on a silent scream of shock, despite it being something I had been expecting, thanks to his slight warning.

But then this whole experience was like watching a horror slasher movie. The type when the nervous looking girl goes searching around the abandoned house asking stupidly, 'is anyone there?'. Then the moment the music changes, you know something is coming. Meaning that every corner she walks around, you then expect the fright to jump out and catch your breath with a scream. That was exactly what being in Hell was like, only instead of lasting minutes as a scene in a movie, it was...*All. The. Freaking. Time!*

Although, right now I had to say that being like this, in Lucius' arms and with him holding me so tight, it felt like I had finally been rescued from this awful place. Of course, it helped that he no longer held that cruel glint in his eyes. As all I had to do now was close my eyes and pretend that I actually had my Vampire King back, which was precisely what I did.

But then as the air pushing back against my face eased, I knew my brief moment of comfort was at an end, something that was confirmed when I had no choice but to open my eyes again. And the second I did had me nearly screaming once again, as I was left looking down the height of a skyscraper. It was so high that if I had still been stood at the bottom then I would have looked like an ant!

I was about to question why he stopped, clinging onto him until my muscles ached and my fingers actually started to hurt. This was because I found nothing soft for them to grip on to, having only the hard edges of his amour to anchor myself to. I instantly started to miss the tee and jean's version of Lucius I usually had to cling onto but then like this…well, he couldn't have been further from those fond memories, as they were oceans apart.

"Holy shit!" I shouted when the fear got too much to ignore. This made the sadistic bastard chuckle, only when coming from his demon it sounded deeper and more like some beastly purr. I tightened my limbs around him and braved another look down only to find that the staircase had come to an end. The last fallen shard had met with a large platform and one that led to an arched open doorway. An archway that was created by two thicker shards creating an upturned V shape that crossed at the top. It was so big that you could have driven a bus through there. This was the same as the other doorways, ones that I could now see were intermittently situated down the spiral of stairs. It didn't take a genius to assume that these archways must have led to different parts of the castle. However, the one closest to the top was only a few invisible steps away from the hovering form of Lucius and I, and being that it was the very last one, it marked the end of the staircase.

I looked up and saw that at least another hundred feet above me was where the top of the building started to narrow and taper off into the tip of the shard. Its walls were more jagged and dangerous looking, as the cluster of deadly spikes got thicker.

"I have no intention of letting you go," Lucius informed me in response to my crying out in fear, and on hearing his words, I allowed myself the slight shudder at the double meaning I found in them. I didn't know if he had felt it or not, as after this his wings simply forced us closer to the edge. Then when close enough he simply stepped onto it, folding his wings the moment only one full foot was applying weight. This meant that I couldn't help but hold my breath, because despite trusting him, in my mind he was still far too close to the edge when he decided his wings were no longer needed…not even keeping them at the ready for a 'just in case' scenario.

"I guess I should be glad you're not clumsy and in danger of dropping me then," I grumbled under my breath and of course, he heard it because he replied on a rumble,

"Dropping you wouldn't be a problem, Pet…" He paused a second before he actually dropped me, making me cry out in surprise. Thankfully, I landed on my feet and watched wide eyed as he walked passed me and at the sound of my annoyed huff, he looked slightly behind. Then after he shifted a wing to the side to be able to see me, he finished his sentence,

"…not when I still have you on a leash." Then to emphasise these words, he let the metal spine leash unravel from his arm. This caused part of its length to clatter to the floor and echo around the gigantic, hollowed out shard tower. I looked back over my shoulder at the invisible sound travelling down the staircase before I felt the tugging at my neck. This was naturally

to force me into action, and a harsh prompt to continue following him like I had done before our swift and frightening flight up here. I had to say that this was also where I was quickly hitting my limit, despite my hurried steps to follow him. Rushing now so he couldn't pull again on the leash forcing me to match his pace, which admittedly was more like jogging.

The moment I caught up with him, he granted me a brief look over the side of his shoulder, looking mildly entertained with me trying to keep up with his long strides. I also noticed that he took this into account when holding the spiked leash, keeping it taut and on a short length so it couldn't catch on my skin. Was this done to protect me from it or to keep me close? I couldn't decide, but I did know that when we walked under the archway and he turned that indifferent gaze forward once more, this was when I'd had enough of playing the guessing game.

So, I reached out to him and grabbed his arm, being mindful of the spikes in his armour. The pressure caused him to take notice and he paused long enough to look down at his arm to find my hand there.

"Lucius, please… I can't stand this any…" I started to say in what I knew was a pleading tone, one that had no effect on him at all, when he quickly cut me off,

"You will do well in remembering your place, for you will touch what I tell you to touch, now come!" Lucius snapped, tearing his arm from my hold, quickly putting me in my place. My eyes widened as I stumbled a step and my mouth dropped in shock before that tendril of dread started to weave its way back around my heart. For it was clear now that I had been wrong. Lucius hadn't been putting on a show at all. For if he had, then where were all the people to witness it now?

Because up here, at the very top of one of his towers, there was no one around us left to fool, other than that of my foolish heart. One that had stupidly held on to the hope that this had all been an act of some kind and as soon as we were alone, then the old Lucius would come back to me. A man who seemed so far gone, I worried if I would ever have a chance at getting him back again!

In that moment, I will be honest, I had never wanted to cry so badly as I had since first setting foot in this Gods' forsaken place. But my fears had been right, the witch must have got hold of him and somehow made him forget who he really was. But if this was so, then the only thing that didn't make sense was why had he been hunting me? And in his right-hand man's words, tearing up the entirety of Hell to find me. Why did he want me so badly and why did he think that I was his Mortal Pet?

Had she planted fake memories or something?

Gods, but there were just too many questions and unfortunately, from the looks of things, Lucius was going to be the very last person who was willing to answer them. Which also meant that at some point I would have no choice but to try and escape him...if something like that was even possible?

Because I knew one thing, that staying here and facing I don't know how long as some mortal sex slave he cared little about, wasn't going to save his people, or those I held dear to me, *Lucius included*. But then one look at the new space he led me into and the startled gasp that escaped became the backdrop song of impossibility and astonishment.

How in the Gods was I ever to escape such a place?

This new panic was settling in deep and growing by the second all from the sight that faced me now. The long and terrifyingly narrow walkway was one of many and one that I had seen from below when first entering this dark, sinister castle. I remembered thinking then that they looked like veins connecting organs to the heart of the building we were now leaving. Because this was when I started to understand that the main building I had first entered, had been nothing more than a colossal tower of stairs and an impressive throne room beyond. It almost acted like the lobby and was a way for you to get access to all the different sections of the castle. Doing so as we did now by the walkways that connected each of the surrounding buildings to the staircase we just came from.

Meaning that this was where I found myself now, walking towards one of those buildings. Only one look down and it was enough to make even the bravest being gulp. I didn't know how high up we were but seeing as it was the highest of the bridges then I couldn't help it when my legs turned to jelly. Especially when the bridge started to turn from the white marble stone that the inside of the staircase had been cut from, to a black ominous glass that wasn't quite opaque enough to see through.

The sight below was enough to turn my stomach and it didn't help that although fully encased from all sides and above, the cracks weren't exactly making the seven hundred foot drop any easier to cross. It looked like a giant hollowed out shard of black crystal, and the cracks that marred the carved walkway looked like lightning bolts had struck it and branded the glass. I almost expected to hear the pop, grinding, or thunder-like boom you would when ice starts to crack beneath your feet.

This was why I was suddenly frozen to the spot, unable to go any further. This was also why Lucius suddenly felt resistance on the leash as I pulled my weight back after first saving my neck the pain of doing so by holding onto the ring around my throat. Lucius looked behind him and I could see the scowl on his face as he was about to snap at me but then something shifted in his hard gaze when he took in my obvious fear.

"I...I can't." I told him with wide eyes, ones pleading and begging for even a shred of humanity and kindness. One that eventually came in the form of a growl of annoyance, before he stalked back to me and just before he looked about ready to throw me over his shoulder, I put my hands out in front of me to stop him,

"If you do that, you will kill me!" I shouted in panic as I nodded to his spiked armour that would have made me into an Amelia flavoured shish kebab! He rolled his eyes, and said,

"I am not of simple mind, human." Then to prove this, his armour on one side started to seep back down his chest, adding to the plating there and now leaving one shoulder bare.

"Oh...Ah!" Was my lame reply and one that ended on a shriek when I found myself in the air and being lifted with both hands on my waist as I was literally thrown over his shoulder. Gods, he was so strong he didn't even bother bending into the action. But then, this caused its own problems as it not only left my head hanging down his back, in between the middle of his wings but it also ended up putting me closer to the sight of my fear. Naturally, I screamed, taking in that of my terrified reflection and the sight beyond it that caused that terror to build. I quickly tried to scramble my way up his back, using whatever I could get hold of, which ended up being the folds of his wings and the bones that connected the leathery skin between.

"Be still!" he snapped angrily.

"AHH!" I shouted ignoring him and still squirming in his hold as I managed to pull myself up. I did this by hooking my arm around one of the massive horns that his wings were connected to at his shoulders, using the crook of my elbow to keep me anchored there so I was upright. I heard another growl of annoyance before he gave in and shifted me, letting me slide down the front of him. But then before my feet touched the floor, he swept them up so he was now carrying me in his arms.

"Oh Gods, thank you," I muttered making him huff before telling me,

"Fucking Gods had nothing to do with it, for they don't

carry the burden of you!" This was snapped without looking at me and I flinched at the hurtful words, a reaction he obviously ignored. No, instead of giving way to my feelings, he took sure and long strides towards the end of the walkway, one that was too far away to see what awaited us. But then, after a longer stretch of silence fell between us I was surprised when he not only was the one to end it, but it was what he said to end it that surprised me the most.

"You never feared heights before," he said in what thankfully seemed like a slightly less pissed off way.

"I never feared you before either…*things obviously change,"* I blurted out before I could stop myself. And boy, did I know my mistake when suddenly I found my feet back on the floor and my back being pressed against the cracked sides of the walkway. I was quickly caged in by the angry demonic King, as his wings spread wide and his horns butted against the fragile looking wall at my back, making it crack around the tips.

"AH!" I cried in fright as one hand then joined the tapered points of his horns as he slammed his palm against the wall, making cracks branch out angrily next to my head before his other hand fisted my hair. Then he yanked it back, forcing me to look up at him and the bite of pain made me hiss out a breath. It also made me do as he silently commanded for me to do so as the pain stopped, becoming now nothing more than a firm hold of me.

After this he snarled down at me,

"You will fear what I want you to fear, girl!" I swallowed hard and decided in that moment not only to be brave but to be what many would have considered suicidal! Because my own temper, the one that had been simmering under the surface for too long now, suddenly couldn't be contained any longer. And he knew it as my eyes narrowed and my back straightened despite the hold he had on me, or the hurt it caused to do so.

Because down there in his throne room I had reason to side with caution, thinking that pushing him in front of his Kingdom would be forcing his hand when that hand didn't want to be forced.

But as for now, well that hand was currently fisted in my hair, doing so of its own free will despite us being alone. Which meant my reasons for reining back my anger were no longer facing us as a sea of demonic faces all eager for that show of domination from their King.

Because Lucius wasn't my King or my Ruler.

He wasn't the Boss of me or my Master.

He was my Chosen One.

Which was why I had to know. I had to know that even if in Hell he was still that to me. That he was still my Chosen One down here and the only way to know fully was to push him. To push him enough just to see if he would hurt me or not. I knew it might have seemed slightly crazy, but I just had to know.

I. Had. To. Know.

So naturally being me when I pushed...

I pushed hard.

CHAPTER FIVE

PRISONER OF MY MIND

"I will fear what I damn well want to! My mind is not your slave, Lucius. You can't control what I think or how I feel…especially about you!" I said this in words that were nothing short of a verbal lashing and it was one I was surprised to see him even flinch from. It was the barest of movements, but it was enough to tell me that what I had said meant something to him. However, whatever that was, there was only one way he reacted to it, *with a demon's threat and anger.*

"I own you!" he roared, and I closed my eyes as I shook my head, but it was useless. Especially when the hand that had been against the wall by my head started to move to places, that right now, I really didn't want it to go. This was despite the moan that escaped me the moment that brutal hand softly ran the backs of his talons down my bare arm at the same time telling me,

"I own every part of you…" his hand then rose back up my arm and started to skim across my collar bone before dipping down in between my breasts, making me suck in a fearful breath.

"...This beating heart..." he said before I felt the tip of his claw tug at the material and I yelped the moment it nicked my skin, creating a sting. It was such a contrast to his softly spoken words that my eyes flew open and were met with his crimson gaze blazing into mine. He then made a show of lifting his talon to his lips, before licking his tongue along its length. Then once clean, he told me with dangerous calm,

"...This blood that pumps through it..." another pause and then he suddenly clamped his gauntleted hand over the bottom part of my face, proving that even in Hell it was possible to be lured into a false sense of security. Meaning that with my jaw in his firm grasp and a hand still fisted in my hair, he held my head prisoner with both hands, using both now to bring me closer to him. Only then when inches apart did he finish his sentence,

"....*Even the lashing of your tongue is mine!*" he growled before dragging me up the rest of the way to meet his lips, at the same time having no choice but to lower his own. And this was when he started something he couldn't stop. Something that started with sucking my tongue deep into his mouth and holding it there with his teeth before letting it go. But this was when his next actions must have caught even him by surprise. As instead of letting me go like I knew he had first intended, he started kissing me. No...not just kissing me, because it was so much more than that. It was a blaze of fire igniting us both the moment he touched his lips to mine. It was the power of reunited souls that recognised the Hellish abyss that had come between them.

Both sides of the coin sinking away to reveal true beauty on the inside as two faces finally meet and forge a deeper secret connection at its centre. His heated, possessive growl merged with my own moan of pleasure, one consumed by his kiss as his lips dominated my own. A warmth spread throughout my body at the same time arousal pooled between my legs. I found myself squirming to get closer still as the burning continued to rise up in my core, thanks to the skilled way he plundered my mouth. And he was right, he claimed it completely, owning every inch of it!

I also found myself too affected to do anything other than let him. Not that there was much else I could have done, not with the brutal and unyielding hold he still had upon me. One, that at the moment was shamefully adding to the arousal, as his immense strength had always been a major turn on for me and even when coming from his demon, this was no exception. But then the hand on my chin left me and slammed once more against the glass at my back as his body bowed further into my own. Meaning that the flinch of my body was one that was barely felt by Lucius thanks to the cage of his body, as it pressed himself against me. It was as if the whole kiss had affected him in such a profound way that he was struggling to control himself against the power of it.

However, that fire he ignited wasn't of the eternal kind as a frustrated growl later and the flames were being doused in our reality, doing so just before either of us could get burned. Because just as quickly as the kiss had happened it was gone, now being ripped away by a demon's doubt. And well, the look on his face said only one thing…that he had been shocked that he had allowed it to go that far at all.

He had been trying to prove his words of ownership and kissing me like that had obviously steered him far away from making his point. Because by making him lose control like that meant that he wasn't the only one with the power to claim. With one look and he knew it, which was why his next action was to continue to try and reaffirm what he started. I knew this when his hand left the glass and was suddenly at the small of my back yanking me hard to his frame, telling me,

"I own every inch of this fuckable little body, one I will take a great deal of pleasure in soon punishing and then...*claiming it!*" This ended when he suddenly cupped my sex and dangerously scraped the tips of his talons up along my folds. And with nothing between us but the thinnest of material, I ended up crying out when he grazed against my throbbing clit. He growled low, a rumble I felt all the way down to my toes. Then, with his fist still locked in my hair, he pulled back even more, so my neck was stretched taut and ready for the taking. He then shifted slightly to the side snarling down at me, doing so against my cheek whilst his hand turned palm up so he could use the less dangerous side of his claw against me.

"...and I will prove just how much I own this fucking mind you think to deny me," he said with a snarl of words before I could silently question how he would do that, knowing that he had no control over my mind.

I whimpered against him and this was because the back of his talon flicked over my soaked clit, making me suddenly reach out and grab hold of him. The second I did, he started not only rubbing against the bundle of nerves but vibrating his talon against it. It was as if he was giving life to his armour once more and making it react the way he wanted it to. Which meant that it took about thirty seconds before his name left my lips in a breathy plea for him to stop...

"Lucius, please...I can't...I..."

Unsurprisingly, this was something he didn't listen to but instead only increased the sensation. Doing so until it had me gripping him harder, closing my eyes and crying out just as it was close enough to roll over and take me to a place I was desperately searching for. My legs spread wider in a silent invitation for him to take me there...to take me all the way...

To take me to that sweet home of sexual oblivion.
One he suddenly denied me.

"You will not find release until I demand it of you!" Lucius ordered making me cry out,

"NO!" I had been so close but damn it, he was right. As no matter how I tried to defy him, it was a fight I just couldn't win, not when demons never played fair! Because as much as I had denied the possibility, I found a soft stroking at the edges of my mind that was snatching the sexual release away from me. Almost like my mind was a dark forest and there I was, in the centre of it all, on the floor naked, legs spread with my hand cupping my sex and my own fingers working me until I came. But then came the whispered voice echoing through the trees, the voice of Lucius pulling my own hand away from me and forcing my compliance. There was only his command that mattered. Only his voice to follow. And in that moment,

I hated him for it!

I cried out again in frustration and when I hit a clenched fist against his chest his demon actually chuckled. Then I felt him get close, as his talon stopped vibrating, and slowed to a gentle motion, one definitely more maddening and closer to making me lose my fucking mind.

"I told you, Pet, I own every fucking inch of you… including this defiant, stubborn mortal mind of yours, one I will soon bring to heel!" At this he inched even closer, and proved the level of control he had on me once and for all in this Hellish realm he told me,

"Now open your fucking eyes and see me, see your Master, girl!" he shouted making me flinch and then just as I was about to try and pull away, he pulled me closer, lowered his head enough to speak against my cheek, as he demanded more softly this time,

"This is when you come for me, my good little Pet." Then

the back of his claw barely even touched me and that gentle whispered voice in the woods starting roaring for me to come. Not a second later and I found myself screaming out my release with only one name that felt worthy of the power behind my cries of pleasure,

"LUCIUS!" My screaming of his name was answered with his hand tightening in my hair making the pain morph into an even deeper orgasm as he snarled demonically against my cheek,

"You. Are. Mine!"

Then he yanked hard on the leash so that this time it snapped from where it was linked to my collar and he released it to the floor with a tinkling sound of metal on glass. After this his words of ownership catapulted me into an even deeper abyss, whereas the only sound that followed me down was the deafening cries of my own pleasure echoing in my mind.

It was a release that rolled straight on until the next, claiming me, body and mind one after the other, until I wasn't sure it would ever end. I wasn't even sure I would survive it for it was one so powerful, it felt as if it had the power to rip me apart! An endless pleasure that was tearing a piece of my soul from me and handing it over to the demonic hand of my Master like he demanded. It wasn't a shock then as my legs buckled and I would have sunk to the floor, in what felt like a useless puddle of mortal mess, had it not been for his quick actions.

I was soon swept up into his arms again, with my body still convulsing, doing so now within his tight hold on me. After this he didn't say anything, but then again, he didn't really need to, as I think it was obvious to both of us that he had made his point. In fact, if I hadn't been too lost to the euphoric aftermath, then I would have mustered up the feeling of embarrassment and shame. But like I said, I was too busy lounging in the field of bliss for that to take effect yet. Besides, his reaction wasn't really surprising, as even when Lucius was the man I knew him to be in my heart, then he was still controlling and dominant in the bedroom.

So really, it was foolish of me to expect anything else of his demon. And thinking about it, then it wasn't as though he had hurt me in any way, other than a nick to my skin and a pull of my hair. As nothing hurt now, other than the slight tenderness at my clit, something that was to be expected. Something that also made it difficult not to squirm in his hold.

"Behave, little Pet," Lucius warned, this time in a softer tone, one that I held on to. For in that moment of vulnerability and weakness I found myself treasuring it enough to hold on to him tighter. This was something I knew he noticed as he granted me a brief glance, but his thoughts remained his own as he didn't comment. No, instead he continued to walk towards the end of the covered bridge, one I no longer feared now as I was safely in his arms.

The arms of my Demon.

But then something caught my eye as we made it past the halfway point, it looked like a sudden storm had gripped the Hellish landscape. I frowned as I stretched a little so that I could raise myself up enough to look behind him, something that was hopeless thanks to his huge wings in the way. Of course, he noticed this too, and turned briefly to look for himself at what had taken my attention. This new position allowed me the quick glimpse from where we had come from. Allowing me to see that it was as I first suspected, the storm was one we had seemingly stepped into, not one that was raging around the rest of the castle.

"What is…" Lucius turned back to face the way we were headed and answered in a hard tone,

"You will soon see." Then he continued on, now with what seemed like greater purpose, cutting the space more quickly.

Which meant that his long angry strides soon got us to the end and what faced us now wasn't like any doorway I had ever seen before. And well, considering where I was, then this was hardly surprising.

To be honest, I even found myself questioning if this was a door at all as there wasn't actually any real entrance to speak of. No, instead, what there was looked more like at least forty souls all reaching for their chance to escape, one that had been made impossible when turned to stone. Eighty plus arms were all squeezed tight through a centre gap that was lost to stone flesh. Each arm was bent at the elbow and grasping for whatever the surface was beneath them, with their fingernails embedded there like they were trying to scratch their way free.

In fact, I found the sight quite haunting and hoped that whatever was beyond this unusual door, was not symbolic for what faced me now. Lucius stopped and then set me down, doing so now more gently than he had the previous times. Then as he stepped away from me, it gave me time to cautiously look to the sides of the bridge.

The storm outside raged with even more ferocity than when I first noticed it and taking a step closer, I peered back towards the other towers. As I expected, the air around them appeared clear, unlike the one we would soon enter, as it was the only tower consumed by a strange red storm. It was like a massive tornado, and at its core you could just make out the black sides of the tower through the breaks in the dark reddish cloud. Flashes of long, forked lightning blazed like fire, and deafening thunder quickly followed, sounds that split the sky with a booming roar that naturally made me jump.

My small frightened sound must have caught Lucius' attention as he glanced over his shoulder and ordered,

"Come here, Pet." Another bolt of fire was again chased by the thunder seconds later and it was enough to make me hurry back to his side. This was because I was also very aware I was still on the precarious looking bridge, and didn't fancy being close to the sides when fate decided one of those lightning bolts was destined to try and crack glass.

Once Lucius was obeyed, he lifted his right hand up at the same time the gauntlet started melting away to reveal a hand I knew intimately well underneath. He raised his hand to his mouth, released his fangs and bit down hard, cutting into his wrist. He then lowered it enough so that the blood pooled in his cupped fingers without spilling a drop, seeing as it was obvious that he needed it for this next part.

Then, once he felt he had enough, he threw his arm out and let his blood travel through the air until it splattered against the stone hands. The second it made contact, the limbs all seemed to ripple as one, like they all belonged to the same tortured creature. Then slowly one at a time they started to retreat back through the gap and with each arm that disappeared, more and more of the door was revealed beneath. It was only when ten remained that these hands reached for the large wrought iron rings that could now be seen framing both sides of the double doors. As they started to pull back on the doors, they folded inwards and both the hands and the wooden panels started to sink into the centre, quickly disappearing from view.

I frowned in question, one that was just on the tip of my tongue when suddenly the two door panels reappeared after seemingly being flipped around completely. A new set of double doors that were covered in a glossy red paint faced us now, and the crimson coating was one that dripped down from the top and had looked to have dried that way.

Surely it couldn't have been blood?

I didn't ask, and if he saw me shiver because of the thought of it, he didn't comment. No, instead he motioned for me to precede him with a nod of his head. I came close to saying, 'no, no, after you' but decided against looking weak. After all, I'd had enough of showing him what little backbone I had down in Hell, so instead I did as I was silently told.

But as I approached the doors, I couldn't help but look up at the sheer size of them in a questioning way as I wondered if I even had enough strength in me to push them open. Especially seeing as they were the size you would have expected at the end of a drawbridge. However, I didn't get the chance to ask as Lucius' hands shot out and pushed from behind me, marching me forward at the same time. So, it wasn't surprising that I found myself with no other option than to enter, not with the mountain of a demon at my back pressing against me like a moving wall.

In fact, I was just about to stumble forward when I felt a hand grip my waist and hold me steady, telling me that he at least cared enough that he didn't want to see me go flying on my face. Talk about clutching at straws in the hope department…geez, easily pleased or what, Fae!

The space he walked me into was dark, and for my puny mortal sight, too weak to see where I was going. Something, I gathered Lucius knew too, as it was most likely the reason he still hadn't taken his hand away from gripping my side. But then, I felt that hand shift to now put pressure on the small of my back, pushing me enough to step away from him.

"Stay." This one worded command came out in a hard, demanding tone and I shamefully felt the growl of this single word ripple to my sex. After this I felt his dominating presence leave me and was left standing in the dark feeling vulnerable, holding myself around my stomach, totally unsure of where Lucius had brought me. The sound of the storm still raged around us, and I couldn't tell whether this was more of a comfort or not, as being stood here in total silence wasn't something I would have liked to experience either.

However, the storm cracked and thundered, along with the high-pitched whining sound as the wind whipped around the shard tower we stood in. But despite the power of the storm, I was also surprised when you could hear the slight sound of sparks crackling in the air around me, wondering what made them? I turned around, and even blind without the light, I tried to trace the sound and discover the origins. I turned again just in time to see as light erupted from behind what looked like a giant red crystal. It was one that stood vertical and tapered into jagged points like the castle itself. It looked as if it had been hacked off a larger piece and mounted into a wrought iron cage that sat on demonic metal feet.

It was stunning, even if it did start to cast an eerie glow around the room, because it wasn't the only one. No, this turned out to be the first of many, as seconds after this had been ignited, the next one to it followed. My eyes travelled their journey as one by one another crimson crystal would light up and cast out that same Hellish glow on the room. Although, if you could actually class it as a room, I wasn't sure. In fact, it was very similar to the top of the tower that held the staircase. This was in the way that it looked like a colossal glass shard had been hollowed out, only this time, this one wasn't white…*it was all black.*

It made the walls look sinister and more like a glassy version of a person's Void. Almost to the point that if you touched the walls you would be surprised when your hands felt a solid structure beneath your palms. Of course, you could just make out the storm passed the surface, something which helped create the illusion of movement, as if the walls weren't actually there. As if I could just swipe my hand right through them and escape like a ghost passing through the walls.

But then as I continued to follow the crystals igniting one by one as they lined the circular room, I ended up turning to take in the very last one behind me ending it on a scream. This was because Lucius was now stood behind me where I didn't expect him to be. However, after my shock had calmed, I started to really take him in, and this was when my new reality started to sink in.

Lucius had changed.

His wings had gone, along with the horns that held them connected to his back. His demonic armour had also disappeared which now left him in simple black trousers and bare chested. The dark veins around his eyes and those that shadowed his features had disappeared leaving pale unmarred skin beneath. But as for his eyes, they still held the hints of crimson and were all that remained of his demon. And with this change, one I wasn't expecting, he soon added words to aid in the shock of which side of him I was faced with now,

"Hello, Princess," he said and the second he did, my reaction couldn't be helped as I felt my hand rear back, knowing nothing could stop it now. I let it fly through the air as my anger hit the pinnacle point of no return and connected with his handsome face. A face I knew far better now than the one before it.

His face cracked to the side as the sound of my palm connected with his cheek and echoed louder than the storm.

After this he slowly looked back at me, gifted me with a devilish grin and said only one thing,

"I guess I deserved that."

CHAPTER SIX

LUCIUS

UNFORGIVEABLE

Days ago. Back in the Temple of Souls…

"I lost you once, don't make me lose you again, Amelia, please don't fucking do that to me." I said this in what I knew was a pained way for my fight at getting Amelia to see reason was one I was losing by the fucking second! I hated that I was back here again with her. That it seemed like one emotional hurdle after a-fucking-nother to somersault over.

I had barely even come to when I first heard the truth being spoken and it was one I had worked her entire lifetime at hiding. I thought back to the extremes I had taken just to keep my past actions from her and now knowing it had all been for nothing was a bitter sweetness I never expected to feel. For she had been shown it all, despite my pleas for her to save herself the pain.

But then my utter shock came when seeing her reaction. For once she had been made a secret witness to it all, stepping back through the linked memories the Keepers had shown her, the outcome had been the very last reaction I ever expected. No, what I had expected had been her hatred, her heartbreak, and her declaration of never trusting me again. I had expected this to be the one final thing that made her run from me. To want to throw away everything we had been through for the belief that it had all been built on lies. After all, gaining her trust in me had been a personal battle of mine from the very beginning.

However, in true Amelia fashion, she surprised me yet again and for once it wasn't in a good way. Because none of what she had just discovered was what was making her leave this time and in truth, I actually wished it was. I wished it was because that would mean she wouldn't have been running towards danger when leaving me and I had a better chance of winning her back along with her trust.

But like I said, this wasn't the case, for what I could see she was planning now was a battle I would lose the moment she stepped into Hell and into a place no mortal could conquer. And despite my own anger towards her for what I knew would be a disastrous and potentially deadly decision made, I knew that it was one, at the very least, she struggled with. The way she sucked back a sob at the sound of my pleas told me this. But if it was begging she needed in order to prevent her making a foolish decision, then my pride could go and take a flying fuck, for I would do anything right in this moment to stop her. It was fucking suicide for Gods' sake...didn't she understand that!?

However, I liked to think that my pained actions had a chance at getting through to her, as a glimmer of hope soared within me. This was especially so when she closed her eyes because I knew then that the guilt of her decisions weighed heavily on her heart. I simply prayed to the fucking Gods that it was to the point where she would rethink this madness. For I knew that when it came to Amelia, guilt would be my only weapon to use against her and if all I needed to do was add a little more, then call me a bastard and so be it. Because just so long as it was enough to stop her from being her usual reckless self then ego be damned, I would do it.

I fucking begged!

Oh, I knew why she thought she had no choice, being like her mother in that way. Always at the ready to save the fucking day! Something which usually meant setting off a chain of events that only ever had one of two outcomes…death or a survival labelled 'dumb fucking luck!'

But then that guilt was harder to deliver when she still refused to even look at me, meaning that I knew I was close to losing the fight. An instinct that was only proven right when she spoke and the moment she did, I found my own eyes closing due to the strength and heartache of her words,

"I love you so much, Lucius, by the Gods, I do." Fuck the Gods if she thought this was her goodbye! For they would have an avenging half angel, demon pounding at their door if Hell took her from me!

I took a deep breath and with a strength I didn't know had been buried there, one named patience, I told her in as calm a tone as was physically possible right now,

"Amelia, sweetheart, then prove it, prove it by just giving me your hand, that is all I ask." I watched as her shoulders slumped, making the sight of her in that moment look even smaller than she usually did. Gods, but seeing her from behind like this, made me grit my teeth, for she looked like a child who had just had their dreams crushed. I clearly wasn't the only one suffering an internal battle, one that she didn't realise yet was a war none of us would win. She wanted to do what she believed was right, but she also knew that if she did, then she would sacrifice my heart in the process as she must have known what such actions would do to me? For how could she speak of her love for me if she didn't?

My answer unfortunately came in the cruel form of her walking away from me and towards the Tree of Souls, and what was a permanent portal into Hell. And all the while she utterly refused to look back at me, knowing that if she did then the sight of my pain would have been my last and only power against her determination. Which was why I found myself soon roaring out in desperation, hoping…no, praying to any fucking God that would listen to take pity on me and grant me the same amount of power they had to stop her.

"NO! COME BACK HERE!" I bellowed in rage, although it was no use as my demanding words were lost to a stubborn mind that refused to hear anything other than her misplaced beliefs and ironclad resolve. I knew this when she continued to voice a love for me that in this moment she refused to back up with her actions.

"I love you so much, that I would go to Hell and back for you," she said in a way that I knew she was already lost to me. I knew it. I felt it. I fucking hated it, which is why I quickly shifted my focus on my last hope at stopping her.

"I DEMAND YOU FUCKING LET ME INSIDE NOW!" I thundered like a wild beast, knowing that the sound was that of half man, half demon. That the Hellish part of me was an echoing rage that vibrated around my body and mind as if my demon had the power to rip me apart by the seams. To tear apart the shreds of my humanity and take control over the parts of my mind that keep him contained.

But containing that Hell was what I forced myself to do because I knew no good would come of letting that part of myself free, not when I needed to keep a level head. A level head in place of the pounding, furious rage that I could feel beating against my vessel. One that would have only managed in getting me knocked on my ass the second my demon foolishly tried to fight us both through the barrier.

I couldn't afford for that to happen.

However, the Keepers of Three simply shook their heads at my threat, signing their own death sentence. For when I finally made it through this fucking thing then I would sever all three heads from their warped fucked up body!

Amelia glanced their way, obviously worried that they would have no choice but to grant their Master his wish. Even in my rage I could see the way she tensed as if readying herself for my granted entrance but then relaxed when she saw the unfulfilled outcome thanks to their silent refusal. Because she didn't know that the Keepers weren't a slave to their Master, whose life they were connected to, but they were a slave to the Tree of Souls, one that was connected to mine.

Fucking semantic bullshit!

It was the sacrificial roots of my heart that Lucifer had forced to beat with his own blood. I owned every soul whose essence was symbolised as a silver leaf on that tree. A soul that became infected, turning back to its original state of a mindless, bloodthirsty being. This was as the infection grew up its roots, like veins pumping deadly blood back to the heart. Soon it would reach me, its source of new life and that would be the end of my people.

But of course, I knew this already, even without seeing the tree and without once more finding myself in the Temple in which my vessel took its last breath as a mortal man. Our memories merging from beginning to end and finally a rebirth that I now knew Amelia had witnessed as if she had been there herself.

This was why she now believed that she had the power to stop what I had started decades ago. A chain of events that at the time was necessary in preventing the end of all life, not just that of my own and those connected to it. A cruel twist of fate that now brought us to a new threat and one that I had no intention of letting Amelia become entangled with, just like her mother had the first time. Now all I had to do was convince her of that fact before I had no choice but to imprison my Chosen One in the depths of Castle Blutfelsen. But then again, she would no doubt find a way out of Blood Rock, for she had seemingly made a skill out of getting herself both into trouble and out of it again. However, this time her guilt was once again evident as she hung her head and confessed,

"I am so sorry, Lucius, I hope one day you will forgive me."

One day perhaps but today…fuck no! Which was precisely why I let loose a string of lies, just by the Gods be damned praying that they were strong enough to stick and stop her in the midst of this insanity,

"NO! No…no I will not! Do you hear me, Amelia! If you do this, I will never fucking forgive you!" I watched as the entirety of her body tensed as if my words had the power to freeze every cell within the vessel of my troublesome mortal angel. This was when I knew my words had at the very least some power left and as I opened my mouth to say more, she got there first, dousing that hope in ice.

"I'm sorry," she said as she looked up at the tree and it was like receiving a double edged blade in my gut as it also sounded like a premature apology for what she could sense as being her failure. Gods, but why did she feel so responsible for my kind? Was it because of her mother? Had discovering the truth from the Keepers of what really happened that day now managed to warp her good sense of preservation…if she ever had any to begin with!

Fuck, but if she actually did the insane thing and walked through that portal then I would be fucking beyond furious with her! Something that was looking more likely by the second as I followed her gaze and saw that now she was looking directly at what was easily seen as the most important soul to me on there…

The crimson rose of my Chosen One.

The soul I had stolen that day and had bloomed into a beautiful flower, doing so even when I had denied the existence of what it had truly meant to me, for I had known better the moment it had happened. I had known what fate had in store for me and despite being determined to run from it, I knew that one day the inevitable would catch up with me. Because to deny what she meant to me was not only to deny my own heart, but to deny the other part of my soul she had unknowingly infused herself with that day. And now she wanted to tear that side of herself from me, for how could she ever hope to survive Hell alone?

I held my breath, as for a single moment she seemed unsure, a hesitation I was desperate to see grow but then in the next heartbeat that damn flicker of hope was ripped from me when a single leaf fell and fluttered to ash. This becoming the only reminder she needed to solidify what she believed was her mission, hardening her resolve like a crust of duty wrapping around her heart.

"AMELIA, WAIT!" My thundering voice had the power to shake the walls, but not enough to stop her as she took her first step forward…*I was powerless*. Nothing more than a broken whisper of words the moment she finally gave in and looked at me over her shoulder. But it was no use, for the second I saw the unshed tears in her eyes I knew it was nothing more than a goodbye.

"You said you wouldn't run again," I uttered with my voice

near breaking, making her take a deep shaky breath. Then she told me,

"This isn't me running, Lucius." I snarled in anger unable to help myself as I gripped the sides of the tunnel feeling the stone crumbling in my demonic hands. Hands that were changing as my restraint was at an end.

"But don't you see, it is! It fucking is, Amelia, and you know it!" I snapped back at her with a clench of my teeth and a prick of my fangs as they grew quickly against my bottom lip. The taste of my own blood was a bitterness only reflected by the battle I was losing. For I watched as she straightened her shoulders in that determined way, telling me that I had just lost any slim chance I might have had and therefore had to start planning for the worst. Her next words were just a confirmation I didn't need or fucking want at this point!

"No, this me choosing to save our world," she replied and I shook my head as I felt the leather of my glove start splitting as it gave way completely to my demon and the symbolic sight wasn't lost on me. Not considering it was merely a reminder of what started this fucked up road fate decided to force us both down.

"Amelia, I fucking swear to every Gods be damned being out there, that if you do this…"

"But I don't plan on doing this alone…" my threat was cut short the second she declared this, and my breath caught up in what felt like a throat full of thorns. To the point that I felt powerless to speak when she carried on and cursed me with the full extent of her plan…one that she didn't yet know would never fucking work,

"Don't worry, if this all goes to plan, then the second I step through this portal, the barrier will drop and it won't be goodbye for long, Handsome…*As I will see you on the other side."* I barely got out a growl of anger before it was turning into a demonic roar, one powerful enough, that this time when the walls shook, dangerous cracks appeared,

"NO!" I roared in blind fury.

But it was no use, for she had simply stepped…

Straight into my personal Hell.

CHAPTER SEVEN

DEAL WITH THE DEVIL

The moment she disappeared was the moment that my demon erupted, doing so just at the very second the barrier evaporated, and my Hellish body responded by storming inside the Temple. Unsurprisingly I was ready to tear the whole fucking lot down with my bare hands if need be.

"WHERE IS SHE?!" I roared as my body leant forward into the bellow of rage, with my wings now stretching out behind me. The Keepers of Three were at least wise enough to flinch away from me as I advanced on them with a fury, that this time, was one that felt like it lit my veins on fire. But their stumbling steps weren't enough to escape my wrath, for I grabbed a fist full of the robe that the mangled body of three men merged was wearing.

"King of Blood!"

"Lord of Souls!"

"Mmgatser mof mmellish!" they all said in unison as I started to force the tall deformity to walk closer to the entrance of Hell ignoring the struggles of a mass of gnarled muscle and bone.

"TELL ME!" I thundered but the second they all started to shake their heads as one, with what little movement the prison of flesh would allow them, I took action. I kicked out hard enough that it broke bone and shattered the knee cap of one of the strongest legs standing. The Keepers of Three landed hard on the broken floor, one that had been cracked due to the Hellish roots of the Tree of Souls from its growing infection. Two of the three heads howled in agony as their own splintered bones tore through their flesh, and at any other time the sound of pain coming from a being that had wronged me would have been a sweet sound of satisfaction...*but not today.*

No, gone now was the usual arrogant, cold-hearted bastard, for now I was beyond fucking panicked! Which was why I grabbed the top head, using one of the Keeper's own hands that were forced into ripping their own ears away, as was part of their cruel twisted curse. This meant that by adding pressure, it caused them to tear further enticing another cry of pain from them. At the same time, I grabbed the one whose fingers were embedded in the eye sockets belonging to the middle head. I then used this punishing hold to position them closer to the portal that had moments ago consumed my Chosen One.

I did this knowing what would be waiting for them should I lose my mind and challenge the Hellish Fates Keeper, in a way that would certainly make them take notice.

But fuck it, if war with Hell was what it would take to get my Chosen back, then so be fucking it!

"Nnnoo...my Lord of...ahhh" I cut off the stuttered and strained sentence with another dose of pain. This was before dragging them even closer, being nothing more than just a thread of fate away from throwing the fuckers back to Hell and letting Lucifer deal with what would be left of his abomination.

Because the Keepers of Three had once been men just like I had, and their new beginning had been even more brutal than my own. After I had been turned by Lucifer, it soon became clear that I hadn't been the first one...I had just been the only success in his warped mission for what he classed as perfection.

In fact, it was unclear just how many failures there had been before me, but I knew for certain that the twisted body of three combined most likely could have been considered the first. However, these were factors I had only learnt many years after my turning, naively believing there were only two of us. Two survived successes with only one of us being suited to rule of the Vampire race.

But then, like most things that included Lucifer and his demonic creations, I couldn't have been more wrong. The proof of which was currently squirming in my deadly grasp, reminding me of an important lesson...*never to underestimate the Devil.*

As for the Keepers of Three, I had done my research over the years and like most of us, naturally they hadn't started off life this way. In fact, they were once known as some of Rome's greatest warriors. They were named the Horatii and were triplets, which in itself was a marvel of the ancient world due to the higher death rates of multiple births in those times. But then, as legend told it, they weren't the only ones, for they soon had no choice but to face their Alban counterparts, known as the Curiatii on the battlefield.

This happened almost six hundred years before my rebirth and at a time known as the Kingdom era of Rome. This particular moment in history was during the reign of Tullus Hostilius, who was the third king of Rome, and in a time known as the regal period. It was the earliest period of Roman history, when the city and its territory were ruled by what was considered royal blood. But just like the rest of the ancient world, the power of Kings didn't come from the blood of Gods but came from the blood spilt on the battlefield from the wars they waged and armies they were so eager to sacrifice in hopes of victory. Mortal lambs often led to the slaughter, dressed up in blood-soaked armour and with nothing more than a blunt sword in their exhausted hand and all in the name of their King. But I had seen enough wars fought to know that the real Kings were those who charged head on into battle, leading the way for their men.

War was a bloody business and not one often fought with the risk of losing its ruler. Men were thought to be expendable and Kings were not. However, this time Tullus Hostilius and its neighbouring city of Alba Longa, both agreed that fighting on the battlefield would be a costly war and would leave the door open for an Etruscan invasion. Neither could take the chance of that happening with what would no doubt have been a great loss on both sides. So Mettius Fufetius, who was the dictator of Alba Longa at the time, decided to appeal to Tullus Hostilius with another idea. A duel to the death, telling him that the conflict should be settled between the Roman Horatii triplets and their Alban counterparts, the Curiatii.

This meant that they met on the battlefield wedged between two armies as their countrymen looked on. And the outcome from such a fight was that all three Curiatii ended up being wounded. However, the losses were far greater on the other side, for two of the Horatii triplets had fallen, leaving only one to fight alone. His name was Publius, the most cunning of all three, using the skill of wit over brute strength. This was put to the test when Publius found himself alone and surrounded by the three Albans.

However, unlike the other triplets, he was uninjured and used this to his advantage, as he knew that he stood no chance against all three at once. So, he turned and ran, using the strength he had over the others to make his way across the battlefield. He did this because he knew that they would have no choice but to pursue him. This achieved two things, both to his great advantage as this chase not only weakened the brothers, making their injuries worse but it also split them up so he could then face each one alone.

His plan had worked perfectly. He turned and launched a furious attack on the first, before easily catching up to the second and killing him. Doing so as the last brother was left standing and with no other choice but to helplessly look on as his brother was slain. Now spent from both his injuries and the chase, it was said that he died with the honour of confronting a known death, doing so still standing and facing Publius even when knowing his fate. Publius declared that he had killed the first two Curiatii for his fallen brothers and that his last kill was for the Roman cause and what would be their rule over the Albans. A declaration that ended by thrusting his sword down the Alban's throat before then taking the armour of his slain enemies as the spoils of his victory.

After this the Alban dictator Mettius honoured the treaty and Alba Longa briefly had no choice but to accept Roman rule. However, this was not where the story ended, for the reason he was cast into Hell, damning the memory of his brothers with him, came upon his arrival home. You see, the part that was left out of the tale told by historian Titus Livius, who was famous for his retelling of the monumental history of Rome, was the part that no human would know…

The Horatii triplets sold their souls to the Devil.

This was because they knew that they could never win against the other three, knowing of the Curiatii's many victories and the rumours declaring they were descendants of the Gods. However, jealousy ran deep within the three, and each wanted to be known and remembered as the famous brothers of three for defeating them. So, they made a deal with the ruler of Hell that promised them victory should they sign over their souls as payment, something they did all too eagerly, never imagining that only one would survive and slay the rest.

But the deal was that should even one of them sin after defeating their enemies and killing the Curiatii triplets, that it would condemn them all to a life in Hell the moment the last brother fell. Feeling sure that this wouldn't happen, they made the deal and Lucifer kept his end of the bargain, for fame was theirs.

Fuckers should have read the small print on that one, I thought with a grimace as I looked down at what had become of them. And why, because their brother had damned them to this life when Publius committed the sin of killing his sister upon his return to the city. This was because not everyone welcomed him home as a hero. Camilla, his sister, had been engaged to one of the Alban triplets. Meaning that the moment she saw her brother's spoils of war over his shoulder, a cloak she had woven as a gift to her beloved, one now covered in his blood, she cursed him in a fit of anger and grief. She cried out his name and proclaimed that no Roman woman should mourn Rome's fallen enemies and in return, Publius killed his sister on the spot.

For his crime he was condemned to death, however due to his recent victory, he used the Roman tradition of allowing the condemned to appeal their sentences to the populace. This was naturally to end in his advantage, seeing as he had just done Rome a great service in his victory against the enemy. Therefore he cheated death.

However, no one cheated the Devil.

Which meant that when he did eventually die shortly after, due to unknown circumstances I could very well put down to the Devil's hand, Lucifer was right there ready to take possession of all three souls. He even had their bodies at the ready, and trials of his abomination began. Now if there had been any before them, I had no idea, I simply knew that what was left of the Horatii triplets was currently at my mercy. At my mercy and close to being thrown back into Hell to face the wrath of their maker once more.

For reasons unknown to anyone but our joint father of Hell, the three weren't destroyed after this failure but instead the Fates intervened and awarded them Keepers of The Tree of Souls. But seeing as the sins of one damned them all, it was made so as not one could live without the other. For their punishment became dependency, seeing as they had failed to depend on one another in the Afterlife. A decision that ultimately led to their Hellish demise.

Now just look at the heroes of Rome, I thought with a sneer.

"Now tell me, Horatii...*where is my Queen?!*" I growled this last part of my demand taking note of their pained sound at being reminded of who they once were. It was no doubt a name they hadn't heard in over two thousand years, unless of course Lucifer himself was ever in the mood to play tormentor and pay his failed attempt a visit. Sinful, jealous brothers who the Fates had strangely deemed worthy enough to be bestowed a new name of Keepers of Three. This for reasons that would no doubt never be known to me.

"The gateway to Hell is forever changing."

"It is fated where she will be."

"Muhuss..."

"Don't fucking bother saying a word, cretin!" I snapped shutting up the one with his brother's hand in his mouth having no fucking patience for it! But of course I didn't, my girl had stepped through the fucking portal believing that I would simply be stepping through it right after her. Foolishly doing so thinking all she had to do was wait for me on the other side. She had no idea that the Tree's portal into Hell didn't work like that. In fact, most gateways into Hell didn't unless they were in the Temple of Janus. It was what made the Temple so important to our world and it was also why not everyone had been granted the good fortune of being allowed to enter it. Power was key, that and the hard to come by Janus Coin.

No, you had to earn that rite of passage... I thought this on looking down at my demonic hand that had ripped away the leather that once concealed it the moment she stepped from my sight. And now she was in fucking Hell, no doubt wondering where the fuck I was!

I am coming for you, my Queen.

"You may not know the destination, but you do know which realm of Hell she was transported...*I know you fucking do!*" I threatened and to emphasise this point, I pushed their combined heads closer to the swirling abyss of crimson fire. An ominous sight that looked like an eternal hole of oblivion. Of course, this was only a glimpse as to what awaited anyone foolish enough to enter through it and think that they could conquer its Hellish world by simply surviving it.

A foolish mortal like Amelia.

Fuck! But how could she even hope to endure such a place?! There was no time to waste, which was why my grip tightened and I pushed further, watching as all limbs tensed and tried in vain to scramble away. So, I kicked out again, forcing the Keepers mangled torso closer to the floor and dragged them the last few inches until they believed I had truly lost myself to madness.

"No, you can't...Lucifer...!"

"He will kill you...You mustn't!"

"Ffffobthin!" This was when I lifted them up close enough so I could whisper to the second head, the one who still had the use of his ears. Then I said in a dangerous tone...

"He can fucking try!" Then I grabbed one of the wrists that was free enough from the mangled body and to prove my point I held it out, forcing it into the portal. I did this knowing it wouldn't last long being imprisoned between the two worlds.

"AAAHHH!"

"NNNOOOO!"

"GGGRRAAAGH!"

"Now tell me, what fucking realm took her?!" I barked at them the second I pulled it back, ignoring the stench of burnt flesh from what was left of their meaty hand. I let them go and watched with a sliver of satisfaction at the way they cowed back away from me. But the sight of them scrambling was only wasting my time and stoked the fury inside of me,

"TELL ME!" I roared making them flinch as one.

"She is on the edges of your realm."

"The Kingdom of Blood and Death."

"Ssshth othnkn yyyonn." I frowned at the one unable to speak and cocked my head his way.

"He said that she is searching for you," the brother said in response to my silent order and the moment he said it, I couldn't help but flinch myself, doing so enough to close my eyes as the pain of that statement lanced through me. My girl was looking for me and I was fucking here! I let my anger snake through me, feeling the demon side of me rippling against my skin at the thought of what could be happening right now.

I would fucking kill anyone that touched her and rip Hell in two to find her! I would destroy all that Lucifer had built and tear his world apart if I found anything had happened to her! For that was my vow!

I turned around to face the portal, and paused when the Keepers shouted out for me, sickening me with their continued loyalty after what I had done to them. For even now I wanted to do more…*much, much more.*

"My Lord! The Tree of Souls…"

"She is the key, don't forget that!"

"Mybbkbdke!"

I snarled, letting my fangs grow again in length at the same time the full change in me swept through my vessel like I was being stroked by the Devil's hand. A caress that caused a crackle of pain I was not only used to but welcomed as I was about to step back into my natural domain. It was akin to being injected with some kind of demonic serum, as I could feel it surging through my veins as it filtered through to every cell in my body. I clenched my fists and looked back over my shoulder at yet another one of Lucifer's sickening failures.

Then I told them before stepping into Hell…

"She belongs to me…and as for the Fates…"

"Fate, can go fuck itself!"

CHAPTER EIGHT

BOUND TO REALMS

The second I step into Hell I found my first breath one that instantly eased my demon. However, it was a relief that was short lived, as any hope that I would find my Chosen here waiting for me was dead after a quick scan of my surroundings. But then this wasn't exactly surprising as I knew what Amelia hadn't known when stepping foolishly into Hell. Firstly, portals into another realm didn't work like she thought they did and secondly, time passed differently depending on where in Hell you were. It was like time zones when travelling the world, only here it was dependant on the level of Hell you found yourself in.

An hour topside could equal to days here, or even months the deeper you went. It was the same for each of the many realms the supernatural beings that didn't belong to Hell or Heaven called home. For the fabric of time was an entity all by itself when stepping from one world into another. The realm of the Elementals especially, for this was where most of those that were not quite demon and not quite angel resided. There were many races of creatures that were derived from both sides of Heaven and Hell, creating subspecies whose origins blurred the true lines of descent. Pip for example was an Imp and was known as an Elemental being who descended from the Hell side of life. However, it was obvious to say that she most definitely preferred to live topside with human life than with that of her own kind.

Not that I blamed her, as many parts of their world was like stepping back through time. Or in some realms like being caught in some technological cross over between modern magic and steam power cities of the 17th century. It was also renowned for being as ruthless as Hell itself in some parts, these depending on its ruler of course. It was also a place that demons were naturally unwelcome, vampires included and that was just fucking fine with me! As I had enough shit to deal with in my own world than having to deal with my people crossing over into theirs.

However, that didn't mean that the crossover didn't go both ways as many of my people were of an Elemental breed. But seeing as I was far from being racist to these kinds of beings, I often welcomed the loyalty offered, Pip being one of them. Something that quite often offered an interesting addition to my power force, something that I was about to rely heavily on when looking for my girl. But then my rule here was quite different than that of the mortal world. Which was unsurprising really, given that Hell wasn't exactly an easy place to rule. It also was the reason I was known as the Tyrant King of Blood and Death, a title only earned through brutality as was the nature of Hell. Because down here money didn't talk, *pain did*. Pain and death were used like a currency and what you were buying was only ever one thing…*Power.*

If there was one important thing my demonic father had taught me was that the more powerful beings you ruled over, the stronger you were in that rule. Of course, it wasn't like mutiny never happened, for in this, Lucifer had learned this lesson more often than not. The worst of which being less than fifteen years ago. He had also proved why it was dangerous to have any weaknesses that anyone may be able to exploit. A hard factor for a being like Lucifer to face, especially when he learnt just how much of a weakness claiming his Chosen One could be. A lesson I myself had learnt, and for a once cold-hearted bastard of a King, finding fear was never easy to face or to conquer. A battle of the heart for a warrior only built for spilling blood on the battlefield and being a bringer of death, wasn't easily won, for it was mainly a war fought within yourself.

But I had played the selfless act for years and now that I had tasted all that was her, there was no going back. The claim had been made, even though I knew the cause of all her danger was me standing at its chaotic core. Which was why I knew that down here I would have to play things differently if I wanted to reclaim her and keep her safe at the same time. For if my enemies were to discover who she really was to me, then I would only end up putting her in even more danger than she usually was when in the mortal world.

This meant that putting every resource I had down here into trying to find her was going to be tricky seeing as I wanted to keep her true identity from this brutal world. One ripe with enemies not to just my throne but to her father's also, for she was a Princess to a hated King by many and a Queen to a hated King by even more.

Fuck, but could things get any more complicated?!

It didn't take me long to realise where I was, and the sight didn't exactly surprise me. After all, I would forever be drawn to this place and whatever portal I stepped through would have recognised that pull of energy. Which was why I was now stood on the border between the forest and that of my castle in the distance. The colossal dark blue obsidian crystal shards had been risen out of the ground by Lucifer's army of witches. Those and any mage that had enough magic that it served him enough to keep them around. Gods, but even the word magic was one that I loathed, and the reasons for this ran deeper than my current hatred for the bitch out to destroy me. But being topside for as long as I had then the word just sounded so juvenile compared to the raw and dark power that could be produced, and right in front of me was the proof of that.

This was my gift, the Devil had said that every King needs a castle and just as much as I was Lucifer's greatest accomplishment, my castle needed to make that statement and to all I was destined to rule over. Personally, I fucking hated the charade and every fucked up part that came with my rule in Hell. Of course, I had joked on many occasions with Amelia about my palace here but looking at it now and I couldn't help but wonder what she would have thought should she be standing next to me. I mean it wasn't exactly the 'welcome home, honey' one would have hoped to present to their intended Queen but then again, I wasn't exactly your poster boy for a conventional relationship.

I turned and looked back at the Forest of Echoes, known as such due to the unique rock formations that are scattered throughout the land. These cluster of rocks created an amplified effect which meant that voices carried throughout the forest, undeterred by the trees that should have prevented most of it from travelling that far.

No, instead it created a warped, ricochet effect making those that were new to these parts believe they were surrounded or that the forest was alive with the voices that were actually their own. Of course, if you weren't far from the rocks then those voices could be heard with more clarity. But that was by the by, for there weren't many that ventured too far in Hell from what they were comfortable with. All but the bounty hunters who had to be fearless to choose such a profession in this dark realm. But then again, it was one that paid well for there were always those who were escaping the wrath of some Lord or King. As for Lucifer, the King of Kings, well then no one escaped him, other than that of his own Queen soon after she was first brought to Hell. And I should know seeing as I was the fucker charged with delivering her!

At the time I didn't know which emotion Lucifer felt more, being utterly enraged or being shockingly impressed. However, that was one time where he broke all his own rules and actually went to the mortal realm to retrieve her himself. This was a time I had no choice but to remember, seeing as I was the unlucky fuck who was charged with ruling in his place for a short time, *one unfortunately not short enough.*

But that was then, and this was now, for it seemed the tables had turned and I was the one now hunting my Chosen One…yet a-fucking-gain! Honestly, at this rate I was half tempted put a leash around the girl's neck so she couldn't wander too far, seeing as she couldn't be trusted not to make foolish mistakes!

Gods, I was fucking furious with her!

It seemed to have been one after another since seeing her that day at the museum and the only one I had approved of had been when she tricked Dante and slipped past his surveillance. Because that had been the only one that had brought her directly to me and what marked the end of years of self-induced torture. Of course, everything after that point had been a combination of street smarts, dumb fucking luck, bad judgement, and even worse rash decisions made on the backs of heightened emotions. Emotional minds, which if you asked me were the worst fucking time a person could make decisions ruled by fear, pain or heartache.

Cold, hard, and calculated was what made a person survive

in my world, and Amelia was none of those things. Yet, here she was, in a place she had only read about in books. Books that right now would have been useful for only one thing, keeping warm when needing to start a fire! Because even though in the mortal world she had been on the run, this was far from needing to be street smart and savvy. And despite needing to give her credit where credit was due, for she had not only managed to escape me, but she had done so without getting herself hunted down by those that wished to use her against me...*This was a different league of survival.*

Fuck me, but thinking back to when she had even gone up against a gangster and his gun happy band of fuckwits was a discovery that had made me proud. And to have even come out of it with the boss actually respecting her, was nothing short of impressive...of course, he had been at the wrong end of the barrel at the time. But like me, respect had to be shown to anyone who had the ability to get the better of someone that high up on the food chain. For they only got there by slaying their enemies and getting the better of anyone who had stood in their way. And this was without taking into account her being a gorgeous, unsuspecting woman dressed like a flight attendant speeding through the doors in a stolen Ferrari.

My little Hell on wheels.

I shook these thoughts from my head and released my wings knowing time was of the essence, and what I needed to do next I wanted to get done and out of the fucking way, quickly. It was time to reclaim my throne and use my title to its fullest, something that had to start first with a meeting with my second in command. The one I had appointed to rule in my absence.

But then again, he was the only one that ever could.

I landed with much more force than was necessary, cracking the stone beneath me and making those who worked at the castle run in fear the moment they saw me.

"Looks like not a lot has changed then," I muttered to myself as I entered my ostentatious throne room that was stark white marble and lengths of crimson displaying my sigil. The grand hall was mostly empty, which wasn't surprising considering there was no particular reason for my second in command to hold court. Of course, when news got out of my return, the place would be packed with those both curious and those too afraid of not appearing and showing their loyalty to their King or fearing my famous wrath.

Truth was, even though my demon side was at home here, it had to be said that when living topside in the mortal realm, that side of me was far calmer than when down here. I think it was because there was always some threat. Some edge to be forced to walk along, even in my own kingdom and down here, it was razor sharp and usually came with teeth waiting for the opportunity to skin into both your flesh and your position.

I ignored the reactions to my arrival as my guards all dropped to one knee and kept their heads lowered with their weapons held in front of them. The sign of submission would have been a welcomed sight any other time but right now, there was no time for an egotistical mind. I was here for one reason and one reason only…

I wanted my fucking woman back!

"Ah, so the prodigal son returns at last, to what do we owe this royal visit?" My second in command said rising from the horn covered throne, one made from the remains of my enemies and a crude reminder to all who foolishly thought about ever crossing me. I made my way across the vast gleaming white space in seconds and took the steps up to my throne three at a time before granting the cocky bastard my answer.

"I have come here to hunt," I told him making him raise a brow in question, but it was one for now I didn't add an answer too.

"Now I am intrigued," was his reply, to which my own response was,

"All in good time, Šeš, but for now, there is only one thing I need...or should I say *three.*" He granted me a knowing grin that morphed into a cunning smile the moment I finished my order...

"I need to call in a vow of those blood bound..." I looked back towards the doors and said...

"Get me, the McBain Brothers."

CHAPTER NINE

FAMILY CONNECTIONS

"The McBain brothers are out on assignment…exactly what is this about?" My second asked the moment my displeasure was shown with my scowl.

"Where are they?" I asked ignoring his question making him sigh as he flicked out the length of his jacket, one I knew was made from the Basilisk he slayed. A proud moment seeing as the King of serpents was wreaking havoc throughout my land and well, in short, was one hard mother fucker to kill. This was because he had the power to cause death with a single glance and therefore had to be fought blind. But then, my Šeš wasn't without his own skills. Meaning that after many had failed to bring the reptilian looking King to heel, he decided to take matters into his own hands. It was only one of the many reasons he was fit to rule in my absence, as he was never afraid to get his hands dirty to do what needed to be done.

He sat back down, now choosing a smaller throne that was situated next to the horned one fit for that of the Vampire King. I would have rolled my eyes at the theatrics of it all, not giving two shits about where the fuck he sat. However, he knew as well as I did that this pretence was needed, for fear was the only thing that kept my kingdom in line down here. But then I guess the same could be said for the mortal world, as take Adam for instance. He was rarely able to be himself in front of me when others were around, being more of a brother to me than anything else. For there were few who knew the real foundations of our friendship, and looking at my second in command right now well, there were even fewer knew who he really was to me.

It was easier that way.

Fuck but not even Dominic Draven knew who he really was, and I had spent most of my years on mortal soil as his right hand man, being to him what Adam was to me. We had once been friends before we were each other's greatest enemy. As for now…Gods, but seeing as he now knew I was fucking his daughter, then really, who the fuck really knew what was going on in his mind. I was still expecting the brutal bastard to try and kill me when I least expected it. In fact, if it hadn't been that his wife's life was tied to my own, then I knew he would have tried long ago despite killing a whole race of demonic life.

But emphasis on the word tied, for after the Triple Goddess ritual, and Malphas' failure on becoming a God, then we were evenly matched. Even if I hadn't been the only one with the power to manipulate his mind, our fates had made us equals for a reason.

My second's voice brought me back to the reason I was here.

"They are trying to sort out that mess between the rooted soul breeders and Arachne and her army…*again,*" he said sighing in reply to my answer, and even I had to roll my eyes at the hundred-year-old feud between the neighbouring forest lands. But then this was Arachne we were discussing and let's just say the Spider Queen was a title she granted herself. For she only ruled over those she created, her own children.

The two forests were on the border of my realm and therefore it was my responsibility to keep it in check, for their war often seeped out into my lands and involved my people. Arachne had once been a mortal and was the daughter of Idmon. She was said to be the most talented tapestry maker and foolishly, to hold the claim, challenged Athena, Goddess of Wisdom and Crafts to a weaving contest. But that was her downfall for no one challenged the Gods without repercussions and hers ended up costing more than just her mortal life.

This was because when Athena found no flaws in her work the Goddess became enraged, as their egos were everything to them. To be worshipped was what gave a God their power and when one was beaten by a mortal, then that worship always slipped a little, meaning Athena had to make an example out of her to keep her worship intact. Doing so even if it was done through the strength of fear. Because some Gods may reside in Heaven but not all are heavenly and pure. After all, Hell wasn't the only place that used fear as a means of control.

Fucking hypocrites the lot of them!

The Goddess beat her in front of everyone who had once been in awe of her talent and cursed her. Arachne hung herself out of shame and upon her sinful death, the curse transformed her mortal body, forever imprisoning her in the body of a demonic spider she had no hope of ever escaping from. Instead, she was forced to become a breeder for the creature she was given to and as a result, found herself being impregnated every day of her damned eternal life.

In a nutshell, this meant that it was no wonder she was constantly pissed at the world. But the lesson was delivered loud and clear, becoming a cautionary tale in warning mortals not to place themselves on an equal level with the Gods.

However, for me it was, as usual, bad fucking timing!

"Get a message to them, use the eye if you have to." At this my second in command answered me first with a raise of his brow in surprise, for no one was permitted to use the eye, not even him. So, to be granted access to it was soon about to call my bluff.

"The Eye of Crimson was gifted for your use only, which means it must be something very fucking important for you to grant…"

"I am well aware of my position, Šeš, I do not need a history lesson. Just use the fucking thing to get a message to them."

"And that message would be?" His question made me sigh and I knew this was the time to bullshit through my teeth as it was too dangerous to reveal the truth. Which was why I told him,

"A witch is fucking with me and stole my favourite mortal slave." His look said it all and his lips twitching to hold back a smile said a whole lot more.

"I was always under the assumption that you hated mortals and the females weren't exactly to your liking for feeding from either." I swallowed down the urge to snap that I didn't have time for this shit and instead forced myself to play it as cold as I could physically force it to sound.

"There is always the exception to that rule and this one just so happens to fit my cock nicely. I also spent a great deal of time training her to fit my needs perfectly."

"Who the fuck cares, just train another, after all, that is half the fun," he said with a flick of his hand as if he were merely talking about the simple sexual use of a body to fuck. I would have growled and punched my gauntleted covered fist through the nearest wall at just the idea of replacing my girl, but thankfully I kept it somewhat calm enough to keep up the pretence.

"I don't want to train another, what I want is to retrieve what was stolen from me and punish those who dare take what is mine!" I snapped with a bite of frustration.

"How was this mortal even transported here, by all rights she should be dead…unless there is something about this one you are not telling me…fated by the Gods perhaps?" Fuck, but I forgot how perceptive my Šeš was!

"I don't know how, but just before I ram my fist down the bitch's throat I will ask how she managed to send her here…in the meantime I want my slave back and I want her back fucking now!" This time I let my anger flow and hammered a fist down on one of the largest horns at the arm rest, crushing it and making the golden tip clatter to the floor and echo around the large space.

"Alright, I get the point, I will contact the McBain brothers but the Eye isn't necessary, for my mage will contact them, as I am sure finding the only living mortal running around your realm won't be too hard to find…that is, if she is running around in your realm?" His question caught me off guard and I couldn't help but mutter,

"I fucking hope so." He raised a questioning brow at this but thankfully didn't push me into answering why it was so important to me. The truth was I didn't know where she could be, for the Keepers had only hinted at it being in my realm as she wasn't drawn to this place as I was. Hell, it was like he had said, as a mortal she shouldn't even be here. But then again, if it was fated by the Gods, then being mortal wouldn't be a factor, for the power of the Fates was everything in this world.

"You know what they will ask for in return," he reminded me and to be honest, I couldn't give a fuck what it cost me to get her back, I was willing to pay it tenfold!

"If she is returned back to me unharmed, then they can consider their blood vow fulfilled."

"Are you serious?!" He snapped making me grant him a look that told him to be careful in how he spoke to me.

"Are you questioning me?" I warned. He ran a frustrated hand at the back of his neck and took a breath.

"No, I am merely asking you if a piece of mortal pussy is worth the strongest shifters in Hell?" At this I nearly lost it and in doing so would have revealed that she was much more than just some mortal pussy. Thankfully, I had enough sense to wisely hold back. After all, this was all just an act I was forced to play out.

"Those royal shifters have been bound to me for long enough. It is time they start fulfilling their own destinies and there is no better cause for them in doing so now by serving me this one last time. Besides, Trice grows stronger and stronger each passing decade and is fuelled by his bitter hatred for being bound to me."

"You have a point there," he muttered before I carried on.

"Yes and that bitterness will either have the power to destroy himself and his brothers or it will be enough to do damage to my kingdom, either one would be a waste, as it would only end in their death and my annoyance at our having to rebuild...neither of these I have the patience or time for," I said making yet another point.

"Nor I," he agreed even without knowing the full extent of bad timing. Which meant that as my second in command he really needed to be informed of what was happening regarding the witch, someone who was making it her mission to destroy my life and everyone connected to it. I also knew that the sooner I discovered her identity then the sooner I could discover her weaknesses and use them against her. Everyone had a weakness in some way, and up until Amelia, then I had prided myself on having none. Which was why I knew how vital it was to keep her true identity unknown, even from the man I had appointed to run my kingdom. Because as much as I trusted him to rule in my place, I didn't trust him when it came to the one being I wanted to keep her secret from the most...

Lucifer.

"Where is Carn'reau?" I asked after the commander of my armies, the once dark Fae Prince and banished rightful ruler of his Elemental world. The reasons for his banishment were never made known to me and in truth, I hadn't cared enough to find out. All I cared for is that he offered his loyalty to me and with it the army he brought with him that was banished as well. Of course, his loyalty came with some perks on both sides, for the exchange in power was a welcomed bonus. This was because my blood granted him more power than those of his brethren, including his brothers. As for my gain, other than that of his army, were his extreme fighting skills and experience in war, for he was to this date unbeaten in battle.

It was why I made him commander of all my own armies, not just the one he brought with him upon leaving his world. The new training methods he enforced meant that my kingdom was in fact one of only few claimed to be the most powerful in all of Hell. Fuck, but the reason Lucifer was so twitchy around me these last few hundred years was because my strength was only increasing, in both my own supernatural abilities and the strength of my forces. But then that was what happened when you spent your time obsessed with trying to create the most powerful beings to add to your collection...sometimes, *you succeeded.*

"He is as he should be, preparing to charge into battle on the Shadowlands at first light, you know the piece of land we have been trying to claim for the last three hundred turns of the sky." I hissed a curse under my breath and said the unthinkable,

"Postpone the war."

"What?!" he snapped back incredulously.

"You heard me, have them pull back and postpone the campaign." I repeated making his green eyes spark with anger.

"But we are so close to winning this—" he started to argue, one I stopped in its tracks before he went too far.

"You. Heard. Me." At this he sighed and wisely gave up the fight after first looking around the room and realising we weren't free to have this open conversation the way he obviously wished we were.

"And your orders for them?" He asked in a now tense tone.

"I want them to march throughout the towns, search every fucking house, inn, every fucking hole in the ground, I don't fucking care, I just want her found!" I snapped having long done with this conversation.

"And the Shadowlands?" I released a sigh and said,

"Once this is all over, I will speak with their King, for this is a mess he should have sorted out himself by now." And it was, fucking big bastard of a Viking. The King of Shadows and the keeper of the Ouroboros had not long since stepped up to the claim of his chaotic Kingdom. One that had spent its near entirety without a leader and therefore was constantly at war with itself along with everyone else in Hell. It was a huge realm and bordered my own from the North. Which meant I'd had no choice but to take control of what I could and try to claim the rest, a kingdom I did not fucking want!

No, what I wanted was for the big bastard to get his ass down here and sort his own shit out, despite his reasons for not wanting to. This being said, to give him his due, he had at the very least stepped up and accepted his fate, doing so with little choice if he wanted to keep his own Chosen One. But his work was only half done and if he didn't act soon then I would be claiming his land by force once and for all.

One look at his face and I knew my Šeš wanted to argue further on the matter and to be honest, I couldn't really blame him. Not considering we had been planning this for nearly a Hell's year. But nothing was more important than this, and right now, Hell could go and fuck itself for all I cared.

"And do you have any idea where this slave girl of yours is or are we just declaring her the most hunted female in all of Hell's realms?" His question made me grit my teeth and hold myself back from commanding this decree, for I wanted her back where she belonged, and I wanted her back now. But with that being said, I still knew the dangers that would follow in making it known to my kingdom what the importance of finding her would be. For some would find it a rare opportunity to exploit what would naturally be assumed was a weakness of mine. This no doubt only ending in her becoming used as a bargaining tool or even worse, a means for revenge.

Caution was definitely key here and having to balance that and using what resources I had without putting her in jeopardy was going to be a challenge. Which was why I needed to be out there trying to find her myself and doing so whilst at the same time praying I wasn't too fucking late already!

"No, I don't know for sure, but I know one being that might. In the meantime, I want this kept between those bound to me and who I have chosen to be charged with finding her," I told him, knowing that by doing so would cause reason for suspicion in itself, for my second was far from stupid.

"And what of the witch?" he chose to ask instead.

"What of her?" I barked in annoyance, knowing my patience for speaking of that bitch wasn't going to last long.

"Well, it stands to reason should she go this far to piss you off, doing so enough for you to come all the way down here, then surely her limits won't end there…how do we know this isn't just all part of her plan?" I thought on that a moment, for I knew that to go into details right now then I would only be in danger of exposing Amelia too soon. Something I couldn't risk until at the very least she was found and safely back by my side. After that, then we could tackle the next shit thrown our way but until then, I had to be careful. Which was why I gave him a vague answer,

"We don't know that it isn't part of her plan, which is why we act on the side of caution. But even then, the rule stands that the mortal girl is not to be touched or harmed in anyway, for only I will decide her fate and that of her punishment...is that understood?" I asked in a tone that spoke of my anger should these wishes not be carried out.

"It will be known," he replied with the tick in his jaw unmistakable. He too was losing patience knowing that he was purposely being kept in the dark.

"Good," I replied turning to leave and only stopping when he suddenly asked,

"And this being who might know where she is, where will you find them, for if I need to reach you?" I paused and turned slightly to look back at him without my horns getting in the way. Then I told him,

"The Kingdom of Lust." Naturally, my reply surprised him, making me wonder if even that being said had been given too much away. For he very well knew, as all did, who the King of Lust was connected too.

Dominic Draven.

"Now that is interesting," he mused making me grit my teeth and snap,

"The only interest in it I want from you is the interest you show in ways of finding what belongs to me, anything other than that is an expelled energy I will not be happy to hear you have wasted." The moment I said it I knew my mistake for this would only drive him to be more curious, his cunning grin told me this and made the next words out of his mouth a lie.

"But of course, my Šeš." So, I took a deep breath and finally made my point, speaking in a way that was, granted, more suited to behind closed doors. But it was imperative that he understood the deeper meaning he would find in just speaking his name aloud,

"I mean it, Dariush…" I paused, narrowed my gaze and said,

"Don't fail me, Brother."

CHAPTER TEN

PORTALS AND POETS

I left my brother, no doubt to ponder my words and stew on my reasons given. Again, he wasn't stupid and could no doubt read between the complicated lines of my being here. But then, deception was no stranger to either of us. For keeping up the ruse of him merely being nothing more than my second in command was a necessary evil in our world. The fact was that we both decided that living this lie was an important element for our combined rule to work as smoothly as it did.

No one knew about Dariush, other than Keira, for she discovered this during her time travelling trip to the past where she first encountered him. He was without doubt my best kept secret, as this was what we both agreed was for mutual benefit. Hence the reason not even my former King, Dominic, knew of his existence. And as far as I knew, Keira had kept my secret out of respect for my wishes for her to do so. After all, I was her maker.

Now, at some point I knew that I would have to explain about the history of my brother to Amelia. And well, seeing as we were now in Hell together, then that time would likely be sooner rather than later, after of course I had first found the girl!

In fact, I had expected one of the first things from her lips after being made to experience my past first-hand was to ask me why I never mentioned him. But then it quickly occurred to me that our joint father had obviously kept his word. Lucifer had, at our request, kept the knowledge of Dariush a secret, and in doing so needed to erase that part of him from my life. This was so that even the Fates weren't able to make his existence known. Which meant manipulating Lucifer's first creation, the Keepers of Three. The Fates had deemed them connected to my life, seeing every piece of it as being the ones trusted with the Tree of Souls. But that didn't mean Lucifer didn't still have his influence over their mind.

It was the reason Amelia hadn't seen Dariush in my memories and until that moment I had never known that Lucifer had in fact kept his end of the bargain. But then again, it wasn't like this plan wasn't to Lucifer's advantage either. Especially not when more than two thousand years later he would use this secret son of his to help him in getting his Chosen One back.

But secrecy was the key when it came to Dariush, for his power rivalled my own but only when he was in Hell. You see, Lucifer's goal when creating the perfect being and one intended to rule over the growing problem the Vampire race was creating, was one he achieved in me. But throughout the years I discovered there had been many failures and only two mortals turned successfully. And out of us both, it was only me that was suited to rule, for when Dariush was turned he became something else entirely…

He was the only one of his kind.

It was why his existence was such a well-guarded secret. For Lucifer he was the ultimate weapon but for me, well…

He was my brother.

But both meant that he could be used against us and even though he was tied to Lucifer by blood, it also meant that he was tied to me in the same way also. It was why, if I chose to be, I could quite easily have become Lucifer's biggest threat of power. For Dariush not only felt loyalty to both of us but only one of us had the power over his mind. And well, it wasn't Lucifer as he would have preferred it to be.

Besides, like I said, we were brothers and that came before being sons of the Devil. We had spent time in the mortal realm together, always doing so under the ruse of him being my second and long before Adam was turned. But then, when we found ourselves constantly being forced back to deal with an entirely different kingdom, we knew things had to change. For it was a usual occurrence, as our realm in Hell couldn't go long without being dominated under the hand of a ruthless ruler.

That was when the decision was made for Dariush to take my place. Something that allowed me the freedom to forge my own destiny and eventually pave the way to strengthen my kingdom in the mortal realm. This had been fortunately achieved with great success, much to Dom's annoyance.

And speaking of Dominic and annoyances, it was time to go and visit an entirely different ruler…

The Prince of Lust… Dom's father.

Now all I had to hope for was that the portal into his realm was still accessible, or time will have been wasted. For I would simply have no choice but to go back to my castle to seek aid, as one of Dariush's many talents is he could create a shifter portal to anywhere. His power in being able to summon the doorways seemed endless, creating them both between worlds and the realms they were built up of. It was one of his greatest gifts, whereas others with even the slightest use of the same power could only manage to create a portal a few times a year.

This was because the amount of power and energy it took was astounding.

However, Dariush could create one with little trouble and as I said, he seemingly had an endless amount of energy to offer. But no one knew this, which was why we didn't exactly abuse the talent…at least not in front of others. For the being with the keys into any place in Hell, Heaven, and everything in between, was a dangerous commodity that others would kill to exploit. But then again, he was Lucifer's secret weapon, so his talents weren't surprising to us. And because of this, it was also why I didn't choose to trust him just yet, for Lucifer would always have that hold on him, being his maker.

What can I say, other than it was a fucked-up family dynamic if ever there was one!

Luckily for me however, my worry had been for nothing as the portal that had been created was still intact and wasn't as unstable as I feared it might be. Because without use, then some of these doorways created just didn't have enough power to maintain themselves and simply vanished. Portals usually drew from the energy of the beings that used them and a trip to the level of lust was naturally a popular place for most. After all, sex was sex no matter what kind of creature/creation or being of Hell you were. And should its ruler be feeling generous at the time, then he was usually all too willing to oblige those looking for a hardcore version of the act.

The portal was situated not too far away from my castle and just on the other side of the Echoing Forest, next to a cluster of caves. I could see the energy waves comes from the distorted space of scenery, telling me it was active and from the looks of things, *used often*.

I scoffed as I landed the moment a break in the trees would allow, not exactly being surprised by my people's choice of holiday destination. I took one look at the portal and readied myself for what was ahead, calling forth the rest of my demonic armour that was as natural as allowing my demon to take over my vessel. This included my chest piece and shoulder plating growing until I was completely covered in a hardened black metal. The armour down my arms, legs and feet had already encased my flesh the moment my demon side had erupted back in the Temple. And thank fuck it had because one thing was for sure, there had been no way in Hell I would be stepping through that portal dressed like a fucking tourist and sporting hiking sandals!

I walked the small distance back to the area I had seen from above and without a moment to waste, walked through the portal, ignoring the slither of stolen energy it consumed. For one such as I, it was barely even noticeable. But for those much weaker, then they would no doubt have felt it enough to require rest once they had arrived. It wasn't surprising that down here, it was survival of the fittest and power was everything.

However, one look back as I stepped through and I knew why the portal had been so active…it was like a damn 'welcome to fuck land', the sexual playground for supernaturals for God's sake! I was just surprised it didn't have writing carved into the arch of bodies that said, 'Play hard and stay hard longer'.

"Fuck me," I muttered with a shake of my head, ignoring the not so subtle arch of bodies that were connected sexually. The dip of a male's head was mostly hidden by being at the centre of a woman's legs and framed either side by her thighs. It was as if he had been frozen in time during his sexual meal. The couple looked carved out of wood and then strangely burnt with a blowtorch. The man's feet and the woman's hands were also fused against the boards on the dock that also had that blackened charred effect.

I looked beyond the eternal image of such a sexual act,

trying to ignore the memories a sight like this conjured up. Especially when remembering the sweet taste of my own girl's release on my tongue as I feasted on her.

Gods, but I missed my girl.

The calmness of the black river was a contrast to the surrounding sandstorm that raged around the realm and could be seen in the distance. One similar surrounded parts of my own castle and were an effective way to keep not only enemies out but also that of unwelcomed magic.

I couldn't help but recite what Dom often did when he mentioned that of his father, and I never understood why until seeing that storm,

"But to that second circle of sad Hell, where in the gust, the whirlwind, and the flaw of rain and hail-stones, lovers need not tell their sorrows—pale were the sweet lips I saw, pale were the lips I kissed, and fair the form I floated with, about that melancholy storm. ..." It was by John Keats, named, 'A dream after reading Dante's episode of Paolo And Francesca'. I think it had something to do with the history of his parents as theirs was a tale of forbidden love like no other. The Demon Prince and Archangel were never meant to fall in love and achieve the impossible by creating life. And just like that forbidden love, Dante's inferno told of the story of Francesca and her brother in law, Paolo, who were both condemned to Hell for adultery. Dante was touched and held sympathy for their condemned love and the cruelty of their death because of it. Francesca was portrayed as being compelled by love and unable to stop it, for the power of the heart is an unrelenting force.

As for the Prince of Lust, it was said that the storm that surrounds his kingdom began the day his precious Sarah was taken from him and to this day has never once stopped. The power of the heart was an unstoppable force indeed and had the power to affect us all or so it would seem. And now, one glance back up at the colossal castle that overshadowed the town below, and that power most certainly wasn't in question when it came to its ruler.

The castle was easily the size of a city itself and a towering mass of black stone carved into giant sentinels. It was said to be built from the underbelly of a volcano that mirrored Mount Merapi in the mortal realm. One which was situated in the centre of the island of Java, Indonesia.

I ignored the hustle of demonic life that obviously lived in these parts and was clearly used to the sexual references at every turn. Like the giant cocks that the boats were moored to, instead of simple wooden posts for ropes to be wrapped around. This was the same as the erotic statues that I could see dotted in between the wide wooden clad buildings. They seem to be directions of sorts, as protruding body parts looked to be pointing a certain way, while gleaming white signs were held in their hands. The gloominess of the rising mist rolling in from the surface of the water was cut short and faded away the further from the docks I walked. This was thanks to the naked figures that lined the streets and held glass blown lamps in their bound hands. Hands that were tied above their heads, almost like they were being suspended from an invisible beam above. Collars of gleaming gold around their necks and a single chain dipped from one pierced nipple to the other.

I knew even from looking at them that these were no doubt a mirror image of some of the sexual slaves that could be found within the castle walls. The citizens gave me a wild berth as I stepped further along the dock and onto the black glass cobbled street, that looked like broken pebbles of highly polished flint. My metal boots that were made up of overlapping plates in a sabaton style, clinked against the ground as I walked. Then the second I had the space I stretched out my wingspan and took to the air, making my way quickly towards the castle.

I didn't have time for being polite here but then again, I didn't have the time to fight his sentinels either, so I had no choice but to request an audience with the royal, knowing he would not refuse me. Especially seeing as he loved nothing more than a bit of drama and me being here would most certainly pique his interest.

I took no time at all finding the entrance, being as it was sandwiched in between two of the largest towers. They were the size of skyscrapers, and at its centre at least fifty carved archways stood, like curved vertical steps. These framed a pair of imposing castle doors of stark white that were big enough to fit my club Transfusion through. Next to this was an outpost of sorts, being an unwelcoming looking building made of spiked turrets. It was a place I chose to land before I demanded to speak with their Lord. I felt a fight coming my way, along with a refusal the second the solider put his hand to the hilt of his weapon.

I gritted my teeth at the annoyance and forced myself to be diplomatic, telling them who I was before I made my demands. Thankfully, this was enough to get me taken seriously, and shortly after this a royal representative appeared to escort me inside. He was an overly tall and overly thin being, that despite his seven-foot height looked breakable all over. White long hair was braided back from pointed features and beady, keen eyes of yellow.

"You have arrived at a fortunate time, for my Lord is in the banqueting hall and offers you a great honour in inviting you to sit and dine with him this turn of the sky." The servant informed me surprising me enough to say,

"I believed all of those who served the Prince were only to speak ancient Sumerian." Something I had done moments ago, despite being rusty. But then again, the language was over 5000 years old.

"Ah yes, well his Maru, and our Enki suggested he...how do I say, get with the times." I scoffed at this, knowing the words he used were the ancient language for 'son' and also the name Enki, 'Lord of Earth', was who Dom was known as in these parts.

After this, talk between us ceased and I didn't encourage otherwise. After all, I wasn't exactly here for a social visit, and the moment I was escorted through into what was obviously his banqueting hall, I soon discovered that the Lord of this castle knew it too.

"Ah King of Blood and Death," he said prompting me to reply back in return,

"Asmodeus, Sar Sha Hatti," I said, calling him the King of Sin as was his preferred title. He eyed me from the top of a long, grand table, one big enough to seat at least fifty people. I also ignored the obvious sexual focal point of the room, being that the table was full of naked bodies all covered in food. No, instead I simply focused on the next barrier that stood in my way.

I knew this when the King boldly announced,

"So, you're the one fucking my granddaughter."

CHAPTER ELEVEN

DRIPPING BOUND LUST

After dropping this piece of knowledge like a fucking A-bomb, I was then surprised when it was followed up with him offering me a seat. This instead of trying to rip my head off, stick an apple in my mouth, and add me to his table of fuckery as his new centre piece.

"Won't you take a seat," he offered again with a nod of his head making a servant girl go rushing to pull out my chair. She was wearing nothing but a gold bowtie and a pointless apron that was see-through. Well, that wasn't all she was wearing, as the moment she bent over, a glittering butt plug could also be seen. Naturally she decided to make a show of the act, doing so enough to look at me over her shoulder and wink at me when she caught me staring at her ass.

Had it been a time before my Chosen One I might have taken the time to admire it but as it stood now, she held no interest for me, and my scowl of annoyance told her as much. I therefore took my offered seat briefly noting her disappointment and caring little for it.

However, Asmodeus clearly did care as he chuckled to himself. Then he flicked his hand through the air as if he was brushing off lint and by doing so telling the girl to silently leave me be. I looked down at the plush red velvet seat in a way that made it obvious how little I wanted to sit down. I didn't have time to fucking dine at this fucked up table of sex and sin. But then one look at my 'host' and I also knew it wasn't wise to refuse him this unnatural welcome. For an unnatural welcome was exactly what it was, especially considering he obviously knew a lot more than I gave him credit for.

So, I decided to be honest.

"I am surprised you offer me one given your last statement," I said sitting down anyway. Asmodeus threw his head back and laughed, doing so in a way that was unnerving. Although this wasn't surprising considering who he was, for it wasn't only his looks that resembled his son. Both were renowned for their tempers and both were hard mother fuckers at that, for I was not the only King in Hell to be labelled as a 'Tyrant'.

Of course, looking like an older version of my former King was also playing on my senses. For it was said that he purposely chose to look this way, much to his son's dismay at refusing to yield and change his appearance. Asmodeus had the power to look however he wished as he was mere steps away from being a God. But then he chose his son's appearance merely for the fact that it irked him, something that was renowned to be his favourite past time.

At least in that we found common ground I through wryly.

"Ah nonsense, for if I wanted you dead, I would have done so by now, having Meria here slice you with her fish blade…" he said making me look to the side where the mostly naked servant was stood now holding a platter of steamed fish. She also gave me a wicked grin as she pulled a large curved knife from the now gutted belly of a silver fish and waved it at me.

"…but then again, you are your father's favourite son," he said making me scoff,

"I doubt that." At this he looked genuinely shocked and raised a dark brow.

"You believe he has another?" he asked making me tense for a split second before forcing myself to relax, with my mind now running wild with questions. Did Asmodeus know of my brother or was this a test because he merely suspected? Either were possible because his skills in manipulation and control weren't solely used or saved for the bedchamber, but throughout the rest of Hell as well. After all, he was the eyes and ears of Lucifer, being that Asmodeus was his closest friend. If there was something to discover in Hell, then Asmodeus would make it his mission to find it.

"I simply point out that my growing strength isn't unknown to him and he believes it could one day become a threat," I said as calmly as I could.

"And will it?" he replied coming straight out with it. I swallowed hard and after grabbing a goblet of what I could smell was 'swine wine' I told him,

"Not unless he does something foolish like trying to take what belongs to me."

"You mean like my granddaughter who you boldly claimed as your own?" he came right out and said it.

"No, for that wouldn't just be foolish but more so deadly," I replied knowing that my warning would be loud and clear and one that would get back to him quickly. Then I took a drink of the amber liquid, named as it was due to fermenting of the swine berry. This was named such for its foul smell when the Hell grown plant flowered. Its taste was a bittersweet flavour that clung to my tongue and made me thirst instead for the sweeter blood of my Chosen One.

"Duly noted, now please, enjoy my hospitality," he said

splaying an arm out towards the tangle of bodies all lay upon the table and displayed like flesh coloured platters for the different dishes we were expected to eat.

There were folded slices of meats arranged on bare muscular chests, following the natural dips and contours of the male physique. There were female bodies overflowing with fruit, with slices cut to frame breasts that were drizzled in golden honey. Salad leaves that made one female look like history's depiction of Eve in the garden of Eden. One with the bitten apple she permanently had held in her mouth like a ball gag, was a telling tale, however the cock up her ass, was not. As for the rest, other than the common naked theme, each body was also connected with the next in some way. Every hole was filled if not by flesh then by the food we were expected to eat.

But one glance at the room beyond the feast and it was no different. The gothic opulence of a King was all around us in both what I would have named a gaudy and predictable décor. Statues painted gold were actually two living slaves positioned in some sexual act together that I had noticed changed every five minutes or so. These framed either side of the seven archways along one wall that were closed off from view by thick, dark red curtains of velvet to match the chairs. Glossy black furniture adorned the room, including the grand table that took up most of the space. On the other walls a black material clung to the stone like thick textured wallpaper and was decorated by large sigil symbols, depicting his rule in gold thread.

At the far end a woman was hogtied to a pole and was being filled from both sides by one man at either end. One with a cock in her mouth and one in her pussy. Doing so whilst both were basting her skin with oil, making her pale skin slick, wet and glistening. This was at the same time as the pole she was tied to was slowly turning her around like a roasting pig that thankfully was without the fire.

Next to her was another serving station with a naked girl tied in a cocooned web of rope, hanging from the beams above. She was also suspended at an angle that made her legs higher than her shoulders, with her chin resting on a platform. I suspected this was to keep her head raised, naturally thrusting her chest down.

This was so that the lowest parts of her were her large breasts, a pair of milky globes that hung down and were positioned over the table below. Directly under her nipples were two golden goblets awaiting to be filled and with a flick of their master's hand, two slave girls started to pour jugs of red wine slowly down her body. The wine travelled the length of her arched back, soaking the ropes red that bound her. It continued down until flowing over the sides of her tits and clinging there until large droplets gathered against the hard points of her nipples. It then started dripping into the cups below making it look like the girl was being milked of alcohol.

"I call it Virgin Filtered, if you care for some?" he asked, and my look said it all, meaning I didn't need to voice my refusal. He shrugged his shoulders and simply held out his hand as a silent order for one of the servants to fill a new goblet, now the 'filtering process' had finished.

I had no fucking time for any of this and one sly look at Asmodeus and the cocky bastard knew it! So, I decided to get straight to the point,

"I am here in search…"

"I know exactly why you are here, for you believe you have lost something that belongs to you," he interrupted, before taking a large sip of his fucked-up preference in wine. I opened my mouth to speak again when he got in there first,

"All in good time, but first I must insist we dine." Oh, fuck yeah, this asshole was playing with me. This was confirmed when he suddenly announced,

"Oh, but wait, how rude of me, for we forgot to set you a dinner setting." Then he clicked his fingers and a beautiful redhead in a scarlet silk robe stepped from behind an elaborate screen. It was one that unsurprisingly showcased a silk painting of an orgy that was made up of six framed panels and was where servants stood behind waiting for their master's orders. The redhead sauntered towards me with an emphasised sway of her hips and I inwardly cringed knowing what was coming...

A fucking test.

I knew it the second his grin widened to display a row of white teeth, with only just the bare the hint of demonic fangs. A pair that looked to be at the ready when his own 'plate' was walking towards him. She was an exotic looking beauty, with an abundance of perfect curves covered in silky dark skin and a halo of tight orange curls.

"Ah, my sun in the dark, what a treat licking cream off your cunt will be," Asmodeus said as he held out a strong hand for her to take as she seated herself at the edge of the table where he sat, doing so with a smile. I heard the clearing of a throat, prompting me to do the same and forcing me to therefore unclench my fist.

The redhead took my hand and took her own place in front of me, seating her sizeable ass to the edge. Asmodeus most definitely had a thing for curves that was for sure. However, all I could think about was one woman's body and it wasn't the fiery redhead that was currently flicking her hair back like she was some kind of Goddess. I didn't even bother resisting the urge to roll my eyes, not giving two shits about what the fuck this girl felt about my obvious distaste for her. Or anyone on this fucked up sordid table for that matter.

But then, clearly undeterred, the girl reached behind her and picked a strawberry from the living fruit bowl between a girl's legs. This was done before bringing it to her lips and biting into it, in what she no doubt hoped for was in a seductive manner. Then, as she let the juices run down her chin, she added to the sticky red liquid as it travelled her skin, doing so by running the bitten fruit down in between the valley of her pert breasts. However, the moment she started to circle one rose tinted nipple, coating them in the crimson fruit, I looked around her frame and in a bored tone said,

"I am not here to taste your particular flavour of sin, Asmodeus."

"No, I suppose not since you have recently discovered your own mortal flavour," he replied in a knowing tone that had me gritting my teeth despite how subtle the mention of Amelia's blood was. But even then, my refusal went unheard as he simply signalled for more of his servants to come forward. All were near naked men this time with nothing covering their erect cocks.

The white open waistcoats matched both the stark paleness of their skin, and the bow ties at their necks. Each carried large urns cut from black glass at their shoulders making their muscles bulge. Their eyes had been painted black and the streaked track marks ran down their faces where they had cried through the thick clay-like substance used.

Two came to stand either side of me at the ready with the urns held high and waiting for the other two to do the same. It was like a mirror image across from me, as slaves took the same position either side of their Lord. Then with a nod of his head, they each started to pour the thick creamy substance down both girls' bodies, who had now crossed their legs so that most of the mixture was captured in their laps.

Lush cream coated berries of reds, blackish purples, and blues slid down their skin and each threw their heads back until the last of the contents covered their bodies. I looked towards Asmodeus and his own naked plate to see her near shaking with anticipation of what sexual delights were to come. They both then started to lie back against the table, moving as one as if the whole thing had been rehearsed. They each draped themselves over the bodies behind them before they spread their legs at the same time. This caused the creamy mixture to go gushing down the centre of their bare mounds, coating their eager pussies and literally making a meal out of their sex.

I looked up from the redhead's sexual display and in between her spread legs found Asmodeus staring at me. The bastard smiled and motioned with a flick of his wrist for me to start. However when I didn't he spoke up on the fact,

"What's the matter Lucius Septimus, not feeling hungry?" I snarled in response, one that deepened when he added,

"Or are you just hungry for some other mortal pussy?"

"You play a dangerous game with me King of Sin." I told him making him smirk after what seemed to be a habit of his shrugging a shoulder and replying,

"Ah, but what is the harm in it really…after all, you should know that my home is like Vegas, what happens here, stays here?"

"Yeah, as a fucking sexual prisoner…clearly." I said flicking the large ring on the gold collar the girl was wearing, one now splashed with cream.

"I merely invite you to enjoy yourself, after all, it is not like she would ever know," he remarked sickening me further, seeing as he was speaking about his own granddaughter. So, I told him firmly,

"No, *but I would.*" At this he started laughing and said,

"By the Gods, what a saint my granddaughter has turned you into…oh, how the mighty fall." I fisted my hands at his comment and held back from pointing out his own history. But then I knew that would only be a mistake as no one mentioned her name and reminded him of what he had once lost...not if they valued life.

"That is only coming from the view that love makes you weak," I told him and the second his eyes flashed dangerously I knew I had made a mistake, one that I hoped hadn't cost me.

"Ah, so it is love then is it...? Well, if it is as you claim it to be then..." He paused and my price of honesty soon presented itself the second he said...

"Time to test it I think."

CHAPTER TWELVE

SEXUAL LIMITS

The moment he said this I shouted out in anger, a sound that became lost when I felt every solid surface beneath me sink away into nothing and I slipped through the room like a fucking ghost. I instantly tried to release my wings as I continued to fall, doing so to the sound of high-pitched laughter of those above me. But then when nothing happened, I was only to end up dumbfounded as I felt nothing.

My wings were gone.

Then, before I could think of what else to do, I landed, doing so on a large bed of white silk. Naturally, I quickly scanned my new surroundings, seeing now that I was in a large circular room and at the centre of what looked like an erotic show. The walls were made up of a series of glass doors and behind each one was what appeared to be a sexual act in action. Two women with hands bound behind their backs were lapping their tongues up an erect cock of an overly large demon who looked to be in the seventh realm of Heaven.

Another room held an elderly man being whipped by a demonic dominatrix, who was using her forked tail as the implement of sexual torture. Her victim was shuddering in pleasure, despite the red whip lines that marred his sagging and delicate skin. Others simply held half naked dancers of all shapes and sizes, mortal and demon alike, and each were attached to their single cells with a collar and chain that was bolted to the wall or ceiling in some way.

Then there were those being sexually tortured on a leather clad contraption of some kind. The sound and smell of sex was everywhere. It invaded my senses like a drug, making my fangs ache as they pressed their way against my gums trying to slip free and sink into someone's flesh. I shook my head, trying to rid the need from my mind, knowing now that something else was going on in here.

This wasn't just a sexual playground, but more like a fucking prison...*literally!* It was as if my reasons for trying to want to leave here became muddy and fogged, as I could feel my cock straining against...fuck, but what was I doing naked?!

It looked as if I hadn't just been stripped of my wings, but my entire vessel had returned back to looking like that of a mortal man. I looked back up to see where I had slipped through to find the ceiling above me had been transformed into a glass window. The banquet for one continued and after first granting me a cocky wink, Asmodeus dipped his head in between the girl's thighs and went to work on eating what her creamy pussy was offering.

"Get it the fuck together, Luc!" I snapped at myself having to once again shake my head free of this fucked up control, knowing I was stronger than this. I was stronger than...

"Oh fuck" I muttered as suddenly the glass door in front of me swung open and out walked a line of beauties that made my mouth water. No! There was only one I wanted, and none of

them were her! I continued to tell myself this over and over again, even as each approached the bed and started to climb on. At first, I started to shrug off each hand that touched me, with fingertips trailing their tantalising nails up my legs and over my shoulders.

"No! I don't want this!" I snapped, closing my eyes and trying to break free from this sexual war inside me, one where my body was responding against my will.

"Oh, but you do, my Lord."

"They all do."

"You will see."

"Let us help you relax."

"Let us pleasure you."

All five silky smooth voices seemed to purr this sexual mantra in a string of sentences, ones that all promised the thing my body wanted the most. That sweet release by sinking my cock into a willing vessel's tight hole, for right now I wasn't picky on which. I just needed it. I just needed to dominate a body, using it in the most sinful way and punishing it as I pushed it to its limits. I just needed to fuck an open wet mouth, gagging them on my heavy cock, one I could feel seeping with pre-come. Blonde, brunette, redhead, or fuck even the white-haired beauty that was rising up between my legs, it didn't matter, they were all ripe for the taking.

But then there was also that nagging feeling in the back of my mind, clawing at me, like when my demon was trying to break free and take control. It became a consistent pounding in my head and the second I reached out and touched one of the breasts being offered up to me, it scalded me. It was burning against my skin when there was no flame to speak of.

I tried to make sense of it all.

"What's the matter Vampire, am I not to your liking?" The blonde asked as she moved to straddle my stomach before cupping both breasts this time and holding them out to me like an offering. I started to shake my head as the feeling of dread began to consume me, making my mind spin. Was I fucking drunk?

Gods, had it been…the fucking wine?!

I looked up to see that Asmodeus was now looking down at me, the cream on his face being wiped off by a napkin in a servant girl's hand. Her other hand was down his loose fitted trousers he wore clearly jacking him off. But he was looking directly at me, as if trying to see inside my soul not simply getting off on the sight of having me a prisoner to his sick idea of a show. My mind started to clear somewhat, doing so enough to turn my head against the breasts that were pressed to my lips. I squirmed beneath the bodies trying to touch me, feeling everything in that moment was wrong.

It was so fucking wrong!

"Why do you still fight it, Lucius…after all…" he paused to raise his glass up at me and said before taking a sip,

"…All is fair in love and war."

"All is fair in love and war." I whispered back to myself after hearing those same words being said down at me, by the only voice I wanted to hear. I remembered it well, as it had once come from my Goddess.

My Chosen One.

"My Amelia," I whispered out loud and unable to help doing so in a pained way. Then one look down, and suddenly I snapped. For it was in that very moment that everything cleared in my mind and the controlling fog no longer clouded me in a sexual haze. As a result, my fangs slipped free and snarled at the bodies that surrounded me. It was a dangerous threat but the one girl on top of me didn't move quick enough. I ended up pushing her from me hard enough that she bounced from the bed and toppled to the floor.

"DON'T FUCKING TOUCH ME!" I roared in a rage so powerful, it cracked all the glass doors that surrounded me, making the girls all scream back in fright. Then I erupted back into my demon side, released my wings and flew straight up smashing through the glass floor to the banqueting hall. Everyone in the room cried out in fear...all except Asmodeus, who didn't so much as flinch. Bodies all scrambled off the large table as food spilt from the ruined feast and the redhead covered in cream foolishly tried to stop me. The second she put her hands out to try and touch me, I pushed her back into the arms of one of the male servants who was trying to pass me, knowing she was lucky I didn't break her neck.

I was fucking livid!

"You dare to pull that shit with me!" I thundered as Asmodeus simply pushed his throne like chair back from the table and shrugged his shoulders casually.

"I thought it would be amusing to try," he confessed making me snarl,

"I am no one's fucking puppet!"

"No, for surely you are someone's if you belong to her?" he challenged, making me lose my shit completely. I grabbed the end of the table and flipped it so hard that it and all its contents went crashing into the wall. This doing so barely missing the girls tied up there and unable to escape my wrath.

"SHE IS MY CHOSEN ONE!" I roared the second after it smashed into the stone arches and quickly became chunks of splintered wood. Finally, at this he released a deep sigh and rose to his feet before telling me,

"Come...I'd best help you find her then." After he said this he turned around and started walking towards the back of the room where he knew I would follow. Especially after finally giving me hope of achieving the reason I had come here in the first place. I ended up following him onto a balcony that overlooked his dark, lustful realm. Sex wasn't just an act to indulge in for Asmodeus, it was what fuelled his very essence and naturally made him one of the most powerful beings in all of Hell. For lust and sex was the same as what hatred and violence did for the Devil. Both sides were some of the most powerful emotions that fed the underworld just as worship, love, and loyalty fed the Gods in Heaven their power.

It didn't make one better than the other, for each side of the divine coin was a gold forged from the exploitation of mortals. But in truth, not one could exist without the other, for the circle of life didn't only spin in one direction. As wars were still fought amongst mortals despite there being enough land for all, just like Gods did in their quest for even more power. Only those that felt something more...*found something more*...were the ones in power that finally said...

Enough.

Their quest for more was finally over and fulfilment came in another form. So right now, the sight of his castle towers simply looking like the cities of the Earth. Only swapping carved stone turrets for metal and glass encasing mortal flesh in business suits. A sight that did nothing for me. It was just another fucked up reminder for me of what I once was.

Before there was her.

Asmodeus flicked out his long robe before leaning heavily against the high black spiral balustrades, and for the first time I had to ask myself had I gotten it all wrong? This sinful life most certainly got stale after a while, for even I knew that after only two thousand years of it. But then for someone like Asmodeus, who had endless lifetimes of not wondering *when* he would meet his Chosen One but instead, when would he ever get her back. Gods, but it must have been a tortured existence, one I wouldn't ever fucking wish for!

Fuck me, but I had been forced to experience merely a few

months without her and I was near tearing my mortal kingdom apart along with my fucking hair out!

"I heard whispers of a mortal girl," Asmodeus finally said.

"Where?" I asked quickly and in a tense tone that said all it needed to about my waning patience.

"You really do love her don't you?" He asked instead of answering my question and now turning back to look at me.

"I do…now tell me where?" I said sternly. He released another sigh and nodded to himself as if deciding something within him, something he didn't share. Then he looked back over his kingdom and said,

"It was said she was wandering somewhere in the forest of rooted soul breeders." Hearing this and my blood started to run cold, as I hissed a pointless plea through my teeth,

"No,"

"I take it that means my granddaughter is in danger?" He asked, finally looking concerned as he fucking should be, considering my Chosen One was about to walk into a fucking war!

"Yes…she fucking is, and we are done here!" I hissed through gritted teeth before releasing my wings and just as I did, Asmodeus gave me one last thing.

"I had to be certain, Luc…*she's my only granddaughter."* I knew what he meant…he was speaking about his fucked-up test of fidelity.

"Only the strongest love ever conquers it," he added, and I growled low before letting my wings take me up into the air to hover about ten feet above where he stood and snapped,

"Yeah, well, next time…*try fucking asking!"* Then I shot through the thick, sinful air, ignoring the pull of lust far easier now that I was putting distance between myself and the castle. I was soon back at the portal and stepping through it after cracking the flint beneath my feet with the impact of my heavy landing.

Because finally it was time to go get my girl and if I had to, then I would…

Start another fucking war!

CHAPTER THIRTEEN

STICKY WEB OF LIES

After stepping back through the portal and into my own realm once more I took to the skies. I knew this was the quickest way to the outskirts of my realm and all I could think to question was if Dariush had got word to the McBain brothers in time. For they had been headed that way to begin with. Now all I could hope for was that they had reached their destination before being ordered to turn back and when doing so, they hadn't been too late in finding her.

Gods, but there were just so many possibilities as to what could have gone wrong and all of them seemed to assault me at once. Doing so to the point that I was nearly a nervous fucking wreck by the time I landed. Of course, it didn't help that when I did, it was in the middle of nothing but the death and destruction left after the war had clearly ended. I looked one way towards the side of the forest that belonged to the rooted soul breeders, and then the other towards the spiteful Spider Queen. It didn't take me long to assess the damage on both sides, seeing as it had been extensive enough that most of the forest had been burnt to a cinder and beyond all life.

I could currently see what was left of the mortal part of the Queen's body, nestled at the centre of a broken a mass of spider limbs and body parts. These sections of what was left of the arachnid demon were surrounded by smaller creatures that were all spinning webs and trying to recapture the human form of Arachne before she could drag herself free. The pieces that had been collected were slowly making their way back to their lair, as they were being dragged by lengths of webbing attached to lines of its surviving children.

Good, there was a mind left to manipulate the truth from.

But then I scented something on the breeze and froze my steps the second I did. It was blood...*Amelia's blood.* I closed my eyes and sucked back a shuddered breath, holding it there for longer in hopes of calming the fuck down. I needed to keep my level head here and I started doing so by scenting just how much blood there was. I followed it towards a broken part of the land that looked as though it had been created on purpose, this along with the melting shards of ice that spread out on the usually dry land.

What the fuck had happened here?!

I flew over to a small ledge and knelt one knee to the ground, finding the source of my current panic. I found a few droplets of blood and swiped them with my fingertip. Then I rubbed it in between my fingers and brought it closer to examine, inhaling deeply as I did. Thankfully, after another quick scan of the ground, I saw that despite it being her blood, there wasn't much of it to suggest she had suffered any major damage. This was good not just for the obvious reasons but also the fact she had been here and had obviously survived, because there was no sight of her broken body unlike the Queen's fate. And one look back at the land's fallen ruler and I knew there had been only one creature capable of delivering that amount of damage…or should I say three combined.

A Wyvern, a Gryphon, and a Cockatrice.

The swifter brothers McBain.

I released a sigh of relief despite knowing there was a small chance at it being premature, which was why I needed to be sure. I looked up from the blood on my metal covered fingers and snarled over my shoulder at the one who could have caused her harm. Then I flew myself over to the twitching form of the losing side's Queen and curled a lip in disgust at the desperate attempt of the spider race trying to reclaim its cursed prisoner.

Oh, there was no doubt putting her together again could be achieved, and that she would rule once again, but from the look of all the children she had lost, along with her devastating injuries, then that rule would take years to rebuild once more.

The moment I landed close enough the few spider children that had survived scuttled away, obviously sensing the threat in me as being one they had no chance of fighting. They had been trying to drag even more of the pieces of the giant spider and the mortal body of Arachne to the cave it called home. And from the looks of things now, then they would need a fucking eternity to become whole once more as the damage was far more extensive than I first thought. The brother's looked to have shifted into their impressive combined form and ripped the bitch apart.

I looked towards the sky as if I half expected to still see the mighty form flying off with what I could imagine was their new charge in their grasp. I also knew they wouldn't have gotten far as one of the downsides to their remarkable power when shifting was that it didn't last long. Meaning that they would only get so far. Well, if they had received their orders from my brother's way of communicating with them, then they would have tried to get as close to my castle as they could. This before being forced to change back to their original form.

Which meant if they were on foot, they would have no choice but to travel through the Kingdom of Death, a place that started with a rickety old town that was full of thieves, brothels, and vagabonds. Among these were admittedly the few just trying to make what life they could in Hell. It was also a place that bounty hunters often used as a pitstop, for it was known as a good way to exchange coin for more than just a meal and a roof for the night. It was also used for information. People gathered it like currency, telling me that it wouldn't be long before word got out about Amelia.

But it was towns like this that were found throughout all of Hell, with fewer cites than the mortal world. In fact, the biggest misconception about Hell was that it was simply filled with tortured souls of the dead and little more. But it actually was a civilisation of many races and demonic creatures, who for most parts co-existed somewhat peacefully. Although one glance around where I stood now, and that statement seemed weak at best.

Arachne made a pained sound that drew my attention back to why I was here and what I hoped to find from her memories. Because I knew it would do little good trying to get information out of her freely, for threatening death would have only been a welcome by one cursed as she. The demonic element of her new being was now in pieces and would no doubt, if they could, be scrabbling to try and contain their undying prisoner so she couldn't escape them. This meant that offering an eternal death would be one she would no doubt have begged me for.

Any other time I might have felt pity for such a being, but not today…not when I knew that my girl had been here, that her blood had been shed. For despite how brave she was, when seeing Arachne for the first time, she would have been forced to face her fears.

She hated spiders.

But then this was Amelia we were talking about, which meant that even if she was afraid, she would no doubt fight with her last breath because that was my girl. I fisted my hand the moment I remembered her blood there and let my snarl of anger ripple through me. Then I set my sights on the one being that right now I could take some of my rage out on.

However, the moment I stepped forward I felt the usual crackle of the air next to me, and having experienced it many times before, I called out,

"It is clear, Brother."

After this Dariush stepped through what seemingly would have looked to others as thin air.

"I thought their plan was to try and stop the war, not burn the whole fucking lot to the ground," he said now being free to speak as he usually did when no one else was around.

"I have a feeling that they had no choice," I replied seeing for myself what they must have been up against. Besides, I cared little for the carnage, just so long as they were able to keep my Chosen One safe.

"Do you know if they found this slave of yours?" he asked making me sigh,

"They found her."

"You look relieved, which tells me there is more going on here than you're willing to say," Dariush commented and it came as no surprise, so I decided to give him what I could.

"The Tree of Souls is infected," I said making him hiss through his teeth,

"Fuck"

"Yes, fuck indeed," I agreed with another sigh resisting the urge to scrub a hand down my face seeing as that would fucking hurt giving the amount of edged metal that currently covered my skin.

"How did this happen?" I ground my teeth, lifted my left hand and said,

"This is how it fucking happened." The gravity of my words hit him hard enough to snarl one name,

"Fucking Cronus."

Cronus had been a God who was thought to be dead and who, before Amelia was even born, tried to bring about his rebirth. This time doing so as a God on Earth and to aid him in what would have been an apocalyptic endeavour, tried to release the Titans. It had been the start of what would become known as the Blood Wars.

We had won the battle that day, but it wasn't without losses on both sides. My own sacrifice made, however, had been the first time we had managed to stop the Titans from breaking free of their once eternal prison in Tartarus. But unbeknown at the time, losing my hand in the lowest depths of Hell had kick started its own chain of events. And naturally the biggest problem we faced now, was how to stop it. Because there was something Amelia hadn't known when stepping into Hell believing she had the power to stop the curse. There was only one way to do that and that was down in Tartarus where this all started. The problem with that was…

Tartarus didn't fucking exist anymore!

It had been destroyed in the second battle against them and the Titans were buried along with their God, Cronus…or so we were led to believe. But of course, the Keepers of Three had conveniently chosen to keep this information from Amelia. The biggest question of all was why. The Fates could not lie, this was true, but what they were pretty fucking good at was keeping shit to themselves and the manipulation of others through choice words spoken. Basically, in short, they were crafty fuckers who couldn't be trusted!

"And what of this witch, do we know of her involvement, as I gather there was more to this magical bitch you weren't telling me?" My brother was most certainly right there, but now was not the time, which was why I told him,

"I will explain later, but all you need to know right now is that she is our enemy, she is more powerful than any other witch I have ever encountered and if there is a way for her to get to me, she will find that way with a blade in her hand." He raised a brow at this, no doubt questioning, like I did, who could possibly come by that amount of power for a witch. Instead he refocused his question on my Amelia.

"And what of the girl, I take it this is also a means of—"

"The girl for the time being is not your concern." I interrupted quickly and now we were alone, this prompted him to ask,

"And what of when it does become my concern Šeš, what then?" he asked referring to what was code for brother and derived from an ancient form of cuneiform and usage of Akkadian language. It proved useful to us for it was an extinct East Semitic language, one that was used in ancient Mesopotamia and dating back from the third millennium BCE. That was until its gradual replacement by Akkadian-influenced Old Aramaic among Mesopotamians by the 8th century BCE. In short, it was one not known in Hell and that suited us just fine.

"The day she becomes a concern is the day she becomes a threat to us but until then, leave her to me." At this he finally conceded and nodded in understanding. I ignored his keen eyes and focused instead on when he asked,

"What are your instructions?"

"Send Carn'reau and my army to the first town when

entering the Kingdom of Death, for it is likely that will be the first place they stop." I told him, after first getting a bearing on where they would possibly land.

"I believe they are shortly to enter the shitty place, for it was naturally the first town to look at being as it is the closest from the wastelands. But what makes you so sure the brothers even found her here?"

"I have evidence to support that theory..." I said as I absentmindedly rubbed my fingertips together again, as if I was able to feel her presence in my realm by a single drop of blood.

"...but as you know, I am nothing if not thorough," I added, making him chuckle as I had Arachne in my sights. Then I left him standing where he was as it was time to discover the truth.

Once again as I approached, what was left of her children scattered, dropping the broken pieces of their Queen after they had been still trying to drag them back to the cave. The battered female form of Arachne lay still with her face down in the ash coloured dirt barely even looking as if any life was left in her. So once close enough I flipped her over with my boot and faced what I wondered if at one time had ever been a beautiful face.

Her dark hair was matted with dirt, blood, and what looked like white vomit caught in fist size globules. This I soon discovered was from being forced to produce a stream of webbing that had first been impregnated inside her belly, before being regurgitated and directed at her foe.

I knew this after I had grabbed the top part of her head, placing my palm to her eyes and forced my way inside her brain to breach her memories. After this...*I saw it all.*

I had been right, my girl had fought, not once giving up despite her fear. But even then, had the shifter brothers not turned up when they had, then she wouldn't have lasted long, for they had protected her and saved her life. A few minutes later and I didn't need to see anymore, dropping my hold on her and ignoring the moan of pain the second I did.

"Was it as you suspected?" Dariush asked as he approached.

"It is," was all I said in a tense tone, for seeing her in danger that way wasn't exactly easy despite knowing the outcome. My brother nodded and told me,

"Then I will return to the castle and wait for them to arrive with the girl, that is if Carn'reau doesn't get to them first."

"I care little who walks her through my doors just so as when she arrives she does so walking unaided, and above all, *unharmed,"* I replied making him smirk in a knowing way.

"But of course," he said before his eyes glazed over in a demonic way as he started to create a portal, doing so with little effort. But just before stepping inside he looked back at me over his shoulder and said,

"And naturally I look forward to meeting her, for then perhaps I will finally learn the truth you yourself are refusing to say." Then before I could respond he disappeared through the wavering air, leaving me scowling at the empty space he had once been stood in.

I gritted my teeth at the thought of not being there when she arrived and being questioned by Dariush who was obviously determined to discover his own answers. Not that I could really blame him, as in the past there hadn't been much I had kept from him. But knowledge of my Chosen One was not for the likes of Hell, which, unfortunately, included him.

Speaking of Hell, I looked distastefully back down at the broken woman at my feet when she reached a shaky hand back up at me and with a strained voice begged,

"Ppplease...kill...me..." I thought back on everything her mind had shown me and before giving it a single thought more, I let my demon take action.

"With pleasure," I said, at the same time my demonic

armour liquefied down my arm and became a solid entity only when in the shape of a large blade. It shot down too fast for eyes to trace as it speared her straight through the neck. Then a quick flick of my wrist was all it took to sever her head completely as the blade twisted. It cut through flesh, muscle and bone like butter and the result was her head now rolling away from her body.

The wailing hiss of agony echoed all around me, proving there were more of her children still left alive than I had first thought. They cried out for the loss of their Queen, one they had been trying in vain to piece back together.

But my real satisfaction came when picking up her head by the hair, walking closer to the cliff's edge and flinging it into the dark abyss below. Then I walked away to the sounds of an entire race screaming as one as they mourned their mother.

Then I told them…

"Trying fixing that, assholes."

CHAPTER FOURTEEN

SLIPPED THROUGH MY FINGERS

This time when I landed, it was in the vast wastelands that surrounded the Kingdom of Death, which was the neighbouring land to the Kingdom of Blood where my castle was. Hence why I was named the King of Blood and Death, for both belonged to me. And speaking of what else belonged to me, it was time to go reclaim my girl.

I narrowed my gaze on the colossal head of a death dealer who had his mouth open as if he was about to swallow the souls of all who dared step inside. I just hoped like fuck she was here, for I was reaching my limit in waiting and this worrying was driving me fucking insane. To the point that my demon side was ready to take over completely just as he had that time back in the silent garden. Which was a thought that only ended with me quickening my steps, deciding against using my wings in case I missed something below.

I also wanted to keep my identity unknown for the moment so I called forth my helmet, letting it materialise in my hand. This particular one was a favourite of mine and usually sat in my private tower with the rest of my collection. It was a continuation of my demonic armoured suit, forged in such a way that it was connected to the blood it had been made with...*my own.*

I slipped the black metal over my head that was the same style as the rest of my armour and cut down over my face in a T shape, typical in some ways of a Trojan warrior. But with its overlapping plates and two large horns reaching high above my head in a U shape, that were tipped in blood red, then that was where the similarities ended.

I reached the steps that lead up into the town, only feeling better once the cavernous space started to open up the further I walked. I ignored the questioning looks of those who no doubt suspected I was some bounty hunter because of the way I was dressed. A newcomer that most would distance themselves from, where others with something to prove would most likely challenge me. To be honest, out of the two I wasn't sure which I was hoping for more, as I most certainly could have done with a good fight.

But did I have the time for that...? *Fuck no!*

Did I want it...? *Fuck yeah!*

Before long I came to the tail end of some of my army that were holding their position and stood waiting for their general's orders. I frowned in question before approaching them, demanding,

"What is the meaning of this?"

"Move along, bounty scum," the soldier said with a mere glance back at me, making me snap at the disrespect despite him obviously not knowing who I was. So, I grabbed him by the throat at the same time ripping his own helmet off his head, before forcing him to his knees. In response, I soon found all those around him with the tips of their blades pointed at me.

Unphased by this, I growled low and dangerous.

"You dare speak such words to your King, for you must tire of the use of your tongue to beg of me in such a way to rid you of it!" I snarled with a rumbling sound of displeasure from my demon at the end. But this statement was enough to have those that once pointed their swords at me now wisely lower their weapons along with quickly falling to their knees. This started a wave of movement throughout the entire army that snaked up the main street of the town, as they first split in the centre before finding the floor.

Well, so much for being inconspicuous, I thought wryly.

I could barely see the end of this river of bodies that were still falling as the presence of their King travelled up the ranks like a fucking Chinses whisper. Which was why I had no patience to make a show of storming through the centre of them all. So instead I took to the sky until I could see the end, where my commander was positioned. But then something else took my eye…*Gods alive but could it really be…*

"Amelia…?" I spoke her name as if she were some kind of myth. Some magical creature that only existed in the realm of hopeful dreams. Gods in fucking Heaven, but she was alright! She was right there, and she was standing tall and from what I could see, was unharmed!

"Thank the Gods," I muttered, closing my eyes for a second as the feeling overwhelmed me, for it was as if my prayers had finally been answered. But then, when I opened them again, I took in the scene in more detail and moved my gaze beyond the sight of my girl.

But even hovering fifty feet in the air above, I could still see that she was stood next to the three brothers and opposite them was Carn'reau upon his beast of a steed. I narrowed my eyes seeing that they all looked to be in what appeared to be some kind of standoff, with the McBain brothers standing guard over the girl against my army.

"What the fuck?" I questioned with a frown. I was about to get to the bottom of it and take possession of my girl when suddenly the worst fucking thing happened! It started when Trice suddenly cried out in anger,

"NO!" but then it was too late, as my eyes homed in on something in the younger brother's hand. It started when the one named Vern had stepped forward to converse with my general and commander. But then the second I eyed the cause of Trice's anger I too seemed to mimic the sound that had come from him, as I bellowed in fury,

"NO!" but it was too late, as the younger brother had thrown a glowing bottle behind him and the second it smashed, it created a portal, that had the power to suck those who stood next to it inside…

Amelia included.

Undiluted rage had me dropping from the sky and landing with enough force it cracked the cobbled street and made the whole town shake. I looked up and snarled furiously before gaining my full height when rising from my bent knee to fully standing. I did this in dangerous, slow movements that had those around me staggering backwards, including the cause of my rage…Vern McBain.

"My King…" Carn'reau said in surprise as I turned his way and suddenly thundered,

"WHERE IS SHE?!" The army behind him responded quickly and the beast my general rode upon whined in an anxious way, sensing the higher power pulsating from me.

"Oh darn," Vern said uncharacteristically before he became the second life I held in my grasp in the past few minutes. I did this by lifting him in the air by his throat, ready to choke the fucker! He clawed at my hand in a desperate attempt at trying to draw breath and I knew that I would have to force my hand to let go if I was to get my answers.

Fuck, but she had been right there for fuck sake!

"I asked you a fucking question, Wyvern!" I growled after first dropping him to the floor and giving him no time to cough through his first few breaths. But I had to give him his due, he was a ballsy mother fucker as he glared up at me and said,

"I haven't a dickybird." I scowled down at him and instead of kicking the shit out of him, because I simply didn't have the time, I instead took control of his mind. His eyes glazed over and rolled back in his head the second I forced my way in there, and because he was in his own right a powerful asshole, it didn't come as easy to me as it should.

However, with that being said, I forced my way deeper and stripped him of his rights to keep me out, seeing it all starting to play out. I skipped over the parts I had seen, that included the battle with the Queen, ignoring how well they had fought in keeping my girl safe.

Because despite it being a factor that would no doubt save his life, I was too furious right now to let him get away unscathed and wanted no image in my mind to cloud that decision. He would feel my wrath, there was no doubt about that!

But then I slowed down those memories when I reached what I was looking for…where they had perhaps purchased the portal orb.

"Necromancer," I hissed letting him go and turning back towards where they had obviously come from.

"No…No don't go…" I ignored his pointless pleas by storming down the street until coming to a shop front I recognised from his memories. The stained glass displayed the name and when I walked inside, I found a girl with navy blue and white tipped hair. She was also muttering to herself about pains in her ass handsome bastards, as she was bent behind the counter arranging something on one of the shelves behind.

I cleared my throat and she snapped,

"Sorry we are closed...*on account of the army standing in the street, dickhead, or did you miss 'em?*" She muttered this last part to herself making me wonder with that attitude how she had any customers at all. But then again, this was Hell and she wasn't exactly dealing with the most reputable clientele. Not especially considering what the witch was selling. I took a few steps forward and when she heard that I was still there, she rose up from her crouched position and released an annoyed sigh. This was all before turning around to face me, as at the same time telling me,

"I said we are closed assho...holy shit!" She ended this irritated comment on a shriek of fear as I was removing my helmet, making her stumble back the moment I revealed myself. Good, I was glad the girl feared me as it would make it easier this way.

"You know who I am," I stated making her nod her head in quick jerky movements and I glanced down in an expectant way telling her she was missing something when faced with a King. Her deep blue eyes widened as realization took hold and she lowered her body to bow in my presence. To be honest I couldn't give a fuck but with half the damn town now watching, I knew it was needed. However, what came next was unfortunate, as I had no choice but to threaten her.

"Then you also know what I want."

"Erh...not really..." she replied in an unsure way and I held up my hand to silence her and snapped,

"The girl, I want to know where you sent the fucking girl!" My growl of anger was easily read for she paled. Then she muttered under her breath,

"Damn it, Vern." This was said off the back of Vern, who could be heard shouting in rage, despite how much like a posh twat he sounded when doing so. But it was clear he cared for

what I was doing in here, as one glance out the window and I could see he was fighting my men. Doing so now with one clear goal in mind, to get to the girl I faced...*interesting.*

He was trying to fight his way free of my men that soon had him restrained to the ground. It was also testament to his strength for he didn't make it easy and much to Carn'reau's annoyance, took at least six of his men to achieve this.

"I didn't send her anywhere, I swear, my Lord," she replied when I made it clear I was still waiting for an answer. So, I took a threatening step forward and warned,

"I will hurt you, woman...and then when I am done with you, I will burn all you built to the ground...now give me the information I want to know!" If I thought she had paled before, then now she had lost all colour, even in her once peach coloured lips.

"I...I...honestly...I don't know what you're talking about... *please."* She held up her hands in fear as I stalked towards her, too afraid to move back and try and run from me.

"The portal orb you supplied the Wyvern, tell me, where did it lead?" I asked again in a tone that said I was closer to following through with my threat. She frowned a moment as if genuinely confused before she cursed,

"Fucking Vern!" I frowned and then heard another roar from the street as he shouted,

"SHE DOESN'T KNOW ANYTHING! LEAVE HER ALONE YOU NINNYHAMMER!" At this unique insult for a simpleton, one I will confess to have not heard since the sixteen hundreds, I halted my steps, tipped my head to the side and commented,

"Your handiwork, I presume?" She awkwardly shrugged her shoulders and replied,

"Uh...maybe...what can I say, he pisses a lot of people off." I took a deep breath and agreed,

"Indeed."

After this I continued to close the distance between us making her cry out for the Wyvern in panic.

"VERN!" she shouted despite the fact moments ago just cursing his name, meaning that this witch had deeper feelings for my new prisoner. She ran from around the counter without thinking about the danger and I snagged her body from getting any closer to the door. She cried out making Vern hear her and the guttural sounds of the fight was obvious as to why.

He cared for her too.

I held her squirming body still, doing so by collaring a metal hand around her throat. She stilled the moment I applied enough pressure to tell her how serious this was, and then I whispered down in her ear,

"I don't want to hurt you girl, but you try my patience."

"But…but…I swear to you, I don't know what he took as he certainly didn't pay for it…*as usual,*" she said in a strained voice more down to the circumstances and not because I was hurting her like I promised I would.

"And what of the girl?" I asked this time.

"Sire?"

"What do you know of the girl?!" I snarled dangerously down at her this time and as a result, I felt the lump pass down my hand at her throat as she swallowed hard.

"Alright, I will tell you, but please…*don't hurt her,*" she replied surprising me. For the reason she held back now was because she was worried what I would do to Amelia. I released a sigh and told her,

"Do not fear for the girl's life, for I don't intend to harm her."

"And how do I know you're not just lying?" she braved snapping back and I had to say, I liked the girl's spirit. Besides, she would clearly need it considering who she had chosen to fall in love with.

"You don't. But then again, I don't need you to, not with your life in my hand…now tell me of the girl!" I said squeezing slightly to add emphasis to my words.

"Alright, alright!" she shouted making me ease my hold after a few seconds.

"So about five or so hours ago they brought a mortal girl into my shop. I didn't think much of it, other than doing as they asked…"

"Which was?" I interrupted.

"They were looking for an elixir to restore their energy, which I gathered had something to do with needing it for getting the girl to where she needed to be," she told me and so far, nothing seemed out of place.

"Then what?" I prompted.

"We went in the back to try and find it when Trice realised Vern had followed and no one was watching her. After this he freaked. By the time we ran back to the shop, she was gone."

"Gone?!" I snapped, seeing that this was the part that was new to me.

"Yeah, well obviously they found her again, only it seemed she was attacked," the girl added making me tense all over.

"ATTACKED!" I roared making the girl in my arms cower, squirming harder now to be free of me. I therefore forced myself to be calm enough so I wouldn't accidentally break her bones, for I was holding her too tight as it was.

"Not by me! Or them, it was by a witch or something… please!" She shouted, and this was when I hit my fucking limit. Once again I ignored the bellowing sounds of a Wyvern's rage beyond the doors and focused on discovering the truth. I did this by spinning her to face me, placing a hand over her eyes and said,

"Fucking show me!" She whimpered at first but then the second I accessed her mind she relaxed in my hold. Then I scanned through her memories and the second I saw Amelia entering inside this room, everything stopped.

I breathed a quick sigh of relief before allowing the rest to continue and it was only a minute later that I ended up hissing out one word like it was acid on my tongue...

"Hex!"

CHAPTER FIFTEEN

IN ANOTHER'S ARMS

"Is that all you have, you ruffian!" Vern said after I broke his nose and he spat blood off to the side. It also didn't take me long into this fight to realise that something was wrong with Vern and if I was honest, it was throwing me off my game.

After I had learnt all I needed to from the witch, I naturally let her go. Not only had she not done anything wrong, but she had helped care for my girl after her attack. Also, from the looks of her memories, she had been nothing but kind to her. Which was why when leaving the shop, I declared the building and the witch under the protection of my rule and a death sentence to anyone who threatened either. This was much to her and Vern's astonishment, but I couldn't give a fuck, for anyone who aided my Amelia in surviving this ordeal, I was indebted to.

As for Vern, he refused to give me any information as to where he'd sent them, despite the beating he had received. I had tried to access his mind and found a blank, for he had only given them a hint of where they should go. Meaning it was Trice who had most likely unknowingly thought of the place the portal had sent them. Which meant that unless Vern was willing to slip up and think back to the actual location, then it was useless.

He was one cunning, ginger fucker!

"I fail to understand why it is you still resist, for what do you hope to achieve from all of this?" I asked after wiping my own blood from my lips, after the few lucky hits he had managed to get in. You see my idea of gaining information from Vern wasn't by tying him to a fucking chair and torturing him. For I didn't do such unless I wanted to deliver a lot of pain as revenge. In truth, I had also needed the fight.

But for Vern, he had kept Amelia safe and protected her, which was precisely why I didn't want to kill him or beat him beyond repair. However, he couldn't go completely unpunished either, as he refused to give information to his King and didn't make it easy when he was escorted back to the castle for questioning.

Basically, the dickhead was doing this to himself. Which was why I decided to give him his chance against me. Any other time and this would have been in a ring surrounded by an audience, as this wasn't the first time I had fought those that needed to be punished. But instead, this fight ended up inside a large prison cell. Because I had no fucking time for theatre of making this a show. This was between him and me and despite his new fucked up way of speaking, I discovered his reason was the promise that was made for all three of the brothers.

They wanted their souls back.

He was basically giving his brothers the chance to deliver the girl and get what was owed to them, the promise of lifting the blood oath of regaining back complete possession of their souls. I also discovered that the reason for his new persona was down to pissing off the shop owner, a girl I learnt was called Nero.

"You of all people, Sir, would fail to understand such trials and tribulations that comes from having one's soul in the hands of another." I released a sigh and muttered,

"Fuck me, but she really did a number on you." I also shook my head before throwing a rag at him, nodding to the deep gash on his head caused from when I hammered it against the wall. He caught it one handed and put it there to slow the blood enough to give it time to heal before he lost too much and passed out.

"You swear M'lady was left unharmed?" He asked at the mention of her.

"You saw her for yourself, did she look fucking harmed to you?!" I snapped losing my patience and finding myself near ready to fight once more. Damn it, but if he just gave me something!

His shoulders sagged just before he staggered into the wall, using it to prop himself up. It had to be said that the Wyvern had given the fight a fucking good go and despite beating him, he hadn't been exactly what I would have called easy. It was why the whole thing had been so satisfying, for it was unusual for me to find such an opponent who never gave up, even after I had broken bones. Of course, he would heal…maybe not as quickly as I would but he would most definitely live to see another fight, for it was clear the cocky bastard was no stranger to being in a brawl.

"I fail to see what the lady could mean to one such as you, on account of her being decidedly mortal," Vern said wincing after it, and I didn't know if it was due to physical pain or the pain his own words cost him, as he obviously hated this new affliction.

"That shit gonna wear off soon?" I asked making him mutter,

"By Joe, I do hope so, dear fellow." The wince this time confirmed it had nothing to do with pain but more the hit to his ego at sounding by all accounts, like a posh twat.

"She's certainly got imagination and talent that girl of yours…fuck, I am tempted to employ her," I confessed making him push away from the wall in clear irritation saying,

"Now just a darn minute, I forbid any such thing…upon my word," he scoffed making me roll my eyes and tell him,

"Keep your britchers on, asshole, I said tempted, not that I would…besides, I have bigger matters to deal with now, like getting you to tell me where the fuck my mortal is!" I snapped making his eyes widen at my slip up.

"Your mortal?" He questioned.

"Yes, *my fucking mortal!*" I shouted back almost about to crack my fist against his skull again. He released a sigh and said,

"If it's the lady's safety that concerns you then I can assure you that she is perfectly safe, especially with Trice becoming so protective over…" He trailed off the moment he heard my response for I started growling like a demonic beast.

"What did you say?" I asked in a dangerous tone, as I could feel the jealous rage rising through me like a red mist was overtaking my senses. I had never really had the need to be jealous over Amelia before, having intervened and ended all relationships with other men before they even had chance to begin. But then that was before I had allowed myself to claim her fully.

Now, however, just at the mere hint of it and I was back to being ready to tear into him once again. He held up a shaky hand, one where the skin was now missing off his knuckles and said,

"Take care for but a moment, good sir, for it is not as it appears." But even then, I could tell there was something in him that seemed more to hope that this was the case, and for his brother's sake that this statement was true. But it was obvious, that despite his words, it was not something he was confident in.

"It better the fuck not be, or you will be finding yourself a bloody cell mate with the same last name as you if it is any other way!" I snapped before forcing myself to leave, knowing that if I didn't then there was a chance the Wyvern wouldn't survive another hour!

After this I left my prison, cracking my fists and popping a dislocated knuckle back into place. Something that had happened when trying to hit a certain well-spoken Wyvern in the face and getting the wall instead when the fast fucker dodged the punch. I quickly became consumed with needing to know what was happening with Amelia right at this very moment. For all I was left hoping for was that wherever they were, they had decided to stop and rest for the night.

I made it back to the grand staircase that connected the main tower to all other towers that surrounded it, including my own. As usual I had little patience for climbing fucking thousands of steps and released my wings to fly straight up the centre. I landed quickly and was soon crossing the glass walkway over to the private part of my home in Hell. This was so I had the privacy I needed to access Amelia's mind once more.

I had made a promise not to do this again but considering she had also made the same promise never to leave me, I think I could be forgiven this once in being allowed to use it to my aid. Because clearly promises were subjective on whether or not the fucking world needed saving! This, I thought with a grit of my teeth, was something I had been doing a lot fucking more lately!

I opened the private door that was guarded by the souls of the condemned and needed my blood to open it. I even remember Lucifer explaining how I would be grateful one day for the privacy and warned me that in Hell, there was always someone watching. A lesson I had taken seriously and kept with me throughout my continued existence.

It was also why, when having his witches build this place, an everlasting storm was created to continually surround it, so it added to the protection. Of course, he was not only thinking of me but more so for what I had been charged with protecting. I had been declared as keeper of the Crimson Eye, and right here in my tower was where it was kept.

The Eye was said to have been born through the rage of Janus, the God of time and ruler of the Fates. As a rule, Janus rarely intervened in the way of life, learning quickly that the slightest change of the past can affect the future. Because knowing one's fate has the power to affect the entire world.

This being said, Janus first had to experience this lesson for himself and did so when he became enraged by man's wicked ways. Romulus, the first King of Rome started commanding the kidnapping of the Sabine women. It was a time in which the men of Rome committed a mass abduction of these young females, hellbent of stealing them away from the other cities in the region. This was because of the dwindling population and the greater ratio of men to women.

Romulus became concerned with maintaining the city's strength and knowing that with their few women inhabitants there would be no chance of sustaining the city's population. The greater fear for the King was that Rome might not last longer than a generation. On the advice of the Senate, the Romans then set out into the surrounding regions in search of wives to establish families with. The Romans negotiated at first but did so unsuccessfully with all the people that they appealed to. This included the Sabines, who populated the neighbouring areas.

The Sabines, like others who had refused them, did so because they feared the rise of a rival society and refused to allow their women to marry the outsiders. Consequently, through this failure to come to terms with the exchange, the Romans devised a plan to abduct the Sabine women instead, doing so during the festival of Neptune Equester.

They planned and announced a festival of games to attract people from all the nearby towns. At the festival, Romulus gave a signal by 'rising and folding his cloak and then throwing it round him again', no doubt looking like a pompous ass at that! But with the signal given, the Romans started grabbing the Sabine women and fought off the men that tried to stop them.

Nearly all of the women abducted at the festival were said to have been virgins, all except for one married woman, Hersilia. She became Romulus' wife and would later be the one to intervene and stop the following war between the Romans and the Sabines. However, before this happened Janus, being enraged by the act of man trying to overrule the fate of the population, intervened. He caused a volcanic hot spring to erupt, resulting in the would-be attackers being burnt and buried alive.

The part of the story that isn't told to mortal man was that after this happened, Hersilia found herself among the dead. She had been captured by one of the men who Janus had punished with death, meaning she was then free to escape. However, instead Janus was touched by her bravery and compassion, as she found herself looking to help any that may have survived, despite what they had done to her own people. This was when she came across a large red stone sparkling in the ash of the remains.

Being one that was worthy, Janus let her pick it up and the

moment she did, she saw a glimpse into the future. The stone showed her that the only way to end the coming war between Romulus and her people was through love not hate. She was shown that through making the King fall in love with her, it would one day give her the power to convince him that war was not the answer. Shortly after this, she went back into the city of her own free will and caught the King's eye. A little time later they were married and history was changed for the better.

The Crimson Eye was created through Janus' brief hatred for mankind. But in doing so, he transferred some of his power through rage and the emotion was forged in the burning core of Hell, forming it into a precious stone of fate. Now, despite it being used for good and bringing about the peace between two regions, Janus also knew it equally had the power to destroy through that same type of knowledge. It is why, as soon as the stone fell from Hersilia's hands, it sank back into the depths of the Hell in which it had been born. This before being spewed up by the volcanic eruption Janus had created in his wrath. Lucifer naturally took possession of it until there was one he felt could be trusted more.

And apparently that person became me.

And rightly so considering I had barely been tempted to use it, having no need to know my future. For I knew what fucked up shit could happen when you relied too heavily on the Fates to guide your life. Not when I knew that your decisions should solely be those based on your own beliefs, strengths, fears and even doubts.

I quickly located my bed and lay down, having no intention of sleeping but only hoping that what I did next was to aid me in finding her. That and also crushing all concerns I had in what was fuelling my jealously. Especially when it came to one Trice McBain, needing to know that he was being as honourable as his younger brother presumed.

The moment I closed my eyes, it didn't take me long to find her mind, accessing it far quicker down here where my powers were far stronger in my own realm. This also brought me comfort as I knew then that she was also still somewhere within my kingdom. Which meant that wherever they were, they hadn't gone too far beyond my reach.

But then the second she felt me entering her void, she responded and when I heard that sweet voice whispering,

"Handsome" I allowed myself a moment to feel revealed. Her sleeping form was mostly shadowed for some reason, even though I could surmise she was lay somewhere on the ground outside. But the darkness around her worried me...*where was she?*

I leant down close to her and whispered in her ear from behind,

"Amelia, where are you, Sweetheart?" She sucked in a startled breath, telling me that I was in danger of her suddenly waking because of it. That was the last thing I wanted to happen right now as it would make it more difficult in finding her. This was because her void was only accessible when she slept, for her mind was too strong when awake.

If only I had taught her how to let me into her conscious state of being, then I might have had a chance at finding her the moment I followed her into Hell.

"I'm here," she whispered, and I could just make out her reaching hand, as if searching for me. But then this was when I noticed the shadow around her started to move, as if it were something cradling her form. A form that soon started to take shape.

"My Khuba...You. Are. Not." I replied in a hard tone, one that I knew sounded harsh when she flinched because of it. But then, despite believing what that shadow could represent, I was at least comforted when she pleaded,

"Please...I am...I am waiting for you..." This was when she finally opened her eyes in her own dream and found me scowling down at her with my arms crossed and no doubt looking furious. However, the moment she reached out once more for me, I forced myself to believe that the reason for the male presence wrapped around her sleeping form had been for her own wellbeing. That it had been to ward off the night's chill.

It was that or death would be the only thing waiting for Trice McBain when he finally walked my woman back through my castle doors.

I released a deep sigh before lowering to one knee so I could get closer to her, unable to deny the pleading look on her face. She opened her mouth as if ready to speak my name when the shadow across the middle of her belly started to become that of another man and I was left with a bitterness like no other.

The deep sting of jealously of the likes I had never felt before made the last thing I said down at her being one she would no doubt wake up and remember.

For it was said as nothing short of a warning…

"You wait for me in another man's arms?"

CHAPTER SIXTEEN

PERSONAL DEMONS

As I sat on my throne waiting for her to approach it took everything in me to sit there and wait after motioning for her to be brought forward. I simply wanted to storm my way past my people and claim what was mine in the single second it would take me in getting to her.

But to see that she was stalling only fuelled my anger further and fed the demon side of me that had not long ago taken over completely. Something that had become a battle I fought with myself since she had awoken and broke the connection to her void. In fact, the only reason I hadn't given into my rage is that during the whole time I was in her mind she had clearly wanted me to find her. She had been looking for me and despite having another man's arms around her, it had been me she had been reaching out for.

So, I had beaten back the demon in me and held firmly onto the rational part of my mind that focused instead on leaving my tower and trying to find her. However, it was all in vain for during this time searching my lands for any sight of her, she had been making her way to my castle. The McBain brothers had done what they had been charged with doing just like Vern had said they would, completing their task to regain their souls.

Which was the only reason I hadn't ripped Trice apart with my bare hands the moment I first saw him. For surely if he had fallen for my girl, then why would he be delivering her to me despite the uncertainty of her fate, for no one knew who she was to me. No, for all he knew, death was what I had planned for her.

Of course, on hearing what fate had befallen her by the time I got back, then it was my brother's life I had in my hands instead of that of another McBain! I couldn't believe he had ordered her thrown into my prison and despite hearing his reasons, I fucking lost it! I had just been about to storm into the prison and get my girl when my brother's words had stopped me...

"I wouldn't do that if I were you, not unless you want our father finding out what she really means to you." I had paused in the archway to my brother's quarters, that acted as an office of the King. But considering he used it far more than I, then it had my brother's tastes written all over it. It was clear with one look at the place that he was still partial to our once Persian existence. Scalloped archways were what framed hung fabrics that represent the sunset over the sandstone of the walls. There was also a carved desk that showed Persian soldiers fighting the Romans, something that throughout history, happened often.

He was a sucker for the old days.

However, today was a new day and in it he was pissing me off.

"Is that a threat, my Šeš?" I asked in a dangerous tone.

"I do not speak of me!" He snapped, angry at the insinuation he would go behind my back and speak with our father.

"Just think about it, if you do not act like you would with any other prisoner, then how long do you think it will be before the whispers start?" I snarled at the idea and tore my gaze from his to find the tiled floor adorned with Persian rugs in reds, creams and hints of blue. Fuck, but I hated that he was right!

"Then what would you have me do?" I snapped back.

"What you would with any other. Demand their presence where you are sat upon your throne," was his response.

"Look, I have no idea who this girl really is to you, but I am no fool and know she is more than just some slave for your cock, despite your claims." I released a frustrated sigh before telling him,

"Now is not the time."

"That may be but even so, you told me of this witch and I acted when seeing the Hex upon her skin, for I was not to know this was even the girl which you were looking for. You said that if the witch had the means and found a way, then she would…"

"Yes, yes, I know what I fucking said!" I barked back, knowing this was partially my fault, for my brother was only acting according to what he saw and what little information I had given him.

"Fine, have the girl brought to my throne, but I want her cared for." He raised a brow but didn't say anything more, knowing I was on edge as it was. He simply nodded his head and watched me as I followed through with an idea that came to me.

I might have to be forced to put on an act, but Amelia didn't know that and knowing her, then she would surely challenge me the moment she saw me acting masterful and cold towards her. Therefore I needed to get word to her somehow, so I grabbed what I needed from my brother's desk. I tore off a strip of parchment from a map of our realm, grabbed a quill and wrote a small note.

I then entrusted it to Dariush, telling him to include this in with the food I wanted sent her, along with some new clothes. My girl needed caring for, especially as it seemed she had spent the night sleeping on a forest floor.

But again, if Dariush had any thoughts on this, I didn't know as he wisely didn't comment. Instead he simply nodded and took the note. Now all I had to rely on was that she would find it and more than anything, she would act on it.

After this time with my brother, I left him with his task and was forced to wait for my own act to begin, which was one I would still be forced to play until I had her safely inside my tower.

However, this was all until I discovered what had happened during her time down in the prison and something that was only brought to my attention moments before she was brought to my throne room. Hence why, by the time she did appear, I had erupted fully into my demon and was near shaking with anger. Something that didn't help when she was stalling to make her way to me.

But then I tried to view her trepidation by looking at what she faced now, for she hadn't exactly spent much time around my demon side. My armour had formed into something more intimidating and my face was no longer that of the man she knew. But then there was also the setting in which she was being forced to walk down, surrounded by the creatures and demonic beings of my court. Gone were the days of me in jeans, casually lounging on the sofa with her watching some geeky show she would talk all the way through.

She had well and truly entered my world and in it, I was a cruel, heartless, demonic king.

A tyrant.

I was not her Lucius and one look at her now and she knew it. So, it was regardless of whether she had found my note or not. Her fear in coming to me now was not part of an act I had asked her to play along with. She truly was looking fearful of me. She even nearly stumbled and would have fallen had it not been for my general's quick actions. But when he didn't remove his hand quick enough I found my anger replacing my gratitude pretty quickly, snarling some threat at him to let her go.

But then she finally reached the steps leading up to my throne and the second she started looking up at me with those big blue eyes, doing so like some frightened doe…well, then it took everything in me not to react. In fact, I think I was scowling down at her and motioned with my fingers for her to not keep me waiting any longer. Something my general also warned, for she wasn't helping matters.

However, the second she finally made it to the top of the steps I couldn't hold back my reaction to her any longer. I suddenly stood which startled her enough to take a step back, forcing me to act the moment her clumsy steps would have meant a broken neck. Meaning that I ended up grabbing her quickly, and hauling her back to me, holding back from taking possession of her lips like I wanted.

Instead I found the only tenderness I could grant her in that bitter sweet second was a simple caress of the back of my talon running down her cheek. She closed her eyes at the gentle touch and my name was whispered from between her lips like a lover's kiss.

"Lucius"

I found my head starting to lower, like a natural pull towards my Chosen One as was the power she held over me. To take those sweet lips prisoner like I was desperate to. In fact, I only just managed to stop myself in time, knowing this was precisely what I shouldn't be doing! This then meant that when she finally opened her eyes again she found my gaze narrowed and my lips curling in a snarl, off the back of my frustration.

Unable to stand witnessing her fear and now her disappointment, I spun her around to face my people, deciding now was a good time to make my point.

She shuddered against me and my instincts snapped, collaring her neck in a heartbeat. I didn't want to hurt her, or scare her for that matter, but instead using it to bring her a step back and closer to me.

She was going fucking nowhere!

After this I lowered my head so I could speak directly in her ear but keeping in mind those that had the potential to hear me.

This was when I gave her my warning…

"Found at last, my little human."

CHAPTER SEVENTEEN

AMELIA

DEMON'S NATURE

Back inside Lucius' tower…

The moment I saw that my Lucius was back to the man I knew, so many emotions slammed into me all at once, with anger being at the very top of that list. But just beyond the upset, I was also mainly relieved to have him back, which was why the second after I slapped him, I threw myself into his arms, whether he was ready for it or not.

But of course, *he caught me.*

"I…I…was…so worried," I said as I buried my head in his shoulder and let the flood gates open, pouring out my emotions through the tears that were now soaking his skin. I felt his hand cradling the back of my head as he held me to him, whispering words of comfort in between trying to gently stop my crying.

"Ssshh, now sweetheart, I am here...*I am here.*" He whispered this last part into my hair, giving me a squeeze as his left arm was wrapped around me. It was only now that I also realised that he had left the gauntlet on that hand, as I felt the strength in his hold at my side through his metal clad fingers. Although, it had to be said that like this, he was definitely considerably gentler with me than he had been. Which was what caused me to suddenly rip myself out of his arms and go back to being pissed off.

"And there she goes," he muttered dryly to himself, but it was after putting space between us that I heard this and turned back around to face him.

"I think this is the part you start explaining what the fuck is going on, Lucius!" I snapped making him cross his arms over his bare chest, making his biceps and shoulder muscles bulge. Doing so in that frustratingly sexy way that made me want to drool, damn him!

"And where exactly would you like me to start, sweetheart, when you decided to do something totally fucking stupid and reckless by stepping through that portal or every *single fucking thing you have done since?*" He growled this last part proving that I wasn't the only one who had something to be pissed off about. But then I wasn't about to admit that, because come on...whoever admitted they were the one in the wrong to start with at the start of an argument. No, the truth was I had enough guilt about that already. Meaning that if this conversation started at that point, then I would never get to the bottom of everything that had happened since being shown into that throne room.

"Right and you're so innocent eh...um, let's start with when you decided to make me feel like a fucking dog at your feet in front of your whole Gods be damned kingdom!" I shouted making him at least look slightly guilty. Well, at least I got a sliver of this reaction before his features hardened and he informed me sternly,

"Everything I did was done for your safety." He started to turn away but paused when I snapped,

"Bullshit!" He looked back at me over my shoulder and warned,

"Careful Pet, my demon is still on the fucking edge because of you." I narrowed my gaze at him and was just about to speak when he interrupted with a warning,

"Don't push it, Amelia, not unless you enjoy the feeling of your body in chains." I swallowed hard at the threat now knowing that he was more than capable of putting action into his words. Which begged the question as to why this was?

Wisely I let it go and I released some of my anger on a sigh. Then I asked more calmly this time,

"What the Hell is going on with you, Lucius?" At this he laughed once without humour and dragged his right hand through his hair whilst his back was to me. Then he turned back to me and snapped,

"Hell is the right word there, sweetheart, for that is precisely what you put me through and what happens when my demon is forced to come down here looking for my Chosen One…one who ran from him…yet, a-fuckin-gain!" He shouted this last part making me flinch before defending myself,

"Alright, so I understand why it may have seemed that way but…"

"It didn't seem like anything, Amelia, it was…Just. That. Way!" He argued back emphasising those last three words with a growl. So once more, instead of letting anger rule my words, I deliberately took another deep breath and told him,

"No, it wasn't. I stepped through that portal with the foolish belief that you would simply follow me through it."

"Yes, fucking foolish indeed!" he bit back.

"Lucius, I..." He quickly cut me off,

"But like always, your arrogance and stubborn nature decided it knew fucking best as fucking usual..."

"Hey, that's not fair!" I snapped. But then he just quickly stepped back towards me and his angry strides made me start backing up, finding myself steered towards what looked like a seating area.

"No, what isn't fair is being forced to watch as the person you care for and love most in the fucking world does the one thing you ask her not to do! Someone who disregarded any thoughts or feelings for what I was forced to endure by your actions!" I winced at that and at the same time my footing lost its balance and I started to fall backwards, something this time, Lucius let me do.

I realised why the second my landing was soft as I had fallen back into a huge armchair that in that moment the only details of it I could take in was the black velvet material it was covered in.

"I had no choice," I said in a small voice that was close to breaking as I knew Lucius was right.

"Oh no, you had a fucking choice, Amelia and guess what..." He paused before leaning in close and doing so by bracing his hand on the back of the chair.

"...You chose fucking wrong, my girl!" He snarled these words and I shuddered against the power of them. Gods, but he was so angry, and quite honestly, considering the amount of worry I could see I had put him through, then I wasn't surprised by it at all. But still, I knew I had to at least try and get him to see why, even if I knew he wouldn't ever accept it. I had to at least try and make him see that my decision hadn't come easy, nor had it been made on a whim. I had truly believed in my cause and he had to know that, if nothing else.

So, I braved raising my hand to his cheek, and the instant I touched him, he closed his eyes, as if savouring my touch.

"It was something I had to do, Lucius, and you…" At this his eyes snapped open and the twin crimson depths darkened before he tore himself away from me,

"You didn't have to do shit!"

"Lucius, please…" He ignored this and carried on,

"And if *you* had just given me a fucking shred of insight as to your actions and a second's chance for me to explain why it was a fucking colossal mistake, then I wouldn't have just needed to tear Hell apart to fucking find you!" he shouted making me take a deep breath and remind him,

"Yes, and if you had the chance, *you* would have stopped me."

"You're damn fucking right I would have! In fact, I would have tied you to a Gods be damned—" It was my turn to interrupt him as having him holding on to his anger and unwilling to let it go only managed to fuel my own.

"What, Lucius…what would you have tied me to…a fucking rock or the Tree of Souls? Because you sure as shit couldn't have done much else, Lucius!" He snarled back at me, but I ignored this and carried on,

"As the way I remembered it, our options were pretty bloody limited seeing as we had a witch and her fucking army above ground waiting for us like a fox at a rabbit hole!" I snapped back, with no chance of holding it back any longer.

"I would have thought of something had I first had the chance to!" He argued.

"Lucius, don't you see, you are answering exactly why I didn't give you the opportunity to stop me, whether that was right or wrong, it doesn't matter now as we are both in Hell. We are both in a place where we can stop the Venom of God together." At this his head snapped back around and the look he gave me was incredulous.

"You're fucking insane if you think I am letting you do anything, let alone help me to sort this shit out!" My eyes widened, and I felt my jaw go hard as my shocked gaze quickly turned into a frown.

"Sorting this shit out? Lucius, this isn't just some misunderstanding we can have a meeting with the Gods to discuss, this is…"

"I know precisely what this is, Amelia, for I was the one fucking there, remember…"

"Lucius, come on…" I tried but was shot back down the second he said,

"Forgive me, Princess, but I don't recall seeing you there that day losing your fucking hand!" At this I flinched as if he had struck me. Because clearly now he knew exactly what I had seen, this meant there was no holding back on his past. It was obviously no longer a concern…and evidently it was something he cruelly chose to throw at me.

But then, one look at my face, and he knew he had gone too far. He knew it the second he saw the pain his words had caused me, for he could see it in my eyes before I turned my face away, no longer caring to look at him.

His deep regretful sigh was all I heard moments after the extended silence that followed.

"I am angry," Lucius admitted in a deflated tone making me snap back sarcastically,

"Uh yeah, thanks but I got the memo on that one loud and very fucking clear, Lucius!" But his response surprised me as it was no longer an angry one. Because the next thing I knew I had him crouching by the chair next to me. Then he took hold of my chin so as he could turn me to face him, telling me at the same time,

"Give me those pretty eyes, my sweet girl." After this I made it easier on him by looking his way and no longer having the fight in me to refuse him.

"Do you have any idea how worried I was?" He asked me with his voice only giving more weight laid against his words.

"Lucius, I…" I tried but he shook his head and continued,

"Do have any idea the blind fucking panic you caused me?" This time when he asked I gave him what he needed and that was the time to get it all out. Of course, my guilt tripled!

"I had only just got you back," he added and finally I shackled his wrist with my hand and squeezed before giving him what he needed,

My understanding.

And as Han Solo would say, I told him…

"I know."

CHAPTER EIGHTEEN

MY DEMON'S BEDROOM

The moment I agreed with his pained statement in just getting me back he gave me more.

"I nearly lost my fucking mind!" He told me and this time the guilt of what I put him through made me close my eyes and whisper,

"For that I am sorry."

After this his hand left my chin and cupped my cheek before threading through my hair until it was at the back of my neck. Once there he pulled me closer to him as he tipped his forehead to mine, holding it there as he whispered,

"I know you are, my brave foolish girl." Hearing this made me lose hold of my breath, making it come out in an emotional shudder.

"Is that why you acted that way towards me?" I asked making him release me so as he could pull back and tell me,

"You think I would take revenge against you in such a way?" He asked making me admit,

"Well…yeah." At this he surprised me when he burst out

laughing. Admittedly, I had to say the sight nearly brought me to tears as it was one down in his throne room, I thought I had lost. That deep relief hit me again and I sucked in my bottom lip to stop the emotions from turning to tears. This was because I could barely believe that we were both here, we found each other at last. Because there were times that I feared it would never happen. That he had been taken by the witch and I would only end up having to fight to get him back. But it was also that hopeless feeling too that I had been made to go through when down in his prison, believing my life was possibly at an end.

But then looking at Lucius, and well, Hell was unsurprisingly something that had obviously taken its toll on both of us, only in different ways. As I knew my own story, but what I didn't know yet was Lucius'.

Hence the reason I asked,

"Then why did you treat me that way?" At this the humour left his eyes, along with the crinkles that appeared at the corners whenever he smiled.

"Because this is my world you are in now and trust me when I say it is nothing like the one I rule on Earth's plane." At this I would have scoffed, 'yeah, no shit' but stopped myself choosing instead to say,

"And in this world, you can't be seen with a Queen?" At this his gaze softened and he reached down to run a thumb over the apple of my cheek before grazing it across my lips.

"No, in this world I can't be seen to have a weakness, one that would be used against me by my enemies." I frowned in question before he walked away putting distance between us so he could sit opposite me. This gave me the opportunity to glance around at the space we now occupied to find it surprisingly comfortable considering where we were. Shards of black glass curled up like wrought iron spindles to create the sides of both the single chair I was sat upon and also the large sofa Lucius chose to sit on. The back rose up higher than my shoulders and curved around like a large ominous wave to give a place for the crimson cushions to rest against. In fact, I didn't know whether it belonged in the Adams' Family house or in some art gallery on display.

"But then again, I am not the only ruler in Hell who has enemies that would jump at the chance to take advantage of the opportunity to claim you." I frowned at this, naturally needing that statement clarifying.

"What do you mean?"

"Your father is no saint in this world, Amelia, and has many a time played judge, jury, and executioner to his own kind. And where do you think those that do wrong get to spend what is left of their lives…where do you think they get sent for punishment?" He stated as it wasn't a question.

"Ah," I replied in short.

"Yes, ah indeed and remember, eternal life is a long time to hold a grudge, Pet…a long time to lie in wait, merely biding their time until such an opportunity for revenge presents itself." Right, so I would be that opportunity for revenge then, I thought with what I knew was no doubt a grim expression.

"So, it was all an act to keep me safe?" I asked gathering as much but his answer surprised me.

"An act? No, not at all."

"But you said…" He held up a hand to stop me before adding more,

"I said I needed to keep you safe and I did that by naming you as a runaway slave of mine that needed to be found and punished by my hand. As for the act of making it believable, well, let's just say that my demon was easily provoked since you disobeyed me and walked through that portal into Hell, for I wasn't the only one furious with you," he said referring to his demon as if he were almost a separate entity.

"So that was what exactly, your demon's version of punishing me?!" I shouted getting annoyed at the idea.

"Oh, you know nothing of punishment, my dear girl, you can trust me on that!" He snapped back.

"So that show was…"

"Wasn't a show at all," Lucius finished off for me and my scowl deepened.

"But I don't understand?" I admitted making Lucius release a sigh, as he dragged a hand through his hair again.

"It is harder to control that other side of me down here. The rage, the power, the need to control and dominate all those beneath me…I am too close to the surface and as for you…" he took pause and I couldn't wait.

"What about me?"

"My need to control you has never been greater. To bring you to heel and keep you there is all that consumes our joint need. You ran from me too many times, that the demon in me knows that down here such a thing will not be tolerated." With the stern tone in which he said this, I could do nothing but take his words seriously.

"And what of the other part of you, like the man I see now…what of him, Lucius?" I asked not liking what I was hearing at all.

"I am furious with you, Amelia," was his obvious statement.

"Yeah, I get that but…"

"No…no, you don't," he said cutting me off.

"Lucius." His name passed through my lips in a way that told him I didn't like where this was going. Naturally, being Lucius, it was one he ignored.

"Your decisions over these past months have done nothing but continually put your life at risk, placing yourself in danger…"

"But I—" Again, he didn't let me finish.

"Do not think me a fool and ignorant of all that has happened to you since stepping through that portal!" He snapped getting angry again and well, if what he said was true, then I couldn't blame him. I had been reckless, *I knew this.*

But then also knowing that he had discovered everything that had happened was also something I had hoped to save him the pain of. Obviously, Lucius had his own methods in discovering the truth, and my hopes of brushing past it all and focusing solely on us being back together and reunited had been a foolish wish. But even knowing this, I couldn't help but try to defend myself.

"It's not like I intended for any of it to happen!" I snapped back.

"And what did you expect exactly, taking a trip to Hell was going to be like a trip to a chop shop in Daddy's stolen Ferrari?" he threw back at me, making me sound like some spoilt, foolish Princess!

"I didn't do this for fucking fun, Lucius! I thought you would come in after me, remember!" I argued making him cross his arms again, so I continued,

"I waited, Lucius! I waited for you to follow me through but then I got scared and realised I couldn't just sit there and wait forever. That was when I realised my mistake, all of about two minutes after I made it through!" I told him making him at least let go of some of his anger.

"Portals don't work like that, Pet." He told me, and I felt like rolling my eyes but wisely refrained. I did however say in a sarcastic tone,

"Yeah, I kinda got that Hellish memo, like I said about two minutes after I realised my mistake! So yeah, I might be what you would call foolish and reckless and stupid or whatever else you called me, Lucius, but I gathered as much just before the panic set in…but thanks for pointing out my mistakes like I didn't already know and suffer from them!" I said adding this last part in a tone that said it all, making him not as cautious as he rolled his eyes before saying,

"Yes, well despite your lax in that famous intelligence of yours, I at least tried to cling on to the knowledge that you believed in your noble cause and were being led by it." I gritted my teeth to hold back the insult and instead went with another round of sarcasm,

"Oh geez, thanks," I mumbled making him frown at me.

"Is that why you were an asshole to me back out there, even when we were alone?" I asked making him growl,

"No, my demon was like that with you because you were still in danger of being discovered had I been the foolish one and reacted any differently towards you."

"What do you mean?" I asked looking back towards the door that strangely from this side just looked like any other castle door. Where the mass of souls were? I didn't know. Although, what had I expected exactly, for them to have all been in here like one big party to welcome their Master home. Yeah, 'cause that wouldn't have been weird at all, I thought wryly.

"There may have not been any of my people around but there are those that are still able to spy on us no matter where we are in my castle…everywhere except this room." I frowned in question and looked around the unusual space. It didn't exactly look like your typical bedroom, that was for damn sure! What with the flaming shard torches and the black glass furniture seemingly merging into the walls. Even the floor was ominous looking, like some frozen black lake that any minute you expected to crack and send you to an eternal watery grave.

But then my eyes rested on the largest structure in the room, making me question its purpose. It was like a raised platform, high enough you couldn't see the top thanks to being surrounded by the jagged mass of black shards rising up like giant clawed fingers.

"And what is this room exactly?" I asked needing to be sure that the room I was in was in fact Lucius' bedroom and not some secret sexual dungeon he planned to 'punish' me in. Gods, but what was wrong with me as just the thought alone and I couldn't help it as a sexual shudder rippled through my body.

"It is my bed chamber…and that you have been staring at is my bed."

"Oh," I muttered at the sight of such a thing, wondering how you would even get in something like that…oh right, but of course…*wings.*

"The reason no one can access this space is because the storm that forever continues to rage around the tower protects it from anything getting through. It is drawn to the heart of the Crimson Eye at its core," he told me and piqued my curiosity enough to ask,

"Crimson Eye?" He smirked as if he knew I would ask, for my inquisitive nature wouldn't have let something like that pass without questioning it. But then disappointment followed as he told me,

"That is a conversation for another time, Pet. All you need to know is that the storm protects this tower, which is also why it was made my personal quarters as no one can enter or leave without my command…" He paused a moment so he could rise from his seat and get closer to me. Then he leant down over me and warned me softly in my ear,

"And that, Pet, my little prisoner…

"Includes you."

CHAPTER NINETEEN

IMPRISONED

"What exactly are you saying, Lucius, that I am looking at my new cell?" I snapped making him grin in a way that was solely sinful. Then he took hold of my chin in his hand, lifted my head back and told me,

"Amelia, my sweet little troublemaker, after what you have put me through, then you should be thankful to find yourself free of your leash." At this I'd had enough and stood up to face him, something he clearly found amusing.

"You can't keep me here as a prisoner!"

"And why not?" He asked arrogantly, still grinning,

"Because I am your girlfriend, that's why!" I told him, and this was when he closed the small distance between us and fisted a hand in my hair to hold me to him,

"No, Amelia, you're not…"

"But, Lucius I…" I uttered in a pained tone, hating to hear this coming from him. But then before my mind could stay haunted on those words, he finished his sentence, growling it out like a promise to the Gods,

"...You're my fucking Queen!" After this he crushed his lips to mine and kissed me, one that this time, made my shocked gasp end on a deep and blissful moan. This was because the kiss was most definitely one between reunited lovers, and instead of the few days apart, it felt more like it had been years!

It was a kiss I felt in my very bones and it lit up my insides as if I had barely been living before it. My hands fisted in his hair unwilling to allow him even the remotest chance at pulling back and putting space between us.

Gods how I needed him!

"Lucius." I muttered his name, one he tasted and responded to by growling before once more deepening the kiss. But only seconds after thrusting his tongue inside, he was taking it away again and I couldn't help the needy reaction.

"No, please." I could tell with the way his eyes burned a deeper crimson that he liked the sound of this coming from my lips, something he shared with me verbally,

"Easy, Pet, I am not going anywhere. You, on the other hand," he said before quickly sweeping my legs out from under me and carrying me up to the highest point in the room. The small mountain of jagged glass had a hidden staircase sectioned off and was at least thirty steps up the mass of black crystal. It was only made obvious as to what it was when we neared the top and I could see the hollowed section in the middle that was surrounded by deadly shards. These all ranged between four-foot high and at least ten-foot, and once again I was left questioning how a person like me would even get in a bed like this.

These taller shards were grouped together at the corners which created the illusion of a four poster bed as if grown from the ground of the tower itself. But then this also presented a problem seeing as it looked impossible to not just get into but more importantly...*get out of.*

Was this Lucius' idea of my prison?

Once again, the idea of that should have annoyed me more than what it did do, *which was turn me on.* Because even at the lowest point of the bed, it would have been too high to climb into, and well, dangerous at that. Especially given that each cluster of shards ended in a row of deadly tips.

However, this proved not to be a problem for Lucius as he lowered his hold on me a little before literally throwing me up in the air and tossing my body over the killer tips. I landed safely in the huge bed with a double bounce.

I looked back up in time to see Lucius grasp a shard not far from the top with his gauntleted hand before catapulting himself over them with startling ease. Again, his landing made my body bounce and it didn't stop until he had lowered himself down over me. He continued to get closer, until his lips were once again to mine but before he continued his kiss where he had left off, he finished proving his point,

"And now, *you are going nowhere.*" And with one look around what now essentially looked like a spiked cage, then yeah, I guess he was right…

I was going nowhere.

After this I didn't have much time to take in anything else, other than the bed was firm, the sheets were a red so dark, they almost looked black and they didn't feel like any material I had ever felt before. Almost like a mix between satin and suede. It was also at least three times bigger than any other bed of his, in both length and width. Unsurprising then, that it made me feel even smaller than I was, especially with Lucius' big body caging me into it.

I could feel the heat coming from his body, and he could no doubt feel the trembling need coming from mine, something his bad boy grin told me he enjoyed. But instead of finishing the kiss, like this position silently promised, he first teased me by running his fingertip around the metal ring still at my throat, one he had stretched so it hadn't been resting against my bruised neck.

However, in this position gravity took it right back there and I felt the weight of it pressing against the tender area, something Lucius didn't like. I knew this when he suddenly grasped the front of it and used it to bring my head up to meet his lips as they crushed to my own on a possessive growl.

This was when Lucius finally gave me what I wanted and started kissing me again and this time, *he didn't stop.* Because he had no need to stop, I was already captured and now, I had just found my cage. But then his kiss also felt like something more. Like a promise of something, perhaps that he would never let me go again. As if he was trying to brand the taste and feel of me to his very soul.

Although after what we had both just been through then this wasn't surprising. As, just for me alone, with the way he held me to him, as he claimed my lips in a bruising kiss, well it was one I never wanted to end. Not when it was one that ignited that bloom of lust inside me that felt like it was quickly turning into flames. One that had me grinding myself against him in a desperate need.

But from the looks of things, I wasn't the only one affected by this. Because I could feel the hard erection pressing against the top of my thigh, long, hard, and heavy…*By the Gods, I wanted it!* His hand that had started in my hair soon gave up the control of my head to trail down my spine. Then it continued to follow the curve of my back, whilst gathering up the back part of my dress, ridding the thin layer between his skin and mine. He continued to do this until strong fingers dipped down underneath me and grabbed a handful of flesh, making me moan. The tight grasp of my ass had my head falling back against the covers, and that moan turned into a cry of pleasure when he claimed it further with the bite of his fingertips.

He then dug in a little lower letting me know without words what he wanted of me. So, I hooked a leg over his hip, at the same time he slid further down to line up our bodies. I let my head loll to the side when I felt the first roll of his hips pressing his solid length against me. Having him applying delicious pressure to the bundle of nerves he had not long ago abused, my mouth opened, and a breath of pleasure whispered out. I found myself closing my eyes and arching my back, just to try and get even more of him. In response the bastard chuckled arrogantly, before he started tutting.

"Not so fast, Princess, for your pleasure has to be earned." My eyes shot open before looking at him wide eyed and questioning.

"But I..." He lowered himself closer so he could whisper over my lips,

"Earned through punishment, my little Šemšā." After this he straightened, putting his knees either side of me whilst sitting up.

"My punishment?" I questioned quietly, after first swallowing hard. The sound of trepidation in my voice was one I knew he got off on, as his grin said all it needed to say...

He was going to enjoy this. And as for me...well, despite this being Lucius, someone who I knew was skilled with every inch of his body in the bedroom, then the chances were high. But then, I was also in Hell. And this was after making him more furious than even the first time I ran from him. Down here he was a scary ass King who openly admitted that his demon was far too close to the surface whilst here. So, yeah, I could only hope I was going to enjoy this.

Because it was time for his demands.

"Spread your legs, do it now," he ordered sternly, and I

swear his words shot straight to my core, making it quiver again. He lifted his chin slightly and made a show of inhaling deep, before following the scent of my arousal down the length of my body. Then he lowered over me again and commented,

"My girl likes her Master's command, I see." At this I rolled my bottom lip into my teeth and Lucius' eyes focused in on the action. Then he was at me in a heartbeat, licking the seam of my lips until I let it go so he could warn me,

"That lip doesn't belong to you, it belongs to me and biting it, well...*that's my job.*" I let out a moan as the pain of his teeth taking hold of my lip only managed to turn me on more, and he knew it as the second he let it go, his own tipped up on one side into a knowing smirk.

"It pleases me to know that my girl also likes the bite of pain with her pleasure, for I most certainly enjoying giving it to you...especially after all you have put me through recently," he said making me flinch at the last part, needing no more reminders of the pain my actions had caused him.

"Speaking of which, I gave you an order, Pet," he said nodding down at my legs and waiting for me to comply. So, I swallowed down my shyness and did as he asked, not thinking it wise to push him or test his need for control.

Then once I was where he wanted me, I was forced to watch as he held his left hand out behind him. His metal covered palm now faced one of the black shards that surrounded us. I frowned in question, but it wasn't for long as I soon found myself sucking in a quick breath at the show of power. The shard started to liquify with the outsides of it rolling down itself until the rest followed and the sharp tip was no more.

It continued to flow down as if it was bleeding away until it reached the base and became the consistency of glue, thickening until it formed shape. Then it started to snake across the bed towards Lucius, making me flinch back. But then, just as I was about to pull my leg back to my body to get away, Lucius' right hand snapped out and shackled my ankle before I had chance. After this he merely gave me a look, one that commanded I do as I was told, even if the added words weren't needed,

"Do. Not. Move."

After he was confident I would follow his order, he released my leg and like his armour, he manipulated the strange Hellish substance until it was touching my skin. The second it touched me I had to force myself to hold still as it did. It was cold, so cold that it sent a chill up my body making me suck in a breath through my teeth. Lucius watched my reactions, enjoying the sight as he smirked.

"Enjoying yourself?!" I couldn't help but snap, turning his smirk into a full blow grin before he answered,

"Immensely."

This single word was emphasised when he flicked his wrist as the black glue suddenly hardened around my ankle like a steel shackle. When Lucius looked satisfied, he did the same to the other leg, and this time praised me when I allowed it to happen without him needing to intervene by restraining me.

"You're learning, Pet," he said after he ran his bare fingertips up the inside of my thigh, flicking the long part of my dress aside at the split in the material. I shuddered making his lips twitch in the barest hint of amusement, before that stern hardness took over and he nodded to my arms.

"Spread them wide," he ordered and instead of doing as he asked this time, I pushed up with them, so I was sitting up slightly to look at him,

"Lucius, I..." My sentence was abruptly cut off the second he was suddenly on me, straddling my hips with his knees either side of me. He looked so damn scary and masterful, I swear I stopped breathing. He then framed my waist with both hands and with a quick jerk of my torso, my arms slid from under me, no longer holding me up and making me fall flat back onto the bed.

Then he gripped a wrist in his hand, leant over me and stretched my arm to the side.

After this, I knew what I truly had in store for me. For Lucius hadn't been exaggerating, he really did mean to punish me. My proof of this came when he told me exactly what *I should be doing.*

Proof when he warned on a sexual demand…

"You…should obey me."

CHAPTER TWENTY

SEDUCTIVE TORTURE

"*You...should obey me,*" he advised with a stern tone that added to the warning, as he waited for another shard to liquify and shackle me to the bed. After it was secure, he reached across the other side of me and did the same to the other hand. I knew he was satisfied when that sadistic grin was back. This was after first watching me test the strength of the restraints by pulling on them and getting nowhere for they didn't budge.

Then he sat up once more and loomed above me, meaning I couldn't take my eyes from the sight. His bare chest looked chiselled from the marble in his throne room, with only the warm skin tone that told me he wasn't made from stone. The hard planes of his pecs dipped in defined lines, doing so all the way to his hard-tight abs. The muscles on his sides, like gills, hardening further as he twisted at the waist when running a hand up my leg, all the way to my waist.

His hand continued up and teased the bare skin at the exposed upturned V shape of my dress that was positioned at my breasts. This was before he was running his finger along the crimson stain his claw had made there when grazing my skin back on the bridge.

"My demon was rough on you," he said in a gentle tone that I knew not to trust, as that was all part of his sexual game. Like a cat playing with a mouse, letting it believe it was free for a moment before being dragged back by its claws so it could enjoy the thrill of dominance. He gathered up what blood was left there and brought it to his lips to suck before he had me flinching again with his abrupt actions. Because he let his body fall forward, landing on his hands either side of me but letting me first believe that he was going to land hard against me.

However, he simply pushed his entire body up, doing so with so much strength that it propelled his body back up to stand. Meaning that from his new height above me, he became even more intimidating.

Oh, and didn't he just know it, as the sound that ended this move was a knowing chuckle...*cocky bastard.*

"What are you going to do?" I questioned as he took a few steps back, so now he was stood in between my spread legs, the master of his domain and all the exposed trembling flesh before him.

"You want to know what I am going to do...?" He asked as he started to lower first to one knee and then the other, pausing enough to add to my nerves.

"...I am going to enjoy this, that's what," he said in a dark tone at the same time his hands flicked out at his sides, commanding the restraints to pull tight. This made me shriek out as my legs stretched further out before him, making me look like some damn sacrificial virgin or something!

In fact, the moment the once sticky lengths of black ooze he had commanded hardened at his silent order, it now ended up looking like giant crystal shards that had fallen and landed in the bed.

"Lucius, I can't, please…" I started to say, getting panicked which he let seep into the edges of his control, realising he had to give me something more. So, he skimmed the length of my leg until he reached the top of my thigh and told me,

"Don't worry, little Pet, I will take good care of you."

"But I thought you were going to punish me?" I asked with a tremble in my voice from both nerves and bittersweet sexual anticipation. He started to lower down over me, gathering up my skirt so it fanned out either side of me, leaving my legs bare. Then he traced the back of his curled talon down the centre of my panties. A pair that was nothing more than a scrap of sheer white material the same as the dress. I sucked in a quick breath at the contact and watched as he got lower, so his next words were said just over my barely covered, soaking wet sex,

"Oh, I will punish you," he said with dark promise lacing every word, purred directly over my skin with his eyes blazing up into mine. But Gods, if he thought by him being down there, ready to feast on me was something I would class as a punishment, then he was very, very wrong. Because I had been expecting to be bent over something and spanked until my ass was red raw.

Meaning that now, as his hand spanned my inner thighs, holding them down, I found myself unable to hold back the question,

"But I thought…" His growl stopped me from finishing that sentence, as he suddenly hooked a claw round the inside of my panties, skimming the smooth talon against my opening before a quick tug was all it took for them to snap. Then with a flick of his bare hand, they were out of his way. This was just before he lowered his lips all the way so he could hold my gaze, doing so long enough to tell me,

"You...thought wrong." His words were a heated growl. A snarled rumble all the way from his chest and ending as his teeth latched around my aching clit.

"Oh Gods, Oh Gods, Ohhhh...!" I let out a long, pained sounding moan when it was anything but. Although this was when I really started to tug at my arms and my legs, trying to save myself the onslaught of his punishing mouth against my sex...*it was just too much.*

"Holy shit...*Gods!*" I shouted this time, as he scraped a fang right over the sweet spot and I would have flown right off the bed, had I...you know, not been shackled to it...oh and also, having wings would have helped.

Despite this I still fought with little success against my restraints, as the feeling was too intense, and my struggle was something he enjoyed watching. I knew this when he paused long enough to raise his face up to see me, smirking the second he saw the strain in my features. His jaw was wet and glistening with the evidence of my arousal. I swear the sight of seeing it framing his bad boy grin was one of the sexiest things I think I had ever seen!

"Fucking beautiful," he muttered more to himself before he dove right back in there again, and this time, he added his fingers to the mix. This caused me to arch my back at the same time I let out an even louder cry, for it quickly took me hurtling to the edge where I would soon be chasing that orgasm right off it...*and I couldn't fucking wait!*

"Yes, yes...Gods, Lucius...yes, I am so close..." I told him as a few seconds more and...

I. Would. Be. Right...

"I know you are, Pet," Lucius said the second his lips left me, along with his fingers. I couldn't believe he had stopped and because of it, I cried out my loss.

"No!" I shouted making him chuckle and I swear if I had been free to do it, I would have thrown something at his head!

"Why are you stopping!?" I couldn't even find it in me to be ashamed that this was screeched in obvious outrage, something he smirked at. Then he slowly climbed up my body like a predator savouring his kill, and when his face was directly over mine, he lowered his lips to my ear and told me in gentle, luring way,

"Because this, my troublesome beauty, is what's called… *punishment."* He growled the last word and then, licked the length of my neck right up to my cheek, now savouring the sound of my horrified gasp. Because now I was left only eating my earlier thoughts at the same time he lowered back down to resume *eating me.* Having him do this to me, bringing me to the cusp of orgasm only to rip it away from me, was a far worse punishment than spanking me as he had done in the past.

This…*was torture.*

No, spanking my ass red raw was a piece of cake compared to this! And this thought only entered my mind after the second time he brought me to the brink, only to rip it away from me just as cruelly as the first time. Just before I could fall into the pool of bliss that Lucius was already swimming in! Because he was having the time of his fucking life watching my desperation!

"Please, please…oh Gods, *Lucius please!"* I begged the third time round when he had brought me to the edge again, doing so quicker this time. He achieved this by finger fucking me until I was screaming at the insanity of pleasure, for it was simply maddening!

"Mmm, how sweetly my bird sings for me…*sweet, sweet, begging, my Pet…"* Lucius said, after leaning over me so he could once again tease me with his words and his lips at my neck.

"...Now again." The moment he said these next two words in my ear, I was crying out once more,

"NO!" However, this echoing plea was answered only with another amused chuckle and a very firm,

"Yes."

Then once more he latched himself to what felt like every inch of my sex and I was again, bending my spine trying to escape all that was him. But then he placed a firm, cold metal hand against my belly and barely had to even push before it was held down flat against the bed.

Then like a good little fucked up bird, I was soon singing for him once again.

"Yes, yes, fuck! Lucius please, not this time I am so…NO, GODS BE DAMN IT!" I shouted trying to yank out of the shackles just so I could pound my fists against his back. This was as I felt the vibrations of his sadistic laughter against the inside of my thigh where he was kissing, in between his obvious amusement.

That had been number four.

I swear if he continued past number five, then a light breeze blowing against my pussy would have made me come like a fucking asteroid hurtling up back into space! And speaking of number five, he started slowly this time, and those barely there touches were soon combined with him blowing on my heated, soaked tender flesh as if he had heard my thoughts spoken aloud.

"Sooo gooood." I moaned, hating my weakness at not being able to hold it back and this time when he smiled, I felt it surrounding my clit before he suddenly ended the gentleness by sucking the bud in deep and rolling it between his teeth. I would have bolted upright at that one, had I not been restrained by more than just his hand that was still positioned at my belly.

I think this lasted all of three seconds before I was about to come and this time I tensed, as I tried to hold back any indication that I was as close as I was, just so it could sneak up on him. However, the sadist in him knew and the moment his lips left me, I looked down at him and screamed,

"Fucking bastard! Let me come!" At this he simply smiled as if every time he got a new reaction from me, it was like being awarded the next level of achievement or some shit like that!

"You think this is fucking funny!?" I shouted at him, making him bite his bottom lip to stop himself from laughing at my outburst and I hated him for it!

"I confess that I find it most satisfying, yes," he told me, and I narrowed my eyes at him before saying,

"Then it's a fucking good job I am tied up, because I would currently be kicking the shit out of you…oh, and just so you know, it would not have ended the way it did the last time I put your arrogant ass on the floor!" At this he threw his head back and laughed, making his abs tighten in a way I now hated because him being hot right now just pissed me off.

"I think we will save that type of foreplay for another time, Pet, as right now…"

"I am far from done with you."

CHAPTER TWENTY-ONE

DENIED. GRANTED. OWNED.

"I am far from done with you." The moment he said this my eyes widened, and I muttered,

"You can't be serious!" My outrageous cry was met by action as he suddenly grabbed a fistful of my dress in his clawed metal hand and as it tightened the material around me, he replied,

"What do you think?" Then he twisted his claws in such a way that when he tugged, he ended up tearing my dress right off me. I cried out in shock at suddenly finding myself completely naked. Not that there had been much of a dress to begin with but still, it had felt like it offered me something at least.

He yanked the torn shreds from underneath me, tossing them aside and once more taking his usual position, which was obviously his favourite for torturing me.

"You can't do this," I muttered and at this he grinned. Then while still holding my gaze from above my abused sex, he told me,

"Oh yes I fucking can, Princess...besides...*I am still hungry for you,"* he said pausing enough to speak this last part down at my dripping pussy, making a show of licking his lips. Then he dipped his head down and I tensed knowing what was in store for me yet again.

I cried out in protest before it quickly merged into a moan of pleasure that told him I wanted him to do anything but stop. However, stop he did, and again right on the cusp of me coming. I started screaming at him, cursing his name one second and then begging him for it the next. In fact, by the end of the madness, I lost count just how many times he allowed this torture to continue.

But I knew it was taking longer in between times as he knew how close to the edge I was. That most of the time his fingers and lips would only need to be there a minute or two before I was but a gasped breath away from finding my sweet release. And it was one that I knew when it was finally granted, it had the power to tear through me like a fucking tidal wave, crashing through my soul.

Now all he had to do was let me fucking have it, which is precisely why I said,

"Just let me fucking have it!" Yet my demand was met the way it usually was…*with amusement.*

"I have to say…" he paused long enough to clean my arousal off his fingers before continuing in an entertained tone,

"…it pleases me to know that this experience will make you think twice before running from me again." I had to say I was too out of my head space to do much more in that moment than just moan another plea for him to end my suffering,

"Yes…Gods, please, please Lucius, don't do this to me." His crimson eyes flashed a deeper shade before his grin gave me his answer, making his words no surprise.

"This is but a moment in time for you, my Pet, as hard as that may be, it is still unimaginable to the suffering I was made to endure due to your decision to act against me." I cried out in horror,

"So, this is fucking payback!"

"But of course, it is," he replied calmly, making me want to kick out at him, adding the action to my growl of anger.

"How could you do this to me!?" At this he sat up back on his calves and I watched wide eyed like a hungry animal as he freed his hard cock from his black trousers. Then he started pumping the steely shaft in his fist.

Good Gods, but it was hotter than seeing him lick his lips free of my arousal. Which was why my mind could do little but focus on it, and instead of waiting for my answer I whispered a premature,

"Yes, oh thank the Gods!" He chuckled before answering my first question,

"I am no fucking saint, Amelia, I am what I was made to be, born into this life in the belly of the Kingdoms of Hell and that means...*I will be obeyed."* He growled this warning, pumping his cock even harder.

"I will be obeyed by not just my people, but by you also, for you will soon learn that when it comes to keeping you safe, there will be no exception made. *You. Will. Obey. Me."* He said making me shake my head back and forth as my panic at not being granted my release was making me both furious and desperate.

I felt him crawl back up over me, positioning himself on his knees above me, and a hand came to my jaw to stop me from shaking my head. Then I opened my eyes to see his hand fisting his cock against my belly, before telling me,

"And this...I am sorry to say, my Khuba...I regret that this time, *this isn't for you."* I quickly tore my face from his hold and snarled,

"I will hate you for this!" This was when he lowered down

to my face, kissed my neck and muttered with a regretful sigh against my cheek,

"I know you will, Pet." After this he went back to his usual position between my legs. He added his fingers once more, working me both inside and against my clit, as he alternated the two. I looked down to see him also working his cock, doing so first after switching hands and commanding the demonic metal glove to form something less dangerous around his shaft.

This meant that the talons were gone and the sharp pointed plating was smoothed over his hand in his usual leather glove. I found myself trying to tear my eyes from the sight but watching him now as he pleasured himself over my squirming body, my gaze was locked and going nowhere.

But naturally combined with the erotic sight right in front of me and what Lucius was doing with his fingers, then it didn't take long for me to build. Only, as was the way with my punishment, the moment that it did, his fingers would shift to my inner thigh where he could draw gentle circles against my trembling flesh.

"NO! Gods, please no…no, no…please," I pleaded making him growl at me in a hoarse, aroused tone,

"Please what…tell me, sweet girl…what is it you want of me?"

"You know what I want!" I shouted in a pained cry.

"Open your eyes and tell me what it is you want of me?" He demanded, again his voice was thick with lust and until that moment I hadn't even realised I had closed my eyes.

"And I told you…you know! You know! You know…what I fucking want!" I cried over and over again,

"Give me your fucking words!" He snapped, making me shout back,

"I want your cock, alright! I want you to make me come and

FUCK ME!" I roared at him this time, and he closed his eyes as a satisfied look came over him and then he told me,

"Then it is time for you to learn what it feels like when something you want is ripped away from you." I frowned at what this could mean before losing myself once more to the pleasure of when he went back to fingering me. This time however, he did so quick enough that it had my ass rising from the bed as I braced the best I could from the onslaught of sensation.

"Time for you to take my mark, for on this night, what you give me will not be returned…that, my Khuba…*is your true punishment.*" He said and again instead of letting me reach the top of my pleasure, he ripped it from my grasp, as he continued to work himself until unlike me…he found it. And when finding his release, he did so to the sound of my last cry of outrage, getting off on my pain.

But still not wanting to miss out on watching it for myself, I found my angry glare rooted to the sight of his length being pumped in his fist that was held above me. My eyes widened when he roared out his orgasm and streams of cum burst from the glistening tip of his cock. I even found myself moaning as he pumped it out, so that long lengths of semen landed and were now lay crisscrossed over my torso. I nearly came from the sight alone, especially the way he threw his head back and growled up at the jagged crystal ceiling.

The cords in his neck roped under the tight flesh, as his muscles tensed and flexed with every stroke of his cock. His fangs could be seen lengthening with his mouth open and by the Gods, he was magnificent. But then, as he started to come down from a sexual high I craved, his eyes found mine staring at him. A grin spread as they left my gaze and traced the evidence of his marking my body, before heat flooded his eyes at the sight he obviously liked.

But then he watched as I turned my face away, no longer able to stand the barrage of emotions this punishment of his had done to me. He knew it too when I felt his hand come to my cheek, turning me back to face him,

"Have you learnt your lesson, Pet?" He asked and again I tore my face from his and scowled at the side of the bed, giving him his silent answer. But then he gripped my chin in an unyielding grasp and forced me back to looking at him,

"I said have you learnt your lesson, Amelia," he asked more forcefully this time.

"Yes," I gritted out and he released a sigh before placing his forehead to mine and telling me,

"There's my good girl." I was just ready to reply with something sarcastic and even scathing when he stopped me the moment he kissed my hairline and then started to shift down the bed, making me cry out,

"No! You can't...please Lucius, I can't take anymore! I told you I learnt my—"

"Ssshh now, calm yourself," he interrupted softly.

"But I—"

"You are about to get what my good girl deserves..." he informed me, and I sucked in a quick breath, almost too afraid to trust what it could mean.

"And what is that?" I questioned in a quiet voice, one that said all about the vulnerability I was feeling. This was just as he started to run his fingertips through his release that still decorated my stomach and breasts. He gathered some of it up and dragged it down my belly and even further before trailing it through my sex, making it quiver against the slightest touch.

Then he answered me, doing so at the same time as explaining just what it meant,

"...granting her this reward," his voice said on a growl at the same time making my back arch up as he pushed two thick

fingers inside me, ones now coated with his thick cum. He worked me quick and hard, with his thumb strumming over my clit, and when he started to slow down, I nearly screamed at him when I thankfully knew why,

"Give me your eyes and I will let you come." Suddenly my eyes shot open and I did as I was told, knowing that in that moment I would have done anything he asked me to do, just for the chance of this orgasm. One I was in blind desperation for. And thankfully, this time it was one he gave me, as the second he said,

"Come Amelia, come for your King!" This was when I didn't just come…

I. Fucking. Came. Apart!

I came so hard black spots clouded my vision, and I vaguely heard screams of pleasure deafening my own ears and with my mouth open, head thrown back, that was how I knew they were coming from me. The power of it slammed into me so hard I felt as if I wouldn't survive it.

For how could I possibly survive this?!

This was because it didn't slowly come up through me like they usually did but exploded in a sudden attack that consumed my entire body! It affected every inch of me, as wave after wave it continued to roll through my every nerve, as if it would never end.

But then my world started to go black, as the force of it finally consumed my consciousness.

My dark new world with only one man at the centre of it all…

My Masterful King…Lucius.

CHAPTER TWENTY-TWO

CREATING MONSTERS

I only started to come to when I felt lips at my ear and a voice luring me back to my reality,

"Come back to me, Amelia...come back to me so I can take you there again." At this my eyes opened and the second they did, I found Lucius above me, holding himself there.

"There she is," he whispered before granting a soft kiss against my lips, one he didn't yet deepen. But then I felt him sit back and that still hard, heavy cock was sitting at the ready. It was also something he used to rub the tip up the seam of my sex, coating it with the release he had finally granted me. This was when I knew that I must have only passed out for a few minutes. Because it was as if nothing had changed, other than Lucius now looked ready to go back to his punishment.

I frowned down at him, seeing his attention was solely on watching his own actions as he continued to use his cock to rub against me and I just prayed it wasn't just another way to tease me. This was why I uttered his name in question,

"Lucius?" After this his gaze snapped up to mine and that

heat I had seen there was now burning a blaze of crimson in his eyes.

He wanted me.

"Not having you the way I want you, is punishment for the both of us by my own doing..." he said taking pause as if thinking deeply about what he wanted to do.

"Lucius?" I questioned his name on a barely heard whisper.

"Fuck punishment...*you're mine!*" He snarled and then followed his admission with action as he suddenly thrust inside me!

I cried out once more as the pleasure of being reunited with his body had me almost shattering around him at the first stroke of my insides. He roared his own pleasure and with it, he grasped the shards restraining my legs and with a twist of his wrists, he shattered the lengths, freeing me in a second. The moment this happened I watched the dangerous pieces liquify and travel back to where they had come from, so I could relax in the knowledge it wouldn't cut my skin to shreds.

Once out of the way Lucius grabbed my calves and wrapped my legs around his ass as he rested more of his weight against me. Although whilst still rooted deep within me he remained still, waiting until he was ready. For what I didn't know, not until he lowered enough so he was left holding all his weight above me. Now with his gloved hand to the bed next to my head, he threaded the bare one through my hair at the side. Then he lowered the rest of his body, so he could claim my lips in a bruising kiss right after he whispered fiercely,

"Now, I am fucking home." Then he thrust his tongue inside my mouth taking advantage of the gasp, at the same time thrusting his hips up and driving his cock even deeper. Only after this was when he started really fucking me and doing so like a mad man starved of an addiction. His lips, his hands, his body was everywhere, totally consuming every inch of me. He

ran both palms up through his earlier release and rubbed it into my skin, soaking my breasts and trying to mark me all over, as though he was trying to get my skin to absorb it in a way that it would never truly wash off.

In fact, he seemed obsessed with the idea of me wearing it like a primal brand, and I had to say, the act only managed to turn me on more. Actually, my arousal peaked so much, that one tweak of my nipples in his cum soaked fingertips and I was crying out my second release in a long and panting moan. And he hammered into me through every second of it, leaving my nipples and now gripping my hips in a way that I knew would leave another mark, one I got off on just like the first.

His fingers gathered up more of his cum, this time the small pool of white that had gathered in the valley of my breasts, before forcing it in between my lips, making me moan as I sucked it off his fingers and his salty taste burst across my tongue. This he liked…as in…*a lot!* I knew this as his eyes heated yet again, burning at the sight of my lips trapping his fingers as I sucked them deep.

"Fucking love the sight of my girl taking me deep," he growled against my cheek and then his hands went to the restraints at my arms and the sound of them shattering next ended with him whispering,

"Fucking love the sight of my girl, dripping in my cum, when I am about to give her even more."

"Yes!" I moaned and the second my hands were free, he whispered,

"Fucking love marking you, inside and out…*fucking… love…you,*" he said, and my insides quivered around him as he raised my hands up around him, warning,

"Now hold on, I need to take you harder. I need your pain as much as I need your pleasure…need every piece of you… Every. Fucking. Inch!" He snarled and suddenly my head was roughly tugged to the side and his teeth were there at my throat. Then the second he sank his fangs in, I screamed in the pain he spoke about, and then cried out at the pleasure he knew it would turn into. And he was right, he took everything from me, and made it his own.

Every. Fucking. Inch.

I came a third time, doing so almost as instantly as the first one he finally gave me, and his cock drove home as deep and as hard as I was physically capable of taking. This propelled my orgasm into one that seemed to last forever. His cock dragged through me in sync with every pull of my blood that filled his mouth. The way he was drinking me down and consuming me was as natural as being taken in such a rough and unrestrained way. I had never felt so deliciously abused, my body belonging solely to him, signed over by the blood he took and the quivering channel of my core he fucked raw.

He was an animal.

A beast.

A fucking Devil!

And I loved every fucking second of it!

But then, I wasn't the only one as Lucius pulled his mouth from my neck. Then with a rumbling moan, it was one that mirrored my own as my blood still dripped down from him, now coating his chin from a different part of me, as it had exchanged my cum for my blood. Fuck, but he looked so hot, so powerful, so utterly primal!

Then, when he raised up, tensed above me and arched his own back I knew what was coming. So, I held on tighter, as his hips thrust forward one more time, now rooting himself deep inside me, deeper than ever before!

"AH!" I screamed in pleasure, at the same time he exploded inside of me, coating the walls of my sex with even more of his mark. I felt so much of it that it seeped out around him, soaking his balls that were hung against me, along with the hole that held him snug to me, unwilling to let go of its bounty.

Lucius, roared down at me this time, making me close my eyes and savour the sound of his release, happy in the knowledge that it matched my own. After this he collapsed down on me, resting his head at my neck and lazily licking at my wound to clean up the mess he had made. I shuddered, knowing it was one he felt travel along his still hard cock that was seated comfortably inside me.

"Did I mention that I love you too?" I murmured when I had finally managed to catch my breath, doing so with my arms around his neck and combining it with a squeeze. One that was given back in return, only in a way that meant wrapping me completely in his arms and rolling us both to our sides. Unfortunately, this meant me losing his length and I let a moan slip at that loss. He hummed against my neck before lifting his head up and cupping the apple of my cheek, caressing a thumb across it.

"My girl doesn't like to lose my cock."

"No, she doesn't," I agreed shyly.

"This pleases me, along with how well you took your punishment." At this my eyes widened in surprise and he kissed the corner of my lips and said again,

"You took it so well, Pet." I couldn't help but cough a laugh,

"Ha, I think I said I hated you and called you a bastard among other things and might have even cursed your existence, Handsome." He laughed once and added playfully,

"And let's not forget threatening to kick my ass."

"Yes, well, there was that too," I agreed sheepishly.

"I am no fool, Amelia," he stated, making me question back,

"What do you mean?"

"I deserved it all, Sweetheart, just as you deserved all I did to you," he admitted, surprising me.

"You really think I deserved it all?" I braved asking and this was when the conversation turned more serious, starting with his hold on me tightening,

"You fucking left me," he suddenly snarled against my lips, making me suck in a sudden breath at his words, something that he obviously needed to get out.

"Honey," I whispered on a breathy sigh before he kissed me again, only pausing again to repeat,

"You left me...*again.*" I felt my body tremble this time, shuddering slightly in his hold, one that only got tighter the second he felt it.

"Fuck, Amelia..." he said with gritted teeth before kissing me again, as if he never wanted to stop but the need to tell me what he had been through was also pushing at him.

"What, Lucius...what is it...*tell me,"* I said the second his lips left my own and he trailed his kiss down my jawline before paying attention to my neck. Once there he licked, sucked, and bit down, doing so against the part he had not long ago claimed. He also held the tender flesh between his teeth in what felt like frustration. So, I put a hand to the back of his head and shifted my fingers soothingly through his soft hair. Then I turned my head towards his as much as I could and whispered,

"Tell me, Handsome." At this he froze as if a memory was dragging him back under and before I needed to say more his head lifted so I could now see for myself the utter heartbreak I had inflicted upon him. The sheer amount of worry I had forced him to endure, and the punishment he gave me, was the only way he could make me understand it all.

It was in that moment that I really started to understand all that was Lucius. The man he was, the power he held, the position he'd had forced upon him. It had all meant nothing when faced with trying to prevent me from slipping through his fingers the first time. And then there was the second time, only something he would class as another failure. And he had been right, the second had been far more dangerous in doing so. But even if in that moment I hadn't seen it, hadn't realised it for myself, then what Lucius said next it would have been impossible not to understand it. For it not to seep deep inside me and settle in the depths of my soul.

"All my years…by the Gods, there have been so many, for when millennia acts like a century, and century goes by like a decade, until then that decade becomes a year, it all flows into an endless amount of days…and an endless amount of time… and all of it, Amelia…all of it meant nothing…" He paused to place his forehead to mine as he then whispered the last of his words,

"…not until there was you."

"Lucius, Honey," I whispered as I placed a hand to his cheek and held it there as he confessed his feelings for me, ones that rooted deeper inside than in any way physically possible. He pulled back a little to give me space to tell me further,

"In all that time passed and until you, there has never been moments of panic, moments of sheer, undiluted terror to fill my veins, turning them to the ice of mindless emotion that struggled to make sense enough for basic function. I had never felt so at a loss, so desperate. I thought I had felt the limit of these emotions only once before, but now I know it was nothing in comparison."

"You mean my mother?" I asked taking care at the delicate edge of this conversation and not wanting to lose track of anything because of it.

"Your mother most certainly caused enough worry for those who cared for her, myself included," he admitted before going on to add,

"But you have to know, when it comes to Keira, then I..." I placed my hand to his cheek and stopped him,

"Lucius, I know."

"What do you know?"

"That she was important to you and that type of loyalty, I would be a fool to believe that it goes away just because you have fallen in love." He shifted his head back a little more to get a better view of my face before asking,

"And this new understanding happened when exactly...? Ah, but of course," he said answering his own question as it dawned on him what I had experienced before I had stepped into Hell.

"I guess there is still a lot we need to talk about," I said quietly as I saw his features play out the same thought. Because I was right, there might have only been a few days between us but after what I had seen before stepping through that portal, then really there was much more. In fact, there was a whole lifetime of moments that had passed between us. After all, Lucius still didn't know exactly what I had seen or how it had affected me. Something I could tell he wanted to know.

"Then it is time for you and I to have that talk then, as I for one know it is long overdue," he said pulling me up and making me ask,

"Where are we going?" He didn't answer me at first, but instead he raised me up until I was standing with him in the middle of the bed. Then, after he first helped to steady me, his wings materialised as if they had been plucked from some hidden realm they resided in. Now only appearing when they felt the call of their Master. After this he wrapped a secure arm around my waist and told me,

"To clean you up, before the scent of your blood mixed with the scent of my cum on your skin drives me beyond all reason but fucking you raw again." I couldn't help but grin.

"That doesn't sound like a very good reason to get clean to me," I said with a wink and it was one he burst out laughing at, before commenting to himself,

"I've created a monster."

And what was my response…?

"Hell yeah, you fucking did."

CHAPTER TWENTY-THREE

GREED IS A SIN

"I'm not sure whether I should admit this or not, but I think I am clean, Honey," I said with laughter in my tone, one that came out when I heard his playful growl behind me. Then he lowered his lips to the shell of my ear and whispered,

"I disagree, my sinful, little troublemaker." This caused a shiver and being that I was currently surrounded by all that was Lucius, then the smile I felt against my neck was because he had felt it.

This happened shortly after Lucius flew us both over the black crystal bed and walked us to a part of the room that at first glance just looked like it went to nowhere.

However, the closer we got, it was then that I could see the difference, reminding me of some of the walls in the movie Labyrinth. It was in the way the shards were positioned, as from afar, it had been camouflaged. But then sliding behind one section and there was actually an opening to the side that you could walk behind.

Once there I found a set of stairs cut directly out of the

black stone in a rough way that for someone clumsy like me, would have no doubt fallen and broken my mortal neck. Which, needless to say, was why I was thankful Lucius continued to want to carry me, plus…I was still as naked as he was.

Hence the reason that once we reached the last step (and there was a lot of them) I was thankful to see that we were still alone. But what I had found had me quickly blurting out,

"You know I am starting to think that you have a thing for caves." To which he scoffed a laugh before warning me,

"This is where you refrain from making any Batman jokes or I promise you, Princess, I will drop you straight in there." I giggled at his teasing and decided to push it,

"You got it, Bruce." At this he narrowed his eyes at me, and in a few long strides walked to the edge of the large pool of water before holding my body away from his chest and straight over the water, silently threatening to drop me.

"Whoa! Okay, okay, you win…Jeez, don't get your cape in a twist," I said making him smirk down at me. Then, instead of just dropping me like he threatened, he walked us both into the water, making me hold myself tense for some reason expecting it to be cold.

"It's warm?" I asked with surprise making him just wink at me in return. The room wasn't like any bathroom I had ever seen in all my life, but essentially that was what it was.

The stairs led down onto the only flat surface in the whole room, which ended up being the only part that looked even somewhat conventional. This was because it had a vanity slab with a sink carved out of it and a flat vertical piece of rock sticking out. It was a polished piece of frosted glass that showed your image…or just about.

The whole thing looked carved out of the same black stone that pretty much made up ninety nine percent of the place. A connecting wall opposite the unusual sink was where I gathered the toilet was, although I didn't even want to know how that worked, as I didn't exactly see this place having good plumbing.

The rest of the space was taken up by a sunken infinity pool as the water overflowed the edges and into the frame of a slight cavity that I gathered captured all the overflowing water. I couldn't exactly say what shape the pool was as it curved around corners and out of view. It also enveloped around the pillars of black shards that rose up like tree trunks, seemingly holding up the level above us. But this time, these shards were polished so much, it looked like black liquid rising up above us.

This mimicked the carved stone below that held the deep pool of water, and if it hadn't been for the many hanging wrought iron cages that hung down from the cathedral high ceilings, then it would have been in total darkness. But then with there being so many dotted about the cavernous space and each one being the size of an armchair holding a fire pit, then it made the entire cave room glow. I also had to say that the effect of the flames reflecting off the black water was so startling, it was hard to look at anything else.

It was eerie and magical at the same time.

This was because it was such a seductively dark place that I found myself turned on again and without even needing to look at the naked God that had me in his arms. But then it soon became clear that his intentions were for the reasons he first spoke of. As instead of picking up my legs and slamming me down on the length of him and fucking me in the pool, he started to clean me. He did this by grabbing a bar of soap and a sponge like material from a hidden shelf in the floor by the steps he had used to get us in the pool. Then he sat down, turned me around in his arms and went about cleaning me from behind, making me squirm the whole time.

Which brought us to the discussion of me being clean, as it

felt as though he had literally gently scrubbed every inch of me...all except one piece that was.

"Mmm, I am not sure what I prefer, the feel of you squirming wet and naked against the full length of my body or doing so wet and squirming against my face as you beg me to let you come," he said making me groan out loud, unable to help replying,

"I know which one I prefer." He chuckled behind me, kissed the back of my head and said,

"I know you do, Pet." After this cocky statement, he finally got to that 'one piece' as he told me to lean forward. I thought little of it, doing as he asked but only tensing the moment I felt his fingertip gently trace the outline of my Hex, and also my still healing wound.

"Fuck, but I have never wanted to kill a bitch so much in my entire existence," he growled in anger, then before I could say anything about it, I heard a tearing flesh sound before his bleeding wrist was set in front of me,

"Drink me down, Sweetheart, I want you healed." This was mostly definitely a gentle demand as when I opened my mouth to tell him I was fine, he beat me too it and whispered the single word as a stern order in my ear,

"Feed."

So, I did exactly that, leaving myself with little choice, especially when that torn wrist was placed at my lips. I latched on and did as I was told, drinking him down and doing so with greater need with every mouthful of blood I swallowed. I could also feel him getting hard behind me, and because I could feel the chill before the heat hit my body, I knew it was on its way. The great wave of pleasure that would crash into me, making me rock against his erection because of it.

He growled low, a deep rumbling in his chest as before I knew it, I was suddenly gripped around the waist with a band of his arm and turned. I was then quickly being bent over the edge of the pool and I let my lips slip away from his wrist as I moaned,

"Yes." Not that he needed the encouragement. But in true Lucius fashion he did continue to make demands of me as I knew my mistake when he forced his wrist back to my lips and ordered more roughly this time,

"Drink!" I did as I was told and the second I did, I dragged in more of his blood at the same time he thrust his cock deep inside me. This made me cry out around his bloody flesh, as the orgasm coursed right through me. It was just so dark and erotic that I couldn't help but feel it building instantly again. It was the brutal hold he had on me, curling a gloved fist in my hair and forcing my back against his hard thrusts at the same time feeding me his blood.

But then, I wanted him to feed me something else instead and the second time I pulled my lips away, I ignored his growl of disapproval and quickly explained,

"I want you to feed me something else instead." At this his body went still, before I felt him bend over me further, coming to the side of my face so his entire body was arched over mine.

"You want to swallow me down, my sinful girl?" He asked in that throaty way. A huskiness that spoke volumes…*it turned him the fuck on.*

I turned my face slightly to his and he let me, as my hair trailed freely through his fingers after he opened his fist.

"Yes, I want to swallow you down," I told him and at hearing this he growled in a lustful, primal way before pulling out of me. I turned around the second he gave me space to do so, sitting down on the step and watching as his intimidating size took a step up, so he towered above me. This put him at the perfect height and his even more perfect cock awaited me. I licked my lips whilst looking up at him, now faced with the

hard and glistening length, with beads of water dripping off the end. But I didn't want the water, I wanted his cum! I wanted him to mark me a different way, which was why it was time for me to gain some power back, and this time, doing so by making him beg for it.

So, I started off slow, doing so by placing the pad of my tongue at the base of his cock and slowly licking my way to the top before swirling it around the head. I knew when it jerked and beaded with pre-cum that he liked it, no matter how painfully slow it had been. I did this again, and again and before long I was sucking down the length of it from one side and using my hand to jerk him off on the other. But during all this, I didn't once take him all in my mouth…and soon, he knew exactly what I was doing.

Because even when he did try to direct me to take more and should have become frustrated when I didn't, it was then when he chuckled and told me,

"If you think that by having you take your time worshipping my cock is going to get your own back on me, then you are vastly mistaken, Pet, as I could enjoy your talented mouth for hours before giving in to the impulse of forcing it down your pretty little throat to fuck." Gods, but the crass dirtiness of his words only managed to turn me on more and because of it, I threw my plan out the window and decided to go for it! I suddenly sucked him down, making sure my lips were tight around the shaft as I went, and marvelling at the sound of him sucking air through his teeth. Ha, not so cocky now, I thought with pleasure and decided quickly on my new play…*quick, fast, and intense*.

"Fuck!" He hissed, all cockiness gone being replaced by a man I was quickly bringing to the edge of orgasm a lot faster than he anticipated. I sucked him down, hard and fast, using my tongue flat against his length with each drag of my lips,

swirling it around the top of his head before down I went again. Then I reached out and cupped his balls, making him hiss,

"Fuck me…Gods, woman!" I smiled around his cock to let him feel it before I moaned in my own pleasure as I let my fingers slip under the water and work myself. I looked up at him to see him watching me, his eyes hooded and deep into the sexual sight. Then as my next moan vibrated against his shaft, he let his head fall back and muttered,

"Gods, but your fucking mouth…" He said no more but I took it as a compliment all the same and continued with added vigour to my actions. It was only when I heard his tone change did I know I was close, that and a fist in my hair,

"Slow down just a…fuck, Amelia, slow…Gods, fuck…fuck…*fuck!*" Then I only needed to go down on him three more strokes and soon he was roaring out, at the same time his hold on my hair tightened as if fearing that I would stop. But there was no way I was going to stop, not when it was getting me off too, and the second he groaned two things happened. The first was my main objective, when he came in my mouth and I started drinking him down. The second was when I came under the water, after rocking against my own fingers.

I continued to swallow him down the best I could, admittedly choking a little around trying to get it all, and some spilt from my lips. But as it did this I didn't want him to miss the erotic sight, so I looked up at him knowing he would get off on seeing his mark now on my face.

I knew I was right when his eyes blazed down at me but if I had missed the obvious sight, then his words most definitely got the message across,

"Fucking love this sight…sexiest fucking thing I ever saw!" He swore down at me, whilst softy caressing his thumb at my jawline before he pulled his cock slowly from my cum soaked lips. Then once it was free, that same thumb ran along my chin and up to my lips, gathering some of his release I had missed. This was so he could force it back into my mouth. I opened immediately, and he grinned down at me before saying,

"My greedy little Princess."

After that, well then…

I had to agree with him.

CHAPTER TWENTY-FOUR

HOG TIED

After our foreplay in Lucius' strange bathroom, I ended up lying back against him in the pool, whilst he played with my hair and we talked about a few of the things we should have already spoken about…*like his past.*

Of course, this started when he finally asked me what it was the Keepers of Three had shown me, much of which I knew was hard for him to hear. I could understand this, as there were parts that I knew he would have done anything in his power to keep from me, starting with witnessing first-hand how he had come to be the Vampire King he was today.

But with this being said, I also wanted to keep the conversation as light as it could be, as after what we had both been through, well, I think we needed this time between us. Obviously, we had checked hot make-up sex off the list, along with reunited lover's dirty sex off that list too. Oh, and adding to it punishing oral sex which Lucius most definitely won at. But now, with me yawning every five minutes, Lucius was definitely getting the hint and despite me trying to hide it, he was soon lifting me from the water.

"I think I tired my girl out," he said in an amused tone and I replied,

"What? I'm not ti…erred." I said yawning halfway through that sentence, making him chuckle to himself as he placed me back on my feet. This was so he could wrap a lush robe around me. It was dark grey, thick, and like his bedsheets, unlike any other material I had ever felt before. But it was soft, big, and covered me up in warmth that felt comforting. Not as comforting as being in Lucius' arms of course, speaking of which, that was precisely where he wanted me now. And well, I was so tired, I let him without a word of protest.

He carried me back up the staircase and by the time he was laying me down on the bed my eyes were finding it hard to stay open. I felt the whoosh of air from his wings as he folded them away after using them to get us into bed. I felt the covers being pulled from under me, before Lucius rid me of my robe and covered my now clean naked body with the sheets.

"And what do I do if I need the toilet in the middle of the night?" I asked referring to the cage of spikes that surrounded the bed, speaking now without opening my eyes. This was after I first felt him getting into bed beside me. He scoffed a laugh and said,

"Hold it." It was my turn to scoff this time as I opened one eye a crack to find him on his side, with a hand to his face, propped up on an elbow looking down at me. Then he reached out and flicked the collar still around my neck, reminding me that it was still there.

"I think despite how fucking sexy I find seeing my collar around your neck is, I also think it's safe to take this off now," he said before coming over me and this time my eyes opened wide.

"Are you sure you don't want me to keep it on…you could add a little bell to it and everything," I teased making him smirk down at me whilst trailing his gaze from the top of my hairline down to my chin, which followed his fingertip.

"Mmm, that's not a bad idea," he mused making me add,

"Oh, who am I kidding, knowing you it would be a homing device you added, not a bell." At this he grinned big and replied,

"Now that idea I like more."

"I knew you would," I whispered back after raising my face up and speaking over his lips before kissing him. He responded on a contented growl making me giggle whilst still on his mouth. He pulled back to raise a brow at me, silently asking me why I was laughing in his mouth. So, I walked my fingers up his own neck and said,

"Maybe we should get you one, that way we will match." His disapproving look had me bursting out laughing, so he lay back to the bed with a groan and I continued to tease,

"Oh, and I think a bell on you would come in handy too, a big one…" I said trying not to laugh.

"Uh huh," he responded in a growly way as he covered his eyes with his thick and muscular arm. I rolled so I could now be the one to lean over him, loving the way his arm automatically left covering most of his face and came around my back to nestle me closer to his side.

"Yeah, that way I will hear you coming and know when you are trying to sneak up on me," I told him, making him crack an eye open to glance up at me. I just loved seeing how his lips twitched when finding me funny. Then I felt his hand run up the back of my spine until his fingers found their way under my still damp hair by my neck.

"Oh, I think I would still find a way," he replied making me smile against his chest, where I nestled my head.

"High heels then, as there is enough glass, marble and crystal in this place that there is no way I wouldn't hear you coming then," I joked.

"Ah yes, because I have heard men wearing heels is very sexy and would be a great way in Hell to get me taken even more seriously as a leader," he mused sarcastically. But then I lifted up my head, flicked his nose and informed him,

"If anyone could make it work, then you could, kitten." Again, I was rewarded with that lip twitch of his that I absolutely adored. I loved being able to make him smile, but even more so when I knew I could still do it despite him obviously trying to stay serious. His hand curled at the back of my neck tighter as he brought my face closer to his and said tenderly,

"Missed my funny girl." After this there was a clicking sound and the weight I had been getting used to around my neck was gone. Then with his other hand he reached across himself to pull the collar free from my neck and dropped it to his side.

"I will leave this right here…you know…*just in case,*" he said in a teasing way before getting closer to me and growling over my lips,

"Now sleep, *my kitten.*" After this he kissed me in a quick but sweet gesture and guided my head back to his chest so I could stay nestled against him. I breathed deep and let the scent of him wash over me in a comforting way before letting out a contented sigh. Then after a while his breathing started to even out and for some reason my mind was wired.

"Lucius?"

"Umm?" He mumbled in a sleepy way and his brows went up in question even as his eyes stay closed.

"Are you still awake?"

"Clearly you want me to be," was his dry yet lethargic response.

"Sorry, I should let you sleep," I agreed feeling bad and he released a sigh and told me,

"I will sleep easy knowing you can't get fucking far." I chuckled at this and looked back at the bottom of the bed...he certainly had that right.

"That and if you quit being chatty any time soon," he added wryly making me poke him in the ribs. Then he trailed his fingertip across my neck and I looked up to find him now looking down at me. Obviously, something new was on his mind and before I got to ask he told me softly,

"He died too easily for what he did to you." I smirked back up at him and said,

"Well, if it helps ease your mind, then before you ripped his horns out and severed his head in that *easy way* you think he died, then to the memory of his death you can also add the sight of me hitting him over the head with a bed pan about fifty times." At this he chuckled and said,

"Oh don't worry, Sweetheart, that is a memory that will stay with me a long while yet...although, I think we need to work on your hog-tying skills," he said reminding me that he had seen the memory for himself when getting it from his second in command. I couldn't help but blush before replying,

"Um, wonder how we will do that." At this he rolled into me so that I was on my back and he was over me, so he was all I saw when he said...

"The best way to learn anything in life, my dear girl...lots and lots of..." he paused before ending this as a promise over my lips,

"Practice."

CHAPTER TWENTY-FIVE

A KING'S JEALOUS ARMS

The next morning waking up in Lucius' arms and having his fingertips running lazy lengths along my skin was enough to make me believe that my time in Hell had just been one long nightmare, and now it was all over. To the point that I stretched out like a contented cat making me smirk at the memory of calling him kitten last night. Hence why I teased,

"Morning, kitten." His rumbled growl was a playful one and the bite of his fingertips in my flesh as he squeezed my side only managed to turn me on more. Then he said,

"Morning, my little troublemaker, I see congratulations are in order."

"Yeah?" I questioned.

"For not pissing the bed, as I must say, I am impressed." At this I burst out laughing and this quickly became the theme of the morning. This was because we spent it lounging lazily in bed, either wrapped up in each other's arms or play fighting, which I had to say, made super big beds a bonus. But then as soon as my stomach started rumbling he declared it was time he fed his pet human, as the sounds I was making were starting to scare him. Naturally, I laughed at this and called him a baby. To which he whispered over me,

"Just remember, I know what you can do with a bed pan." To which my come back was to get even closer to his face above me and say,

"Yes, and I know what *you* can do with a collar and chain." His aroused growl was unfortunately answered by my hungry one, ruining my chance at morning sex as he became determined to feed 'his human'. Thankfully, I also learned that there were even more secrets to this room of his as the staircase down to the bathroom wasn't the only space the walls were hiding. I knew this when I saw Lucius disappear behind one and come back with a bundle of clothes, along with being fully dressed himself.

He was wearing what I gathered was casual wear for Hell. It was a pair of black wide leg trousers that seemed to tie at the sides of his waist and a tight fitted black jacket that had no sleeves, so showed off his muscles in a delicious way. His bulky arms and shoulders looked ready for swinging heavy swords and the straps across his wide chest and sides, looked ready for smaller weapons to slot into.

"I'm really hoping that outfit you have for me is a little less revealing than the last." At this Lucius smirked and surprised me when he said,

"I was considering a gold bikini with a chain to match but then I know you're hungry and role play sex is more of a human world thing…besides, I left my Han Solo costume back in the mortal realm." His surprising reply had me bursting out laughing before running the rest of the way to him, flinging my robe covered arms around his neck (or at least trying to) and saying,

"You did your homework, I am so proud!" He smirked back down at me and shook his head a little before telling me,

"You're a strange little human." I giggled, raised myself up further and whispered,

"Yes, but I am your strange little human." He grinned back down at me and agreed with a growl,

"Yes. You. Are." Then he kissed me hard and quick before letting me go. He also slapped my ass and nodded off to one side telling me,

"There is a small bathroom over there, hurry and get ready so I can feed my human and get her back here so I can fuck my addiction." Mmm, I had to say, not only did I like the sound of that, I also *really liked the sound of that.*

So naturally, I did as I was told, finding the bathroom easily now I knew what I was looking for, which was a break in the pattern of crystal. Behind the small wall was like he said I would find, a small bathroom with only a seat that reminded me of the first toilets invented and a stone carved sink so I could wash myself.

There was also enough space to get dressed, and I found Lucius had chosen a pair of harem pants. They were a bluish grey colour that fitted tight to my belly with a thick waistband. They also had little boy shorts attached that were ribbed at the sides. This was part of the design and I didn't need to question why the shorts were included as there were large cut out sections of the trousers. This was at each side that went from the waist band all the way to the tight band at the ankle. Meaning that without them then it would have been a bit too revealing when walking around.

There also seemed to be lots of material, that also gave the slight appearance of a skirt. To match this was a darker blue wrap around top that was cropped to just under the breasts. Thankfully, it was tight enough that it held my girls up without them looking droopy, seeing as there was no bra to speak of. It also had a wide scooped neck with a long floppy hood at the back and overly long bell sleeves. These brushed my knuckles at the front and reached my thighs at the back, shaped into points, with one sleeve that was a striped pattern, with the same grey blue of my pants.

To be honest, the outfit was kick ass, despite practically showing off all of my stomach and both sides of my legs. A pair of flat ballet pumps that came with a strange strapping meant that I didn't know what to do with them so left them off hoping Lucius could help.

When I walked out, I was holding the shoes in one hand and not looking where I was going so was about to walk into one of the shards close to the bed.

"Stop!" Lucius' demand made me look up, which meant saving myself.

"Oh, right," I mumbled making him laugh,

"She can fight off a fucking demon in her cell but walking from one place to the next becomes a hazard," he muttered to himself.

"I don't need to use my charm when walking across a room," was my cocky reply. His lips quirked before he crossed his arms and challenged,

"Oh, is that right...*Bitey.*" Damn him, he really had seen everything. So, I shrugged my shoulders and said,

"Whatever, it worked didn't it."

"Not sure you could class that one as a success there, Sweetheart," was his smug reply.

"I survived didn't I...? So yeah, I would call that a huge success." After this he shook his head again and questioned,

"Seriously, a fucking Bitey...you couldn't have come up with something better for a demon whose pussy bites off dicks?" I laughed.

"Oh yeah, and what would you have called it, huh?" I asked when cocking out a hip and making him fight his smirk.

"Besides a hungry bitch or menace to the male populace?" he questioned back making me fake a laugh this time,

"Ha, ha"

"In all honestly, most likely an endangered species, considering I'm pretty sure their kind would have been eradicated centuries ago," he added making me fight a giggle and instead of showing my amusement, I kept up the teasing. So, I asked in a faked exasperated tone,

"What, by you, oh mighty tyrant King?"

"You're damn fucking right!" Was his quick reply and I swear he supressed a shudder at the thought of such a demon. I was actually surprised he didn't grab his member just to be sure it was still safe.

"Erm…I think we are heading off point here," I told him.

"Oh, how so?" He asked, obviously like me, wanting to continue our teasing.

"Oh, I don't know, maybe because Biteys don't exist," was my sarcastic sounding come back.

"Yeah and thank fuck for that!" He replied obviously relieved by this fact. I laughed and admitted,

"Okay, so maybe you're right, the name was lame."

"Maybe?" He said giving me a pointed look.

"Okay, yes…geez, what do you want from me?" I sighed still acting out our game and running my hand back through my loose hair, one I had no other option than to brush with my fingers.

"Other than a promise never to turn into a Bitey, a fucking kiss would be nice," he said in that dominating tone of his that had my insides going all melty.

"Yeah well, don't worry about it as I promise to let you know the second I need to start flossing down there, yeah? But until then…" I paused when he started laughing in that deep timbre, velvet voice of his and with amusement lacing his command, it made for a dreamy sound,

"Come here, Pet" I raised a brow and challenged,

"Are you sure you're brave enough?"

"Well, until I hear the sound of teeth chattering coming from anywhere below your waist, then I think I will take my chances…now come here, Amelia," he said making me laugh, because his comment was funny but the more serious order at the end was what had me biting a fingertip as I walked over to him. The second I got close enough he snagged me around the waist by wrapping an arm around my back before drawing me in as close as I could get. Then I felt him tapping his fingers against my bare side before he told me,

"You look delicious enough to eat." I blushed despite being brave enough to look down at his hardening cock. Then I made a show of licking my lips and telling him,

"Yeah, so do you"

"Sweetheart, if you're hungry to put something in that talented mouth of yours then feel free anytime." I rolled my lips inwards to hold back the beaming grin that wanted to erupt at such a compliment, doing so only so I could continue to play it cool. Something I most definitely achieved when I flashed him a naughty grin and lowered to my knees. Naturally, this…well, it surprised the Hell out him.

Then whilst looking back up at him, I said

"Well, if you insist, my Lord."

Then I had breakfast.

I had no idea how much time had passed by the time we were making our way back into the main tower of his castle, but I knew one thing…I was ravenousness.

"Your stomach is growling at me again, my little slave," he commented with a smirk and a whisper of words as I once again was back to playing the part of his slave girl. Of course, now I understood why this was necessary, I decided to try and have some fun with it. Mainly by teasing Lucius whenever I could, whether it was quietly muttering things or licking my lips and reminding him of what the first part of my breakfast was.

He had said this as he was escorting me back into the throne room which, thankfully, I noticed had fewer people in today. I also had my collar back in place and a different kind of chain attached to it than from the day before. It was one more conventional looking and far less deadly, even though it was still wrapped around Lucius' fist clearly showing his ownership.

"What can I say, My Lord, I must be in need of some more protein," I whispered back making him growl playfully. We walked to the end of the room where his mighty throne sat waiting and the pile of cushions and throws on the floor told me once again where my place would be. His second in command was there waiting for us and I realised I was still to ask who this man was…or more importantly, *who he was to Lucius.*

He eyed me with great interest, and I don't know why but the look he gave me was unnerving. As if he was studying me or planning something nefarious. Although my reaction to him could have solely been based on how he had treated me when I was first brought here. Either way, there was something about him that simply screamed…*dangerous.*

Once up on the high platform, Lucius lowered me down to my nest of material before sitting himself. I could tell by some of the questioning looks around the room that this was an unusual gesture coming from their King. I only understood why when after he had sat down, the rest followed, telling me that the King was always the first one to take his seat. But this time, *I had.*

After this was what I had been waiting for and as Lucius was clearly speaking matters of court to his royal right hand, he ignored the servants who started to bring out platters of food. However, I nearly started drooling as food I recognised could thankfully be seen. It made me want to question where they had got it from or did they in fact grow it down here?

Of course, I wasn't exactly at liberty to ask, so instead focused on the fruits, nuts, bread and cheese in front of me, admittedly ignoring the slices of meat, due to not knowing what they were.

"Your slave certainly has a good appetite." I heard his second comment, making Lucius actually chuckle.

"After last night, then she has need for the sustenance." I frowned at this and would have growled at him had I been able to get away with it. But then I felt the tugging of my chain just as he started to pull me closer to him. I had no choice but to crawl a little until I was against his leg, where he leant down and took hold of my chin.

"Isn't that right my little *cock hungry monster?*" He teased referring to last night and doing this so only I could hear. Then, before I could reply, he brought me in for a hard kiss and clearly it was one he didn't care about doing in front of his kingdom. As usual, by the time he finished he left me breathless and near panting and his knowing smirk also told me that he knew what he was capable of doing to me,

"Mmm, fruit has never tasted so fucking sweet than it has coming from between these lips," he told me after tapping the pad of his thumb over what most likely after that kiss, was my swollen lips. He let me go again, and commanded,

"Eat, my Pet." I could have said one of so many come backs

but then I had promised him to behave when down here and that meant acting the part. And speaking of that part of willing slave, the moment I had filled my belly, and finished downing the last of my water, I was suddenly plucked off the floor. I gave out a surprised little yelp before I realised I was now being positioned in Lucius' lap.

"Erm…should we be…?" I started whispering my concerns when I felt his hands start stoking across my belly and the bare part of my thigh.

"You have finished your breakfast and therefore now it is time for mine," he said not bothering to keep his voice down and I soon knew why, as I was to be his meal. I knew this when one hand brushed my loose hair back off my neck and his head descended. But then I tensed in his hold knowing what usually happened when he fed from me and I didn't exactly fancy recreating the famous orgasm scene from When Harry met Sally.

"Please…we can't, not here."

"Ssshh, easy now…I will only taste and not drink too deeply," he assured me on a whisper no one could hear. Then, after anchoring my body to his with my back held against his chest and his arm across my torso, he grazed his fangs along my tender skin making me shiver in his tight hold. He then made me hiss at the little slice of pain when he pierced the flesh, but it was one that numbed the moment he started to lap me up, sucking on the small cut.

"Mmm, there is nothing better than having your blood in my mouth and your dripping pussy squirming on my lap," he said being purposely crude seeing as this wasn't whispered and he was making a point as to who and what my role was to others.

But then, I knew why he was making a show when a certain three brothers suddenly made their entrance. But I couldn't help but home in on one brother in particular and the anger across his face looked murderous. I tried not to react, but the moment I tensed in Lucius' hold that was when I knew I'd made my first mistake of the day. Because this was so much more than just feeding from me, this was nothing short of payback. I knew this when Lucius growled low and then told me,

'And now it is time that he gets to see you..."

"...In my arms."

CHAPTER TWENTY-SIX

FROZEN ESCAPE

The moment I heard these words, I sucked in a pained breath knowing that it was as I feared…that night he had been there. He had broken his promise and entered my Void.

"Easy Pet, for I am not angry," he whispered, and I would have liked to have said, 'no, but I am'. However, I knew that I didn't really have much right to feel this way, not seeing as he had been the one to discover me in another man's arms. And despite how innocent it had been from my end, then I doubted even with the knowledge of this it had the power to erase the memory. So instead of trying to argue my point, I just made a move to get off him when suddenly his arms went solid and he warned,

"Although that can quickly change, so I suggest staying exactly where you are before I look too deeply as to why you wouldn't want to be on my lap in front of your obvious admirer." I swallowed hard at the same time I stopped moving, although there was no way I could relax like he wanted.

"That's not fair," I whispered back after turning my face into him so only he would hear.

"No, *it was not,"* he replied not bothering to hide his statement this time and most definitely referring to finding me in Trice's arms. And speaking of Trice, well, he wasn't exactly helping matters by giving Lucius what was a blatant death stare. It most definitely had to be said that he was utterly fearless, *that or suicidal!*

The three brothers walked the length of the throne room and only stopped about five feet from the bottom of the steps. I gave Gryph and Vern a little smile, glad to see that the cockiest brother out of the three was now healing. But then this forced me to remember that it was the man at my back who had inflicted those injuries. I had to say, the thought sickened me a little, despite knowing that in Hell things clearly worked differently for Lucius as one of its rulers.

The two either side of Trice showed their respect and started to lower to one knee as they faced their King. However, it was only when Gryph hissed,

"Trice," did he then do the same. Although, when he did, he made it clear he did so begrudgingly. I was actually surprised when Lucius let it go, even though I did feel his hand tense by my side, and I looked down to find it fisted in the material of my trousers.

"Rise!" He snapped making them do so and as Vern and Gryph stood, they both nodded their heads to me and said,

"Lass."

However, it was Trice who ignored me completely and admittedly it hurt, although for obvious reasons I knew it was for the best.

"And to what do I owe this intrusion?" Lucius asked in a masterful tone that may have appeared relaxed, but I knew it was really anything but. He also started wrapping a length of my hair around his fingers as if this was a habit of his.

It was all a show.

"We 'ere tae receive whit was promised tae us," Trice stated in a hard voice, speaking of course about his soul.

"Ah yes, that of your souls…seems like a fitting price for returning another soul I own," Lucius stated making me suck in a hiss of breath and Trice sneered in disgust.

"Relax now, laddie," his big brother warned on a whisper as Lucius wasn't the only one now fisting his hands.

"I would listen to your brother, McBain, for you are lucky that after last night I am in a good mood…*one that will only last so long until she is under me again,"* Lucius warned making me suck in another breath as he continued to act as if I was some kind of whore he had fucked and was now feeling good about it!

I was near shaking I was that furious.

I turned my face away, feeling disgusted and hurt. Yes, I knew that Lucius had to act a certain way and keep up a charade to keep me safe, but this wasn't that. No, this was just a pissing contest between men! Lucius was going too far and before long I knew I would snap. Because a person could only take so much, and Lucius was about to find out just what my limits of this little act of his was. And I could pretty much guarantee that he wouldn't like the fucking outcome!

"I wull relax when we hae whit's due tae us, 'til then..." Trice started to say but Lucius had clearly had enough,

"Till then you are still under my fucking rule and you would do well remembering that!"

"Oh, I remember it a'richt!" Trice snarled back making Gryph mutter,

"Ah Fuck." And Vern muttered back,

"At least tis nae me pissin' him aff this time."

"You have something to say shifter then fucking say it!" Lucius snapped back goading him...hell, but at this point they were fucking goading each other!

"Ye have yer lass, 'n' I am just wantin' mah soul, thats th' only business we hae left," Trice stated with a shrug of his shoulders.

"And you have interrupted me the dessert of my meal, so it is a business that will have to wait," Lucius replied trailing his fingertips down the side of my breast to make his point and it was one I didn't like. As in...*At. All.*

Which is why I snapped,

"Why don't one of you just piss on me while you're at it!" Lucius tensed beneath me and the brothers all gasped, whilst his second in command sniggered,

"Umm, you know, I am starting to like your slave."

"Silence!" Lucius snarled to his side at the comment before turning his attention back to me, doing so by roughly pulling on my chain, so it brought my face closer to his. Then he warned,

"Don't force my hand girl, for you will remember your place!"

"Oh, I remember it...*my Lord!*" I growled this last part making him snarl back at me. Then he turned his angry eyes back to Trice who looked to have taken a step towards me, only was then quickly restrained by Gryph. This was because his hand was still planted on his brother's chest. But Trice looked down at it before shrugging it off and saying,

"Come oan brothers, it looks lik' th' vow of a King isn't whit it used tae be." Then he turned his back on Lucius who took this as the ultimate insult because suddenly I found myself dumped back on my mound of material. Then he was gone. I blinked and saw that Lucius now had Trice in a deadly grasp, after erupting fully into his demon. He had thrown Trice flat on his back with a demonic hand wrapped around his throat.

"NO!" I shouted making Lucius growl back at me over his shoulder.

"You care for this owned life, my slave?" Lucius snarled at me making me take a shuddering breath before nodding, a muttered plea came next,

"Please...please don't do this."

However, during this Lucius was getting a bite of pain back as I could see that Trice's eyes had turned to ice blue, along with his skin becoming like frost. It travelled down his features until reaching his neck therefore touching Lucius' hand who had no choice but to let go.

Then, just before he could take further action against him, Carn'reau came running through the doors at the end and declared,

"My King, there is an army coming from the Echoing Forest!" Lucius snarled in anger, pushed off Trice and snarled an order over his shoulder at his second in command,

"Office...*now!*" He said before nodding at me and I was quickly on my feet, slightly panicking now as to what new shit was happening. Especially when I watched Lucius walk towards his general. And with each step taken, a long and thick black sword started to form down his arm. Then once whole, he circled his blade with a roll of his wrist as if at the ready to take on this new threat.

I took one step towards him, the worry clearly written on my face when suddenly an arm took hold of me and brought me face to face with the one Lucius named Šeš. His beautiful almond shaped green eyes were frowning down at me in question before back at his King as he disappeared through the front doors.

"I suggest you three fuck off before he comes back and as for you, come with me," he said pulling me off to one side despite my struggles.

"Lucius!" I shouted but the moment we were behind a wall hidden from the view of his throne room he swung me around and hissed a warning at me,

"Don't be foolish, girl."

"Why...you gonna throw me in a fucking prison cell again?!" I snapped making him hold me tighter before dragging me off down an empty hallway, muttering about irrational mortals.

"If it had been left up to me, then you would likely still be there, as you have been nothing but fucking trouble from the start." I frowned wondering what he meant by that but before I could ask he opened a door and pushed me inside it.

"If you know what is good for you, then I suggest you stay in here or it will be that same cell my guards will put you in!" He warned, and I could now see the guards he spoke of materialise out of nowhere as if suddenly summoned. Then, before I could say another word, he slammed the door.

I hammered a fist on the heavy panelled wood in my anger before taking in the room with a frustrated breath. I quickly assessed the space, seeing that there was no other way in or out. Not exactly surprising seeing as I hadn't yet seen a single window.

"Fuck!" I hissed before taking in the rest of the room and taking note of its unusual décor. Unusual in the fact that for being in a castle like this, it actually looked somewhat normal and even, if such a thing were possible...*homely.*

But I ignored the Persian colours of my father's ancient world and the fact that this was obviously an office of sorts, focusing instead on the sound of fighting that seemed to be coming from directly outside the door. I knew the sound of a demon's warning growl anywhere and I also knew that it didn't belong to Lucius like I hoped. I then heard the clashing of weapons and the haunting sound of blood being spilled followed by the cry of death.

Oh shit.

I sucked in a panicked breath and quickly looked around for a weapon of any kind. In the end, a fire poker was all I could find, and I held the wrought iron pole as though it was Excalibur itself, glad that at the very least it had a pointed end.

"Seriously, how does this shit keep happening to me?" I questioned just before it all went silent in the hallway outside the door. My gaze was riveted on that handle and I knew the second it moved I would jump a fucking mile and no doubt scream like a girl!

But then when nothing happened I knew I had to check, as for all I knew then the soldiers could have been the ones to eliminate the threat and I was stood in here shaking in anticipation and worry for no good reason.

So, I bravely crossed the room while still holding my pathetic weapon best I could, I tried the door, half expecting it to be locked. However, what I wasn't expecting was for it to be freezing cold!

"Ah, what the hell?!" I shouted as it burned my hand and I stumbled back a few steps. But then I looked back up and saw that ice was now taking over the door, sealing me in for good. I couldn't understand what was happening, as in no time at all I was soon looking at a wall of solid ice!

After this came the thundering rumble like the earth was being split open by Poseidon himself, as not many people knew but he was more than just the God of the sea but also of earthquakes…oh and of horses. But really, how that helped him when supposedly living in the sea was anyone's guess, as it's not like they were great swimmers!

"AH!" I shouted again as the floor beneath my feet shook for a second time and I dropped my weapon with a clatter just so I could reach out and try to steady myself. But then, instead of finding something to hold onto, what I actually found was something living.

I knew this when the solid muscle moved beneath my hand and the second I stepped away from it I found a hand clamped over my mouth. I hadn't even had a chance to turn and face the new threat head on. No, instead I was left looking panicked and staring at my distorted figure in the ice. But this wasn't all I saw as the massive dark figure behind me was hard to miss. What with their glowing white eyes and demonic stare.

Then suddenly as a muffled scream ripped through me everything within me, turned from ice...

To black.

CHAPTER TWENTY-SEVEN

INNOCENT MISTAKES

The second my conscious state started to take in the motion of movement, one that was constant and in that of a rhythm, I knew that I was being carried. The feel of the air blowing through my hair and along my skin was one that started to bring me around quicker. Which meant that when I finally did open my eyes it took me a moment to stop being confused and figure out why I was seeing the sky upside down.

My head had fallen back, making the pain in my neck tell me it had been like this a while when I tried to move. Then when I looked up, I saw a sight I had seen once before.

Feathers.

I looked to what I appeared to be trapped in and saw another sight I knew.

Giant clawed feet.

Naturally, my reaction to this was to hiss,

"Oh fuck." This was when it all started coming back to me.

I had been put into a room and told to stay there. I had heard the fighting. Then came ice.

Trice's ice.

"Oh no...no, no, no, this is bad...so fucking bad," I muttered before looking up at the three sets of wings that were currently flying me away from the one man I had just been trying like all Hell to get to! And why, all because of three brothers who had taken in Lucius' fucking slave act and now they felt guilty they had sold my soul for their own.

Gods, this was bad. No, this wasn't just bad, this was utterly fucked! I needed to fix this! I needed to do something or what could potentially happen next would be three deaths I would forever have on my conscience. Three brothers who I had come to care about. But then I also knew this could end up being an impossible task and that I would have to have a backup plan. Maybe I could somehow get them to my father or even my grandfather for that matter to ask for his protection? For surely Lucius didn't have any claim if they were in someone else's realm? Then again, he still owned their souls, so I was clutching at straws because I had no idea how the hell this worked!

Oh Gods!

Well, whatever it was, I knew that I needed to get them to at the very least stop, as the further away from Lucius they took me, it would only mean the harder it was for me to get back.

"HEY!" I shouted hoping my voice would carry over the wind. The sky around us was a light grey and below us was a dark brown clearing that was surrounded by dark green trees of some creepy looking forest.

"HEY, you kind-hearted but totally wrong BLOCKHEADS!" I shouted finally making them hear me as a Gryphons head was the first to look down at me.

"Hey yeah, remember me, THE GIRL YOU JUST KIDNAPPED!" I shouted again hoping they would get the message and the second one head looked to another, which I think must have been the Trice's Cockatrice, we started going down.

"Oh, thank the Gods," I muttered the closer to the ground we got and all I could hope for was that this time, it was a softer landing. Because breaking anything at this point was only going to end up being the rotten cherry and bitter icing on the cake!

But then I had at least one thing to be thankful for and could be classed as going my way, as when I was but six feet from the ground the claws opened up and let me go. Thankfully, I was ready for it and even though I didn't by any means land gracefully, I didn't hurt myself this time.

So, I pushed myself up just in time to see three majestic creatures all separated in a torrent of power as the air around their beasts was being sucked towards them and creating a side on tornado. Then the second the creatures each landed I sucked in a startled breath muttering,

"Gods."

They were utterly incredible.

I watched open mouthed as that cyclone of energy swallowed them whole and what walked from the centre of each was the figure of a man. This was when I started running, and the moment I got close enough I started on them,

"What the Hell were you thinking!?" I snapped making each of them look at each other in confusion.

"She's gaen bat shit crazy, mist have bin th' fall," Vern said first before Trice folded his large arms across his chest and said,

"I think ye will fin' we wur saving yer ass from bein' a fckin' sex' slave fur th' rest of yer mortal life!" At this I closed my eyes, muttered a prayer and shook my head as the true shit show this had turned out to be really took shape. And well, I was the only one to blame for it all! Gods, but if I had just told

Trice who Lucius was to me when I had the chance, then none of this would have happened.

"It wasn't like that," I told him making him frown in annoyance.

"Aye fur it didnae look lik' that when ye wur sat on his lap collared lik' a fckin' dog 'n' bein' drank from lik' a fckin' meal!" He snapped sarcastically with his accent coming out thicker with his anger. This made me sigh and tell him again with more force this time,

"And I am telling you that it wasn't like that!"

"Bit lassie, ah thought this wis whit ye wanted?" Gryph said, being the calmer one of the group, as Trice then snapped,

"More lik' begged...if I recall, ye wur desperate fur us tae break ye oot of there."

"Well yeah, that was when I thought I was going to find my head on the end of a noose or on some demonic chopping block!" I pointed out.

"Ah bit fckin' th' king 'n' bein' his whore is just bonnie, is it?!" He threw back at me and I ignored Vern's,

"Harsh that be, Brother."

"Trice!" Gryph also snapped, whereas I lost my shit altogether and slapped him across the face before stepping up into him and snarling,

"I am no man's whore!" His head had whipped to the side and before waiting around for his response I turned on a heel and started storming off.

"Fckin' ungrateful crazed Lass...Where dae ye think yer going?!" Trice said suddenly grabbing my arm and jerking me back to facing him.

"To try and sort this shit out that's what!"

"Whit urr ye saying, lassie?" Gryph asked walking past Trice after I had yanked my arm free from his hold.

"Aye, fur a'm lost ere," Vern added.

"I am sorry, but you don't understand, I have to go back."

"Why?"

"Because it's the only hope I have at trying to save you from Lucius." They each frowned before giving each other another one of those silent looks. So, I rubbed my forehead as I tried to think how to put this before just coming out and blurting the truth,

"Look, I was the one that got you into this and now it's on me to get you all out of it again and if I don't do something, then Lucius is going to hunt the three of you down and I won't have any power to stop him!" I said making Trice scoff and say,

"We are nae as weak as ye think we are!" I gritted my teeth at the stubborn response and made my point,

"Why, do you have an army and a whole fucking kingdom on your side?"

"She haes a point there," Vern said rubbing the scruff of a beard on his jawline.

"Besides, right now he may be busy facing off an army but how long do you think it will be before he discovers I am gone. If any luck and I am not too far…wait, what are you not telling me?" I asked cutting myself off as their sheepish looks said it all.

"Thare is na army," Trice declared sternly making me look to Gryph.

"What does he mean?"

"It wis a decoy tae git ye oot of' there." I sucked back a breath, both relieved and not as Lucius would be bloody murderous.

"A decoy?" I whispered to myself as I looked back towards the way we had come, the castle now long gone from sight.

"Aye, that good blue haired beauty, Nero." So, it had all been magic. There was no army and now Lucius would know it too. This was when I started walking, telling them,

"I have to get back to him, I have to…"

"Awright, c'moan now, ye dinnae have tae do this...you can be free," Trice said, this time losing his anger and wrapping his arms around me from behind. I let my head hang down and told him,

"I was already free, you just didn't get to see it." His arms dropped and he turned me back around to face him.

"Ah dinnae understand," he said.

"And you never were supposed to," I confessed raising a hand to cup his scarred cheek.

"What are ye saying ere, lassie?" He asked and just as I was about to explain, I froze as this time when I heard the thundering demonic roar…*I knew who it belonged to.*

"Och, shit," Vern said the second the air cracked as Lucius landed about thirty feet in front of us. This was when Trice made his second mistake by trying to get me to stand behind him, holding me back. Lucius looked up from his landing on one knee, and in that moment he looked like some dark avenging warrior just dropped down from a Hell above not below. He raised his head and snarled low, letting his fangs lengthen, looking ready to eat out the heart of his enemies.

But the second I tried to go to him, Trice again made the mistake of trying to stop me, which I knew my only choice here was to show Lucius where I wanted to be. I needed to pick a side and for him to calm down when he knew it was his. So, I did something that surprised the shit out of everyone. The second Trice went to grab me I yanked his hand down, stepped over the arm and took it with me in a lock that he had no choice to follow before rolling to his back and ending by me putting him on his ass. Then, before anyone could do anything to stop me, I ran as fast as I could to my Chosen One.

"Lucius!" I shouted his name after throwing myself in his arms, meaning he had no choice but to catch me. Thankfully, his armour retracted at the same time so the impact wouldn't hurt and left the man I loved beneath the demonic battle suit.

I had at least managed to tame the beast back.

I buried my head in his neck as he lifted me higher and I breathed him in deep.

"Amelia." He said my name, whispering it in utter relief into my hair at the same time his arms tightened around me. Then, as he lowered me, his arms unwound from me so he could frame my face as if needing to see that I was unharmed.

"Are you alright, Sweetheart?" he asked, and I nodded, hearing Vern's comment,

"Och, I think we hae missed something big 'ere, brothers."

"Aye," Gryph agreed whereas Trice had regained his stance and said nothing, even if his stern, hard features pretty much said it all...*he was furious.*

However, these comments only managed to bring Lucius' attention back to those responsible for taking me from him and the second he looked over my head and growled low in his throat, I knew this was 'oh shit' time. Especially when he didn't even glance down at me before he was letting me go and telling me,

"Wait here!" His hard unyielding, and scary voice told me what was coming next.

"No! Lucius, no…" He ignored me and started walking over to the brothers, forcing me to go running after him.

"Amelia, do as you're told!" Lucius barked at me as I caught up.

"Aye, Amelia, dae as yer Master commands!" Trice snapped after drawing his sword. I looked back at him over my shoulder and snapped,

"Not helping here!"

Lucius shot me a furious look and warned,

"Get back!"

"NO!" I shouted and this time, pushed his chest to get him to stop, something he didn't do. No, instead he grabbed me by the waist and moved me to one side but then the second I was free I ran and jumped on his back. Once there I hooked my ankles around his waist and spun my body round, letting my weight fall backwards so my hold on him meant he had to come following after me. Then when we were both on the floor I quickly straddled him, tried to pin him there and shouted down at him,

"It wasn't their fault! They didn't know!" Suddenly, I was flipped and the roles reversed as he shouted down at me,

"They knew that they were acting against their King!" Then he pushed back up from me and was suddenly producing his own sword and getting ready to strike Trice who already had raised his blade before him. I quickly scrambled to my feet and just before they could start fighting I tried one more thing.

"If you do this…if you fight them and hurt any of them then I swear to you, Lucius, I will never fucking forgive you! NEVER!" I shouted making him finally take pause. He looked back at me over his shoulder in utter shock.

"Please…don't do this, don't make me hate you for hurting them." Lucius' eyes narrowed on me and opened his mouth to speak but whatever he was going to say got lost. Because when he did, that was when I saw Trice trying to use this to his advantage. Suddenly fearful for a new reason my body reacted, doing so in a way like never before. Not even like the day in the Janus Temple with the witch. It was all so different.

Rage. Panic. Pain. It all ripped through me, starting at what felt like my belly, before it suddenly exploded!

"I SAID NO!" I screamed so loud that it felt like it rattled my spine! At the same time a red bloody stream of air rushed from my entire body and travelled like another form of me towards the four men. It was a silhouette that only got bigger and bigger until by the time it hit them, it was the size of a house.

It slammed into all of them and knocked everyone down like they each were made up of air. It threw the three brothers back with only Lucius, who actually fought against it and remained standing. However, even this didn't look easy.

Then after the angry cloud of power had continued so far it started to evaporate, leaving me just standing there utterly stunned. I was panting heavier and heavier until suddenly I couldn't seem to breathe!

"Luc…ius I…" I tried to say as I looked down at my hands that wouldn't stop shaking.

"I am here!" He told me, at the same time taking my hands in his and telling me,

"Breathe, Amelia…just breathe now…calm, calm for me," he said wrapping his arms around me and trying to breathe with me, no doubt hoping for me to follow his rhythm.

"That's it…deep breaths, just in and out again," he said soothingly, now stroking the back of my hair down to my back as he kept me cradled to his chest.

"Whit th fck wis that?!" I heard Vern ask in a bewildered tone.

"Silence!" Lucius growled before asking me once my breathing had evened,

"Are you alright?" I pulled back so I could see him and nodded a little, feeling completely unsure of what was going on.

"Ah thought she wis mortal?" Trice said making Lucius snap,

"She is mortal."

"Aye and she's also yer Chosen One," Gryph added making Vern suck in surprised breath and Trice look pained,

"Yes, she is and if a word of this is…"

"We wull nae speak a word o' this, we care fur th' lassie,"

Gryph quickly assured him and just as I raised my hand to cup his cheek I started to feel strange.

"Lucius, please don't be angry at…I…feel…"

"Amelia?" Lucius said my name and the worry was clearly there in both his tone and in his face. But then that face started to go blurry and soon my mind was finding it difficult to focus on small details.

"Whit's wrong wi' her?" Vern was the first one to ask and I could just make out a blurred form pushing his way through.

"Amelia?!" Lucius shouted this time as my legs suddenly gave way beneath me.

"Turn her around." I could just hear Trice's order making Lucius snap back,

"Why?!"

"Just dae it!" Trice demanded again and that's when I felt myself moving. After that I felt the air hit my back and pain suddenly cut through me like a lance! It was unbelievable and of the likes I had never felt before!

I screamed before it turned into small whimpering cries of pain. I heard Lucius trying to calm me and the hiss of air being pulled through teeth.

"What is it?!" Lucius demanded through the fog and the very last thing I heard was from Trice, who sounded both angry and anxious…

"The hex…tis…"

"Tis trying tae claim her."

CHAPTER TWENTY-EIGHT

HEX OF A TIME

The next time I opened my eyes I had to give myself time to understand where I was and even then it didn't help. For starters I was lying on a bed of ash and the second I focused, I could see the little paper snowflakes of grey falling down all around me. I reached up a hand and let one catch on the tips of my fingers before bringing it closer to my face so I could discover what it was.

But it was only when I finally sat up that I knew something bad had happened here…wherever here was? *Had I caused this destruction?*

It was like a wasteland of grey, with nothing but water in the distance washing even more ash up to the shore like dead skin floating on the surface. I frowned the longer I looked at the desolate place and for some reason an overwhelming sadness overtook me.

I got up from what strangely looked like an old cart that was without any animal to pull it. Where was everyone, had everyone run from the oncoming ruin? I turned around to look behind me expecting to see the same dead land when I could just make out a line of life beyond.

I turned back to where the destruction seemed to be centred around and felt the ash clinging to my hair, like snow that wouldn't ever melt. But then something caught my eye as footsteps seemed to appear out of nowhere.

"What is this?" I muttered aloud jumping a little when my own voice echoed back at me. Then, as if responding to the question, more footsteps appeared as if an invisible woman was walking in the grey sand. I decided to follow it, making sure I wasn't stepping in the same place not trusting what might happen if I did. It started to take me closer to the water that could have been an ocean or just a lake. I just couldn't tell due to the thick fog that obstructed my view. It clung to the water like summoned clouds that needed to keep the edges of this place from mortal means.

Was this some kind of forbidden place?

I left this question unanswered like all the rest and continued to follow the steps until they finally stopped at what looked like something buried in the ash. At first it looked like a dull black stone that was wet from the water lapping at it. Pieces of ash clung to it only to be washed away again with every small wave that caressed it. I didn't know what it was about the stone, but it seemed to be drawing me in. As though what I was looking at was not just a piece of history, but something that was looking for the one single soul that it truly belonged to.

The person with the power to change that history.

I had no idea where these thoughts were coming from, but I knew that I had to have it. I had to take it and protect it from being used. But then the second I did this I saw the faintest ghost of another girl doing the same. I tried to snatch out quickly, intent on taking the stone before she could get it but then the second I touched it something happened. The girl became whole and cried out as she fell to her knees still clutching the orb to her chest. Then it started to glow crimson and when she opened her eyes, they held the same power in them.

After this she said one name and it was one I knew well…

"Janus"

After this I looked around, now seeing the ghosts of a small army of men all dragging the shadows of screaming women behind them, trying to steal them away. It was like being shown the barest memory of history and from the looks of things, it was an ancient one. Then suddenly a blinding white light erupted and cut through everything. I watched as the rest of the memories were also swept away like an explosion of power had brought the wind of time.

All that was left, was the woman standing next to me, looking straight at me. She had a kind young face with sadness in her eyes. She held out the red orb to me that was no bigger than an apple and told me,

"For me love was the key to end this war…but for you hate is the only power you will find there. Hate is what made him. Hate is what failed him. Hate is what you must defeat…" She paused to look down at the orb still in her hands and said,

"Fate has chosen you." Then she held it out further for me to take and the second I did, I suddenly gasped out for breath!

I sat up still clutching at the orb to my chest only to find it wasn't there.

"No!" I shouted in panic and started looking for it only to find that I was no longer in the same place.

"Hey, whoa, calm down, Honey, you're fine…you're fine now, just take it easy." A voice I recognised started speaking to me and I took a deep breath to try and calm the pounding of my heart.

"That's it, deep breaths, yeah?" Nero said who was sat next to me giving me a warm smile. I looked around and this time it didn't take me half as long to figure out where I was…not that I had the first time. But at least for now I was in Lucius' bedroom in Hell and it was a far more welcoming sight.

"Nero?"

"Hey Chicky, here drink this." I gave it a suspicious look and said,

"It's not Devil's Rum again is it?"

"No, it's just water," she said chuckling.

"Oh good, that stuff tastes like demon piss." She gave me another amused look and teased,

"Had much of that have you." I gave her wry look and said,

"You don't wanna know half the shit." And then I left it at that.

"Fair enough," she said shrugging her shoulders in a way that she understood everyone had their personal demons…even for, well…a demon.

"What happened, where is Lucius?" She gave me a knowing look and said,

"Yeah, you kinda missed out the part where the King is your boyfriend, 'cause you know that shit would have been quite helpful." I felt the heat invade my cheeks and said,

"I'm sorry, but I didn't exactly know who I could trust with that one."

"Oh shit, yeah I get it…" she said holding up both hands and continuing,

"If people knew, then fuck me, you would have been on everyone's bounty list! Your fella ain't exactly gonna win any popularity contests but then again, not a King in Hell that would…well, other than Asmodeus, he's just yummy." I choked on a laugh making her give me a questioning look, so I told her,

"He's also my grandfather." At this her navy coloured eyes grew wide before she said,

"No shit?"

"I shit you not," I replied making her whistle and rub a hand through her blue hair, a mass of curls that were braided tight on one side.

"Wow, well you are just full of surprises aren't you, Chicky?" At this point I would have said, 'oh you have no idea' but decided against it and went with trying to figure out what the hell had happened. Because the last thing I remembered was the field and...oh Gods,

"Trice?! Vern and Gryph, are they...?"

"Calm down, they are just fine and were here not long ago." I released a breath before asking,

"They were?" I was clearly shocked.

"Yeah, well they kind of had to be." I frowned at this.

"What do you mean?"

"Trice was the only one who had the power in him to stop the Hex from taking over you. I swear I have never seen anything like this power. I mean I think I have seen the symbol before, but Gods' balls if I can remember where...it's not exactly common, even for a witch." I thought about all this and winced at not just the slight pain I could feel there on my back, but more the idea that Lucius was forced to watch as Trice had to heal me.

"And Lucius let that happen?" I questioned making Nero say,

"Hey, no sweat, men need a bit of healthy competition and besides, your boyfriend might be known as a tyrant King, but man he is undeniably...HOT!" She said making me laugh. Then she nudged my arm and said,

"Don't worry about them, shit will sort itself out." She then tapped the side of her temple and said,

"I know these things."

After this she explained how Lucius had requested Nero as my personal 'lady' to help care for me, because as it turned out, I had been passed out for a few days. Hence why I was ravenous, thirsty and in desperate need of a pee and well basic hygienic needs. So after taking care of the first three I told Nero that I was going to take a bath before Lucius came back. Something she informed me wouldn't be long as he never left me for more than twenty, thirty minutes tops.

So, knowing this and not really relishing the idea of being a sweaty, smelly mess for when that happened, I made my way down the staircase, taking care not to fall and create a new drama for Lucius to be faced with when he got back.

I didn't know what had happened, but I just knew that if the only good thing came out of being on that field was the McBain brothers were no longer in any trouble, then it was worth it. This was because Nero had assured me they were currently all working together in trying to find a cure.

The brothers were at this moment trying to find someone who had the power to remove it. And at the request of Lucius that Trice wasn't gone long seeing as he seemed the only one able to stop it from taking control of me completely. Not that I knew what this meant or what would happen when it did.

Gods, but really...what was next?

And what had that place been I had seen before waking up back here? Had it been something the Fates had wanted me to see? The woman had spoken about hatred being the key or something. But it was more than this, it was that red orb. I couldn't seem to stop thinking about it. Couldn't seem to get my mind off trying to recreate every second in my mind of when I had seen it. Why was I so drawn to it?

I didn't know.

When faced with the water I sucked in a deep breath and

was just about to remove the clothes Nero had told me she had dressed me in. It was a similar outfit that I had been wearing before only this time it was pure white and there were no slits in the trousers and the top was without sleeves. Nero had also brought some more of her 'seeing powder', laughing when I told her what I had done with the last lot. She had been glad it had come in handy but admitted never using it as a weapon before. I also discovered that this wearing off was likely why my vision had started to go blurry when the Hex tried to take over. Apparently, it takes over all magic, which was what made Trice so special, he was strangely immune to magic used against him.

But it had been Lucius who had informed her the powder was needed, making me first wonder how he knew to begin with. Although Nero helped with that also, as she told me how Lucius when looking for me had paid her a visit and searched her memories. Well, as long as it hadn't been done to Trice I thought cringing, or I didn't know what Lucius would do.

I shook my head and was just about to slip off my trousers when something stopped me. Something was glowing in the darkness of the water and suddenly I became transfixed. I narrowed my eyes and muttered,

"What the Hell is…Ah!" I ended this by shouting out the second a feeling slammed into me. It was like being hit with an emotional bat and I found tears in my eyes as the feeling of dread suddenly washed over me.

"I found this too if you get too cold…Amelia?" Nero's voice trailed off and I looked over my shoulder at her to see a jacket falling from her hands and panic was as clear as day on her face. The colour drained away from her skin and she looked…

Frightened.

"Amelia, you need to step back, *right now!*" she hissed not taking her eyes off the water. So I looked back and saw what she now saw. The entire pool of water had just been replaced by blood and it bubbled and popped as if made of lava. But then something overwhelming seemed to take over me and I turned back to her and in a voice that wasn't my own, told her...

"It's alright, Nero...I am the Queen of Blood." Then I proved it by doing something foolish...

I let myself fall in.

CHAPTER TWENTY-NINE

CRIMSON TEARS

The moment I let myself fall into the blood it instantly cleared and turned back into the water it once was. I didn't understand how, and right then, I didn't even want to try. Because my mind was consumed by another thought…

I could feel the orb was near.

I opened my eyes underwater and let the red glow guide me, swimming deeper and holding my breath despite the burning I could feel attacking my lungs. Yet this didn't seem to hold me back as I couldn't think about the air my body desperately wanted. Not when every single fibre of my being was focused only on finding what I knew was hidden down here. It was calling out to me and the deeper I went, the closer I came to answering its pull.

It needed me.

Finally, I could see an arch under the water where the glow was at its brightest, so with the last of my energy I kicked out behind me and swam through it. This was when I saw a bright light above me. I felt relieved when there was a surface as it was a good job seeing as any longer under the water and I would have most likely drowned!

I broke the surface taking in large gulps of air the second I could, trying not to cough too much so I wouldn't pass out from lack of air that my body was fighting me on filling my lungs. Then, once I was calm enough, I looked around to see that I had discovered a secret cavern. Getting excited, I moved my arms around and kicked enough to stay afloat treading water. Then I found a shallow part to climb out of and quickly took note of the pale stone walls that matched the floor.

It was just a cave.

I swam over to the edge and climbed out, pushing my wet hair back off my face so I could take it all in. The space looked like an entrance of some kind, as all it held was another carved arch that I quickly walked towards the moment that familiar red glow was back and guiding me. I had no idea how I knew I was doing the right thing, but something in me was just convinced that my actions were correct.

So I started running, desperate to see it again, I could almost taste it and it tasted like…well, it tasted like…

Blood.

Did I crave it because of what I once was? Because I was born a vampire and at my core had the heart of one? I had told Nero I was the Queen of Blood before letting myself fall, but that hadn't been me talking. So what did that mean and who was this part of me that seemed desperate to get to the surface? Which part of me had been the one to throw that surge of power at Lucius and the brothers that day?

I had no answers, but I knew one thing, the red orb had them, I was sure of it. Now all I needed to do was claim it!

So I ran through the archway and down the glowing red tunnel until I seemed to burst through the other end, only stopping myself by skidding in the loose black sand that seemed to cover the floor. It was another Temple, but one minus anything other than a carved altar in the centre. It was one that even I could see showed the Divine Fates and the Gods that were said to be the first creations of all realms.

But despite how beautiful the altar was, with stunning white figures carved from what looked like giant pearls, it was the glowing red orb at its centre that had all my focus. So, as I stepped forward, doing so in a way that wanted to get to it and also in a way that was too afraid to. Fearing that like last time it might disappear. But then the closer I got I could see the stone was slightly shaped and looked like a heart, one alive and pulsating thanks to the power radiating off it.

"Oh, by the Gods, it can't be…it can't be real!" I turned the second I heard Nero's voice behind me, seeing now that she had followed me down here. She was soaking wet but like me, nothing else mattered but the stone. However, it wasn't as though she was a threat either, so as she approached I didn't suddenly make a grab for it like I had in my vision.

"What is it?" I asked needing to know.

"It's the Crimson Eye." The second she said it I tested its name in a whisper rolling off my tongue.

"Crimson Eye."

"Yes, but I always thought it was a myth," she added, her voice in total awe.

"Why?"

"Because it was always said to be too dangerous to exist." I frowned at that but then again it made sense when she added,

"It is said that it tells of the Fates plans, or at least…" She paused to look at me like she was now seeing someone different.

"What?"

"…it only does to those who are called to it." I looked back at it and knew that it had called to me, what other reason could there be for me being here now and finding it? How would I have known?

"You think it might want to show me something?" I asked being unsure, despite being near desperate to touch it.

"You're uncertain?"

"I haven't really had the best track record for making decisions based on my instincts...coming to Hell is just one example." I said making her sigh,

"Ah."

"But then again, we are here now right," I said quickly.

"Yeah and I mean it would almost be rude not to," Nero added making me smirk at her and say,

"I knew I liked you." She grinned back and then said,

"Back at you, human." I laughed once and then released it on a breath before getting myself ready.

"Well, here goes nothing...tell Lucius I love him," I said before she could say anything in response to that. Then I reached out and grabbed it and the moment I did, that was when I knew what it truly meant. What I had just grabbed hold of...

I was holding a piece of fate...I was holding its heart.

A rush of visions all hit me at once and I found myself gripping on harder to try and cling on to the power of it. Gods, but it was so strong it stole more than my breath, for it felt as though it would have stolen my soul had I let it. But then something in it started to calm as if it had declared me worthy and recognised I meant it no harm. I was not someone that would abuse the Fates.

I didn't need its hate.

I don't know where that thought had been born from, but it wasn't my own mind. I swallowed hard through the emotional journey it was catapulting me through, as if it had been born from too many. As if it had been born from the bloody tears of a God crying because of the wickedness of men.

It was soul consuming and utterly heart breaking!

But then it started to change, getting past it and focusing instead of what it wanted to show me. I sucked in a startled breath as I started to see the witch, the one who had started this all. She too was crying, only instead of the reasons behind it, I was only left to see the result.

She was sat at a broken mirror with deadly shards all around her. Blood speckled on the bathroom floor around the slumped form of her hooded figure. She was sobbing, begging in another language I didn't know. She was also pleading with someone who wasn't there, and I ignored how I knew this. But then I saw it, the quickest glimpse of a shadow swirling in the shards like it was trying to communicate with her.

Then suddenly she screamed and grabbed one of the largest shards of glass in her now bloody hand. After this she turned it back on herself and this time when she screamed it was through pain she inflicted upon herself.

"NO!" I shouted at the same time the howling of pain coming from the darkness in the mirror echoed that of the witch. She stabbed herself in the face and then in a breath, the vision evaporated.

I cried out for her pain, despite what she had done to us. I didn't know why but it seemed like she had been born from bitterness and heartache. *She had been born through hate.*

Just like another.

The darkness in the mirror…I knew who it was!

"No…it…it can't be possible!" I started to say but then my thoughts cut the visions short and I suddenly came back to my own time. I opened my eyes and quickly blurted out,

"I know who it is…I know who it is that is behind

everything!" Nero was looking at me strangely as if she wasn't listening but instead focusing on something else.

"What...what is it, didn't you hear me?" I asked.

"Your Hex was glowing and burnt through your top." I frowned thinking that I hadn't felt anything, but that wasn't it as I could tell there was more...much more.

"Nero?"

"I know where I have seen it before," she muttered, now looking terrified.

"Where?"

"Fuck! We have to leave...we have to get out of here, come on!" She shouted, suddenly grabbing me and yanking me towards the arch I had run through.

"Wait, but why?!" I shouted,

"Leave the orb, come on!" I pulled back, holding the orb to my chest and said,

"What is this about? Tell me, Nero?!" She looked beyond panicked and after scrubbing a hand down her face she said,

"It is not as we thought it was, it is not trying to take hold of you! It was never trying to summon you to the witch like we thought!"

"Then what? What are you saying, if it isn't that then what is it?" This was when Nero grabbed hold of me with both hands on my arms and said with a little shake,

"It was a trap! Fuck girl! They are using you as that Hex, that fucking Hex is to use you so they could be summoned *to you!*" I gasped and dropped the orb to the floor as that sank in. Then I slowly looked down at it and instantly knew what this meant. Although, like most things, I only knew the full extent of that mistake when it actually fucking happened!

Because Nero was right, I had been used to create a portal right to the one place no one knew about. To the place that no one could get inside without Lucius letting them. Inside his tower. The storm, the door of souls, he had the most protected tower in Hell and why would he have that?! Because he was protecting something that's why?! To the one place that no one knew the Crimson Eye was hidden.

And I had just walked them right inside!

"Oh, Gods no!"

"And we thank you for that mistake, Princess." A malevolent voice said as if hearing my thoughts, and the second I turned around I saw the flash of metal before pain exploded in my head as I fell to the floor. The second I did, I heard my name being called before the same thud landed next to me. After that came a halo of navy-blue hair that started to seep into red, its white tips the colour of crimson. Blood pooled around the face of Nero as her eyes turned white as death took hold of her.

"Ne...ro." I croaked trying to reach out a hand to her. One that was suddenly stepped on making me cry out.

"Oh don't worry, I am not going to kill you yet. I have been waiting too long for this moment, little Princess. But as for your friend here, well, I do love the sight of collateral damage," the woman said and I cried out again,

"No!" My shout of pain was all I had left in me, but it was no use as I suddenly coughed through the agony when I was kicked in the ribs.

The woman's voice got closer to me and I was kicked over to see the face of my enemy for the first time.

"My Master can't wait to meet you," she told me and the second she got closer I screamed. A demonic woman with crimson eyes of hatred stared back at me like those of a snake! Her head piece was alive with souls reaching out like fingers crawling at life. She hissed down at me and said,

"Now it's time to welcome you to the real Hell!" Then she punched me in the face and for once I welcomed the unconsciousness. Because that way it took away the pain. The pain of losing my friend. The pain of knowing that I had led them to the Crimson Eye. That I had failed the Fates but more importantly...

I had failed Lucius.

Because now he would never know who it was that was truly behind all of this.

He would never know that he had a brother.

And that brother... hated him.

To be Continued...

About the Author

Stephanie Hudson has dreamed of being a writer ever since her obsession with reading books at an early age. What first became a quest to overcome the boundaries set against her in the form of dyslexia has turned into a life's dream. She first started writing in the form of poetry and soon found a taste for horror and romance. Afterlife is her first book in the series of twelve, with the story of Keira and Draven becoming ever more complicated in a world that sets them miles apart.

When not writing, Stephanie enjoys spending time with her loving family and friends, chatting for hours with her biggest fan, her sister Cathy who is utterly obsessed with one gorgeous Dominic Draven. And of course, spending as much time with her supportive partner and personal muse, Blake who is there for her no matter what.

Author's words.

My love and devotion is to all my wonderful fans that keep me going into the wee hours of the night but foremost to my wonderful daughter Ava...who yes, is named after a cool, kick-ass, Demonic bird and my sons, Jack, who is a little hero and Baby Halen, who yes, keeps me up at night but it's okay because he is named after a Guitar legend!

Keep updated with all new release news & more on my website
www.afterlifesaga.com
Never miss out, sign up to the
mailing list at the website.

Also, please feel free to join myself and other Dravenites on my Facebook group
Afterlife Saga Official Fan
Interact with me and other fans. Can't wait to see you there!

- facebook.com/AfterlifeSaga
- twitter.com/afterlifesaga
- instagram.com/theafterlifesaga

Acknowledgements

Well first and foremost my love goes out to all the people who deserve the most thanks and are the wonderful people that keep me going day to day. But most importantly they are the ones that allow me to continue living out my dreams and keep writing my stories for the world to hopefully enjoy... These people are of course YOU! Words will never be able to express the full amount of love I have for you guys. Your support is never ending. Your trust in me and the story is never failing. But more than that, your love for me and all who you consider your 'Afterlife family' is to be commended, treasured and admired. Thank you just doesn't seem enough, so one day I hope to meet you all and buy you all a drink! ;)

To my family... To my amazing mother, who has believed in me from the very beginning and doesn't believe that something great should be hidden from the world. I would like to thank you for all the hard work you put into my books and the endless hours spent caring about my words and making sure it is the best it can be for everyone to enjoy. You make Afterlife shine. To my wonderful crazy father who is and always has been my hero in life. Your strength astonishes me, even to this day and the love and care you hold for your family is a gift you give to the Hudson name. And last but not least, to the man that I consider my soul mate. The man who taught me about real love and makes me not only want to be a better person but makes me feel I am too. The amount of support you have given me since we met has been incredible and the greatest feeling was finding out you wanted to spend the rest of your life with me when you asked me to marry you.

All my love to my dear husband and my own personal Draven… Mr Blake Hudson.

Another personal thank you goes to my dear friend Caroline Fairbairn and her wonderful family that have embraced my brand of crazy into their lives and given it a hug when most needed.

For their friendship I will forever be eternally grateful.

I would also like to mention Claire Boyle my wonderful PA, who without a doubt, keeps me sane and constantly smiling through all the chaos which is my life ;) And a loving mention goes to Lisa Jane for always giving me a giggle and scaring me to death with all her count down pictures lol ;)

Thank you for all your hard work and devotion to the saga and myself. And always going that extra mile, pushing Afterlife into the spotlight you think it deserves. Basically helping me achieve my secret goal of world domination one day…evil laugh time… Mwahaha! Joking of course ;)

As before, a big shout has to go to all my wonderful fans who make it their mission to spread the Afterlife word and always go the extra mile. I love you all x

Also by
Stephanie Hudson

Afterlife Saga

A Brooding King, A Girl running from her past. What happens when the two collide?

Book 1 - Afterlife

Book 2 - The Two Kings

Book 3 - The Triple Goddess

Book 4 - The Quarter Moon

Book 5 - The Pentagram Child /Part 1

Book 6 - The Pentagram Child /Part 2

Book 7 - The Cult of the Hexad

Book 8 - Sacrifice of the Septimus /Part 1

Book 9 - Sacrifice of the Septimus /Part 2

Book 10 - Blood of the Infinity War

Book 11 - Happy Ever Afterlife /Part 1

Book 12 - Happy Ever Afterlife / Part 2

Transfusion Saga

What happens when an ordinary human girl comes face to face with the cruel Vampire King who dismissed her seven years ago?

Transfusion - Book 1

Venom of God - Book 2

Blood of Kings - Book 3

Rise of Ashes - Book 4

Map of Sorrows - Book 5

Tree of Souls - Book 6

Kingdoms of Hell – Book 7

Eyes of Crimson - Book 8

Afterlife Chronicles: (Young Adult Series)

The Glass Dagger – Book 1

The Hells Ring – Book 2

Stephanie Hudson and Blake Hudson

The Devil in Me

OTHER WORKS BY HUDSON INDIE INK

Paranormal Romance/Urban Fantasy

Sloane Murphy

Xen Randell

C. L. Monaghan

Sci-fi/Fantasy

Brandon Ellis

Devin Hanson

Crime/Action

Blake Hudson

Mike Gomes

Contemporary Romance

Gemma Weir

Elodie Colt

Ann B. Harrison